GLORY
Of the OLIVE

A NOVEL

Susan Claire Potts
1575 West Big Beaver Road, Suite C-11
Troy, Michigan 48084
810-649-2320

The First Sunday in Advent
A.D. 1994

John T. DiNitto
2 Ledge Circle
Concord, N.H. 03301

Dear Mr. DiNitto:

Harlo Printers forwarded your letter to me, and I wanted to thank you for taking the time to write. I'm glad you liked *Glory of the Olive*. The sequel, *Burning Faith*, is ready to go to the printer's and should be available within the year, God willing.

Like you, I believe the events long prophesied are unfolding before us, and it is our great privilege to live in these times, faithful to Our Lord, and suffering with him the agonies of the nearly worldwide Apostasy.

May God grant you strength to bear your disability and to see it always as precious gold, legal tender for grace for you and those you love.

In the Sweetest Heart of Mary,

Susan Claire Potts

(Mrs.) Susan Claire Potts

Susan Claire Potts

GLORY Of The OLIVE

AVILA BOOKS
TROY, MICHIGAN

ISBN: 0-8187-0203-6
Library of Congress Catalog Card Number: 94-77281

Cover Design by Harry Baker

Printed by Harlo Press, 50 Victor, Detroit, MI 48203

To Vincent,
Always and Forever

PROLOGUE

Omnes gentes, plaudite manibus
Jubilate Deo in voce exsultationis

Crowds gathered early in St. Peter's Square on October 13 at the end of the twentieth century. It was the eighty-second anniversary of that rainy day in Fatima when the Blessed Virgin Mary had come from Heaven to Leiria.

Memories of the event had faded, and children no longer learned of the time when the sun had broken through the heavy clouds and plunged toward the earth, and a hundred thousand people trembled and feared that the world was coming to an end. It seemed a fairy tale from the past, but a diligent student could still, if he wanted to know, look up the newspaper accounts in the library and read in *Il Seculo* about the miracle in the hills of Portugal a lifetime ago.

That world was gone. The grassy knolls and grazing sheep and faithful children spoke of a time when men felt their connection with nature and with nature's God. No more. The travellers thronging into the Vatican had come on vacation, not pilgrimage. If they had any religion at all, it was not the faith of their fathers, a Christianity intimate with heavenly things, but a new religion -- a faith in man, in progress, in the inevitable triumph of the human spirit and the forces of evolution.

Most of the travellers believed that humanity was on the threshold of a superconsciousness, a revolution of the spirit which would match the electronic marvels that had transformed human life. The satellite dishes which sat on top of the ancient buildings were the testament of the New Age, the mark of the exaltation of

1

man. Rome would be the center, the heart, of the emerging world. Wave upon wave they came, not from local villages, but from around the world in scarcely more time than it had taken the Fatima pilgrims to walk to the Cova da Ira.

Why had they come? Few knew. Curiosity, perhaps. The pull of history. But deep within them was a restlessness, a disquiet that they didn't understand and couldn't express. It propelled them ceaselessly through the years, a driving subconscious goad that gave them no rest. The artificiality of modern life pressed like layers of lead on their souls and their hearts' yearning had no words.

At noon the sun shone like an amber pendant in the azure sky, burning the autumn coolness from the air. The crowd grew still as Pope Innocent XIV appeared on the balcony, an imposing figure, carrying the weight of his office with quiet dignity. He had the ascetic look of a monk, a thin angular face and piercing blue eyes. His ringed hand rested on his pectoral cross and his white cassock rippled in the wind as he stood silently surveying the thousands of people gathered before him..

His Holiness was not popular; the world was leery of him. He seemed to have emerged from the hidden depths of the Middle Ages. Since his election in August, he had stayed in the Vatican. He didn't travel. He shunned the press. He prayed and wrote and governed his flock. Theologians were apprehensive. Bishops had been called in from Europe and America, one by one. There was a moratorium on publishing. Change was in the air.

It was the first public appearance of Pope Innocent XIV. Television news vans ringed the edges of the square and the high dual antennae were poised for microwave transmission to their mother stations. Impatient journalists, bored with the Catholic Church, huddled together at the back of the crowd.

There had been rumors that the new pope had something surprising to announce. No one in the media cared what it was, but they wouldn't miss a chance for a story. They were eager to keep their ratings up and their advertisers happy. As the Bishop

2

of Rome stood with folded hands scanning the crowd, the reporters looked at their watches, hoping the speech would be short.

A group of Italian newsmen stood in a little cluster, smoking, and two television reporters in tailored pantsuits and silk blouses walked over to them. The well trained voices of the American women carried over the heads of the crowd as they greeted their European colleagues. A heavyset man turned and motioned for them to be quiet.

One of the women glared at him haughtily. "Mind your own business," she snapped, then turned to her companions and mocked the credulous people waiting for the white-robed man to speak. A muscular cameraman, his long brown hair pulled back in a ponytail and his camera hoisted on his shoulder, winked at her. The woman shrugged and tapped her pen on her notebook. She was anxious to take her notes and head to a cafe for some coffee. The Church was an anachronism, but she had a job to do.

The pontiff began to speak in Italian: "...And so this day, We order the suppression of the *Novus Ordo Missae*, that experiment of unhappy history, and the reforms which followed.

"From the first Sunday in Advent throughout the world, the Holy Sacrifice of the Mass will be offered according to the rite codified by Pope St. Pius V of glorious memory, the unchanged Mass of the Ages. We ratify today, like Our predecessors of four hundred years until the sorrowful days of the last three decades, the timeless *Quo Primum*.

"The venerable rites of the Holy Roman Catholic Church are to be restored."

The newscasters and reporters were caught offguard and strained to understand what the pope was saying. The impatient blond American turned to one of the Italians.

"What's he talking about?"

He shook his head and stared at the balcony.

"What's the matter? What's this all about?"

"The Mass, *signorina*. He's doing away with the New

3

Mass and going back to Latin."

"You're kidding."

"No."

"This is unreal."

"*Si, signorina,*" he nodded. "*Ridìcolo.*"

People nudged each other, whispering. Exclamations of surprise filled the piazza. Far off to the left, a low cry of "No!" went up, and the Swiss guard moved closer. The sound swelled, and there was anguish in the eyes of the pope. He paused, waiting for the crowd to quiet down.

The traditions and disciplines of the Church which had been abandoned during the last third of the twentieth century were to be restored immediately. With words that blazed like the tongues of fire at Pentecost, the Vicar of Christ read the papal order, the *Restoration of Tradition.* At the end, he commanded public reparation by bishops, priests and laity for the blasphemies and outrages which had rocked the Catholic Church and pierced the Heart of God.

The secularists were aghast; the few faithful, overwhelmed, as the Roman pontiff stormed the temple and cast out the modern money changers with the whip of his infallibility. In thundering sentences, he condemned the sin and error, heresy and irreligion which had destroyed the faith and imperiled the souls of men everywhere; and his words resounded from every satellite and pulsed through every cable. As Pope Innocent XIV stood on the balcony of St. Peter's in the Vatican and his resonant voice read on, the shockwaves were felt around the world. He had taken his sword and split the Catholic world.

The open undermining of the faith would end. No longer would the modernists and neo-gnostics, the theosophists and New Agers sit like fat parasites sucking the blood of the Church. The division was clear. *He who is not with me is against me. He who gathereth not with me scattereth.* Like the Master Who had given it, the true Mass was resurrected. Everywhere and for always.

The pontiff finished speaking. He leaned briefly on the balustrade, looking past the crowds standing in St. Peter's Square. Suddenly, his eyes clouded over, and the piazza before him folded into blackness. He ran his hand over his eyes trying to clear his vision, then shook his head and blinked, fearing he had gone blind.

A pulsing white light chased the darkness, and Innocent XIV saw, spread out beyond the walls of the Vatican, a scene which caused him to shudder and grow weak: A panorama of bloodied fields and broken cities. Vengeful mobs and unrestrained violence. The world churning like the sea in a hurricane. War on every side. Drought and famine and convulsions of nature.

The scene faded and his vision blurred again. The Holy Father rubbed his eyes, then gripped the balustrade with both hands, steadying himself, as colored light flashed before him for an instant. Through the swirling mist that followed, he saw two lines of clerics -- bishops and priests -- in battle array facing each other on a wide field.

The numbers were unequal with thousands upon thousands of warriors on one side. On the other, there were only a few, and they were grievously weak. They reeled and staggered from fatigue, on the verge of surrender, broken in defeat, disarmed and ready to die.

The great battalion surged forward, shouting in triumph. Their arrogant heads held high and their cold eyes slitted with hatred, they charged toward the final conquest. They forged relentlessly ahead, driving their knives into the hearts of the vanquished priests.

Innocent XIV clutched his papers, crumpling them in his hands. He tried to focus. His face was ashen, and he felt a chill at the back of his neck. He could see nothing but the vision, the unimaginable fighting and the grief in the eyes of the fallen.

The sky over the battlefield grew dark and threatening. Blood red clouds hung low and heavy over the fields, eclipsing the sun. There was a pause in the fighting and an ominous quiet.

The air was still; nothing moved. Suddenly, a huge roar echoed through the hills and the charging conquerors recoiled in terror.

They turned, dropping their arms, and ran from the battle-field, trampling each other, driven by a preternatural and monstrous fear. The ground shuddered and opened before them; and one after another they were hurled into the chasm, legs flying and arms flailing as screams of unrelenting horror tore from their souls.

Tears filled the eyes of the pontiff and he clasped his chest in pain, unable to breathe. He thought he would die; but as quickly at it had come, the vision disappeared. The hills were gone and the bloodied fields, but the image of the men who fought and died would never leave his mind. He knew what the vision foretold: a battle to the death for the Holy Faith.

And the soldiers were few.

Innocent XIV looked out over his people, his face drawn with sorrow. He felt weak, unequal to the task ahead. Bowing his head, he prayed for courage.

A moment passed, and he felt a hand rest on his shoulder. At first he thought it was his imagination, but the steady pressure remained. Slowly, he turned and saw the one who had touched him, the Prince of the Apostles, the Fisherman. Dressed in his pontifical robes, the triple tiara on his head, St. Peter looked into the eyes of his successor and held them for a moment. Innocent XIV felt his strength return. St. Peter nodded gravely and disappeared.

The people fell to their knees as His Holiness raised his hand in benediction.

"Benedicat vos omnipotens Deus, Pater et Filius, et Spiritus Sanctus."

CHAPTER

1

Circumdederunt me gemitus mortis...
In tribulatione mea invocavi Dominum
Et exaudivit vocem meam

Union Station was bustling with people at seven o'clock in the morning; and Catherine Anderson sat quietly at Gate E waiting for the Wolverine, the old Amtrak train that would take her from Chicago on the final leg of her journey to a new life.

She smoothed her wrinkled denim skirt over her knees and laid her book down on her lap. She was tired and a little disoriented from the motion of the train over the past two days and the lack of sleep, and she tried to relax her shoulders to ease the dizziness.

Angie Fortunata had said she was being silly and old-fashioned to take the train; and as she closed her eyes wearily, Catherine thought that maybe she was right. But there was no joy in flying anymore, no civility. Just cramped seats and stale air and too many memories.

Memories of Frank.

She rose slowly when the red-jacketed agent unlocked the gate and announced it was time to board. She dropped her book into her satchel and laid her coat over her arm. Feeling numb, she walked toward the open glass doors into the cold dark air.

The day, like the millenium, brooded over its awakening, dawning reluctantly, damp and gray. To the east of the Windy City, the lake stretched listlessly to the Michigan border, tired and flattened by the icy burden of winter, the pulsing crashing waves gathering strength unseen somewhere beyond the horizon.

7

It was the first week in April, but spring had not yet come to the shores of Lake Michigan. The cold Midwestern air slapped the faces of the commuters getting off the Metra on the next track, and they lowered their heads and pulled their coats tight as they pushed through the doors into the station.

Milling crowds of travellers surrounded her, but Catherine was alone. No one spoke to her. Her purse was slung over her shoulder and she rested her hand on it as she walked along the tracks. She looked at the people hurrying by, wishing for a familiar face, then silently climbed the steps into the train.

She checked her watch and settled into her seat, drawing back the coarse green curtain and gazing out the smudged window as a ragtag group of people hurried to board at the last minute, scrambling up the steps with their duffel bags and carry-ons, their coats and the morning papers. They struggled down the aisle and heaved their belongings onto the rack above the seats, then sat down, breathing hard.

"Ticket please."

Catherine reached for her purse. The conductor waited, his cap tilted back on his gray hair and a metal punch poised in his left hand. Riffling through the papers lying on the bottom of her handbag, she was afraid for a moment that she had lost the ticket. Her pulse quickened, but she relaxed when her fingers closed around the thick folder.

She pulled out the envelope from the travel agency in Colorado where she and her journalist husband, Francis Xavier Anderson, had lived for seven years. Catherine handed her ticket to the conductor and closed her eyes so she could see her little log house overlooking Lake Dillon and the mountains where she had been so happy in those days before the world had come crashing down at her feet.

"Where you getting off?" the conductor asked, interrupting her thoughts.

"Dearborn." It was Frank's hometown.

"Ever been there before?"

"Yes." She leaned back in her seat and he went on to the next passenger.

Life was so hard, Catherine thought. She used to think it was an adventure. But not now. All the joy had been crushed forever that cold dark night in January. Her mouth went dry remembering it, and her hands trembled.

Catherine bit her lip and silent tears fell. She was glad no one had taken the seat next to her as she pressed her fingernails into the palms of her hands, trying to stop the flood of memories. After a minute she slipped her right hand into her pocket and took out her rosary, then laid it across her lap and untangled the silver chain.

She sighed as she began to pray for Frank, her much loved husband who had been dead since January. Dead. The word clanged against the inside of her skull like alien bells jarring the harmony of her life; and the cold truth of his death, the reality of it, froze her soul.

Weeping soundlessly, she prayed for him, for Frank, who had died alone in the mountains of Slovenia as he drove his Jeep on the road to Ljubljana, covering the war in the Balkans. A correspondent for the *American Republic*, he was shot by a sniper in a tree.

Catherine slipped the beads through her fingers, meditating on the mysteries -- the joy of the Resurrection, the glory of the Ascension -- and slowly she found solace in the prayers. There would come a time, she knew, when she would see Frank again. See his deep brown eyes and his wide smile, rest her head against his broad shoulders. She would hear him laugh and speak to her once more of love and joy and beauty. Someday they would sing again.

Death was not forever.

She would not let herself mourn like one who had no faith. She could not. It would dishonor him. She must carry on, as Frank would say, accomplish her mission. She dried her eyes as the conductor walked up the aisle carrying a cardboard box tray of coffee and orange juice

"Coffee, ma'am?" he asked as she kissed the crucifix. She tucked the crystal beads back in their soft tapestry case and snapped it shut.

"Please."

"Cream and sugar?"

She slipped the rosary into her pocket. "Just black."

"There you go."

"Thanks," she said, taking the styrofoam cup and sipping the steaming coffee.

Stanley Tomaszewski watched her. He was curious. There was something different about her, different from the other women who travelled the Chicago to Detroit run. He glanced at the small gold medal of the Blessed Virgin hanging from a chain around her slim neck.

Sensing his look, she brought her hand up to the medal, holding it in her fingers, and he noticed the wide gold wedding band. She reminded him of someone, but he couldn't place who it was. There was something about her face. Her hair was auburn, long and thick, and she wore it in a single French braid which reached halfway down her back. She had the high cheekbones and broad forehead of the Western frontier and her green eyes were wide spaced and bright.

Stan thought she was about thirty and not bad looking in an intellectual kind of way. He didn't mind brainy women as long as he wasn't married to them. He thought of Stella, his wife of forty-seven years, who was as warm and good natured as she'd been when she was sixteen. He smiled thinking of her and how nice things were going to be for the two of them when he retired in May.

He was sixty-seven and had worked for the railroad since he got back from Korea in 1953. He had seen a lot of changes over the years. The work was harder, people weren't as nice. There was so much pressure. He couldn't understand it.

"Can I ask you a question?" he asked.

She nodded.   He balanced his makeshift tray on the back edge of the seat and looked around to make sure no one else needed his help.   No one did.   The beefy man across the aisle had gotten up and gone to the dinette car, and the woman in the next row whose nasal voice shrilled above the seat, grating the nerves of the other passengers, was reading an editorial to her companion, who laughed derisively at each paragraph.   The conductor leaned over slightly, speaking to Catherine in a voice barely above a whisper.

"Are you one of them Catholics the Bishop's having a fit about?

"Which bishop?"

"O'Callahan.   In Chicago.   He don't like what the new pope's doing, making everybody go back to Latin and stuff.   All that incense and mumbo-jumbo, he says."

"I'm not from Chicago. "

"Well, are you one of them ?"

"Yes."

"I thought so, seeing your rosary and the Miraculous Medal.   You don't see them much nowadays."

"No, I guess not."

Stan paused, considering, then spoke quietly.   "So, you're one of them Catholics.   Real Catholics, that's what it is.   Me, too.   Same as always.   Inside, you know."   He tapped his heart.   "We been kicked around too long.   They tried to kill the Church, you know."   He looked straight at Catherine.

"I know," she whispered.

"But they couldn't do it.   All we needed was a strong pope.   Yup, this here's the one.   Innocent's the man."

"God is good to us."

"You're right about that.   Hey, did you ever hear about the prophecy?"

"Which one?"

"About the pope who would fix the Church back up.   You

know, restore everything. The Glory of the Olive. That's the little saying about him."

"You mean St. Malachy's list of future popes?"

"Yeah. Isn't that something? He saw the whole line of them, right up to now. The Glory of the Olive, that's our times. Makes you feel good. Things are going to get better. It's gonna be okay. That's the glory part, ain't it? Everything being put back together?"

"It will be glorious, all right."

"The Church'll grow again. Like the fruit on the olive tree. Ever see that? That's something. Branches filled with olives. First green, then black when they're ripe. I saw some once in the Holy Land. Only time I ever saw olives not in a jar. Nah, I don't care what O'Callahan says or any of them other bishops. Traitors, that's what they are. I'm dumping that new stuff. I'm gonna do what this pope says. Gotta follow the pope, right?"

"Right."

Stan set his chin. "That's what I'm gonna do. Don't nobody know it yet but Stella. That's my wife. Not even the kids. But we talked about it, Stella and me, the day he made that announcement. Remember that day?"

"Yes. It was a day for rejoicing."

"You're right about that. About time, too. We said that junk they tried didn't do nobody no good. When I was a kid, I was an altar boy, back in the old days when Pius XII was pope. You wouldn't remember him. That goes way back. 1945, '46. Things were pretty good back then. The war was over, but man, then the sixties hit. You wouldn't remember that. Maybe your folks told you about it. Those were bad times. Like the devil got loose, I say. Roaring around ruining everything.

"When they changed the Mass I never liked it. All that talking and hugging and calling the priest by his first name. Standing for communion like you was in some cafeteria line or somethin'. We couldn't do nothing about it, so we just kept going every Sunday, but the kids, they didn't like it. Said it was

12

boring.   That was some fight, making them go, especially, well,
especially when what they said was true.   So what can you do?
You say, 'You have to go 'cause I said so.   Besides it's a mortal
sin to miss Mass.'   And they'd go, 'Sister says there's no such
thing as mortal sin anymore.'   I'm tellin' ya, that was some
aggravation."

"How many children do you have?"

"Eight. All grown up now, thank God.   On their own. I got
thirteen grandchildren. How about you?"

"I don't have any."

"Oh, too bad, well, maybe someday."

Catherine shook her head.   "I'm a widow. My husband
died three months ago."

"I'm sorry."

She looked down at her hands and drew in her breath so she
wouldn't cry again.   Turning her wedding band between her
finger and thumb, she looked back up at Stan.   There was com-
passion in his face, and his eyebrows were knitted the way a
father's are when he looks at his tearful daughter and doesn't
quite know what to say.

Catherine nodded silently and Stan walked back to the
snack counter with his empty tray.

As the train rolled through Jackson, Catherine put her purse
under the seat in front of her and picked up *The Chicago
Tribune*, scanning the headlines: **President Orders Troops to
German Border...Navy on Alert in Mediterranean...Draft Talks
Resume on Capitol Hill...Unknown Plague Strikes Africa,
Puzzles Scientists.**

There were wars and rumors of wars. Conflagrations and
riots. Starvation and despair. Anarchy threatened as the European Economic Community neared collapse; and hungry Russia
loomed over the West like a bear over fallen prey. Floods in one
country, drought in another.   Vicious storms and men yet more

13

vicious.

The world seemed to be lopsided and spinning crazily, like a top careening down the sidewalk, flying off the curb and landing hard against the pavement. Catherine shuddered as though to brace herself against the impact, then folded the paper and put it down beside her. She couldn't bear to read about the savage conflict in Europe, couldn't stand to see how many more people had been killed.

The newspaper accounts could not even begin to capture the horror being played out across the Atlantic as America struggled in vain to stay aloof. Seven exhausting years of humanitarian efforts and peacekeeping missions and the fighting went on -- the days pierced by the sound of gunfire and women's screams, the nights marked by the cries of wandering orphans and the untamed barking of dogs, wild again, running in packs down the broken streets.

A smoky haze blanketed the once great cities of Eastern Europe; and to the west, terrorist attacks continued unabated until Paris was in flames and Naples destroyed. Cathedrals of stone and stained glass from Rheims to Seville were bombed in the night by roving bands of guerrilla warriors with an ancient grievance against the Church. Convents were torched and forty-two priories burned. Three hundred fifty-six priests and religious died in the onslaught.

Deep within the Vatican, Pope Innocent XIV knelt in anguish at a prieu-dieu before the Blessed Sacrament to offer reparation to the Sacred Heart of Jesus. There was no peace in the world as Catherine Mary Anderson rode the train to Dearborn that Lenten morning in April.

"Ann Arbor," Stan Tomaszewski announced. "Everyone getting off at Ann Arbor kindly go to the exit at the back, just past the dinette." A young man dressed in jeans and a flannel shirt hoisted a book bag over his shoulder and walked past the conductor.

"Got everything, son?"

14

"Yes, thanks. Well, that's the end of spring break. See ya."

Catherine watched him. He reminded her of her students -- bright, intense,trying so hard to look casual that even the nonchalance seemed driven. Their heads were filled with learning and yet no book had filled the hollow places in their hearts nor the longing in their eyes.

The young man was going back to his school, and she had left hers. Until two weeks ago she had been an associate professor of English at Rocky Mountain College. She had taught for five years, ever since receiving her doctorate from the University of Colorado. When Frank was killed in January, the semester was drawing to a close, and she requested a leave of absence for the spring term, fully intending to return to her classes in September.

But early one evening something had happened to change everything.

CHAPTER

2

Perfice gressus meos in semitis tuis...

It was the Saturday after Ash Wednesday, and Catherine had been sitting alone at the kitchen table looking out the patio window at Lake Dillon and the mountains rising around it on all sides. She had loved the view since the first time she had seen it, the day Frank had brought her from Denver. The vast beauty and the splendid immensity made her think of eternity, of God. She used to sit by the window with the sun shining on her face and let her mind roam back through the ages, century after century until the beginning of the world.

She loved to think of how, like an artist beyond the reaches of memory, God had formed the rocky peaks which thrust upward into the endless blue of the Western sky, and colored them with spruce and pine, softening the ridges with snow. The world was His palate.

She would walk out on the patio and look at the lake curving into the hills, smooth and flat, set into the valley like a looking glass on a dresser top. Scanning the massive range and the still water, she would drink in the beauty with her eyes, incredulous that she could be near such majesty, that she could reach out her fingers and touch it and raise her face and feel the cool dry air blowing down from the mountains.

But that was when Frank was still alive. Now she felt no joy in the rugged beauty of her surroundings. She missed Frank too much. The numbness which had settled over her immediately after his death had worn off, and she was pierced with the sharp edges of grief. It hurt worse after dark when the work of the day

16

was finished, and she was all alone to face the night.

"Oh, God, why?" she cried to the silent room. "Why did You take him from me? Her voice trembled. "Why did he have to die so young? I am so terribly, terribly lonely."

She wanted to pound the table, but she dropped her head and laid her face on her arms. Tears wet her wrists. After a few minutes, she rose to turn on the lights and pull down the shade behind the white lace curtains.

She was standing at the darkened window when the telephone rang.

"Hello," she answered absently.

"Catherine?"

"Yes."

"Fr. Riley here."

"Oh, hello, Father! How good of you to call." Catherine wiped the tears from her face. He was a link to Frank, and she felt better hearing his voice.

The Reverend Thomas Aquinas Riley was a priest from Michigan, the pastor of Holy Martyrs Catholic Church. He and Frank had grown up across the street from each other and had roomed together at Michigan State. After graduation, Frank had left for graduate school at Fordham and Fr. Riley had gone to a seminary in Europe. They were as close as brothers.

Fr. Riley had sung Frank's funeral Mass and his voice had caught in his throat..

"How are you doing?" he asked quietly.

"I'm okay. Each day gets a little better. It's pretty lonely, though." She twisted her wedding band as she talked, cradling the receiver under her chin.

"Yes, I'm sure it is." He paused. "I miss him, too. I said Mass for him yesterday."

"Thank you, Father."

"His mother came."

Catherine drew in her breath sharply. *Frank's mother.* Helen Anderson had not been to church since Advent, 1970, when the New Mass had been imposed. Unlike Catherine's parents and thousands of others throughout the Christian world, including her only son, Mrs. Anderson, Sr. had not joined what later came to be called the "traditionalist movement," but she was united with them in her heart.

She wouldn't go to a Mass that the pope didn't approve and she couldn't go to the one that he did. So for nearly thirty years, she had stayed at home, reading her old missal on Sunday morning at ten o'clock and saying her rosary. Whatever could have happened to move that woman? Catherine wondered. Sixty-two years old and five feet tall, the tiny dark-eyed Helen Anderson had an untempered will.

"I'm so glad, Father," Catherine said. "How did that come about?"

"It's a long story."

"It would have to be." Catherine still couldn't believe it.

"Did you hear that Archbishop Stagniak announced his obedience to the papal order restoring the Mass?"

"No, I didn't hear that. When?"

"Last week. It's obligatory in Detroit. No more options. There's been one change after another. He's battening down the hatches. He's a lion of a man, that Archbishop. I'm not surprised you haven't heard...There are those who want to keep it quiet. People around here aren't real happy about it.

"I can't understand that." Catherine was indignant. "How they can prefer that *circus* is beyond me!"

"I don't know that they really prefer it. I think it's more that they like the freedom of the new ways. There aren't any restrictions on them and they can do what they want. Nobody tells them what to do. No censures. No sense of sin. Did you ever hear the trade-off theory?"

"No, what was that?"

"A friend of mine, Fr. Dan Murphy--I don't think you know him -- came up with it. He said that the clergy and the laity have an unspoken agreement that they made sometime during

Vatican II in the height of their euphoria over the changes. It boils down to this: the people can have their sin if the priests can keep their heresy."

"A real bargain for both sides."

"Yes," he said with uncharacteristic bitterness in his voice. "And they pay with their souls." He was quiet for a moment, then continued. "Anyway, so many Catholics wanted to go along with the modern world. It was the spirit of the times, I fear. They wanted more freeeedom, birth control, divorce and remarriage -- things like that -- so they'd put up with the noise and confusion and the error so they could blend into the rest of society.

"In exchange, the priests and the theologians and the university professors could teach whatever they wanted, make up their own religion as they went along. That was the contract. And each side is keeping its part. That's the only way this thing could have gone on for so long. Everybody who accepted it got what they wanted while Rome slept."

"So now what happens in Detroit?"

"I don't know. Everyone's in an uproar. There's open rebellion, and the Archbishop's suspending priests right and left. He won't tolerate disobedience to the Holy Father or to himself. I thought there'd be more compliance, once the order was clear, but things have gone too far. It's almost like an anti-church has taken root in the soil and now it's an enormous tree, strangling the roots of the true Church. It's going to take a while to cut it down, I'm afraid."

"That's disheartening."

"Yes. If they'd just go and leave the rest of us alone, it wouldn't be so bad. But they won't. They can't stand to see the beauty and the strength of Holy Mother Church restored. The worst part is the nest of hypocrites who'll feign obedience but keep working to destroy the Church from within."

"Like during the Modernism crisis."

"Exactly."

"So now what happens to you?" Catherine asked. Like scores of other traditionalist Catholic priests who had refused the changes in the Church following the Second Vatican Council, Fr. Riley had been offering Mass outside the auspices of the arch-diocese, supported by a steadfast group of people who struggled to keep the faith of their fathers. The Modernists in high places ignored him. The last thirty years had been a bitter and lonely time for those who loved the Catholic Church.

"The Archbishop called me in about two weeks ago for a talk when he got back from Rome."

Catherine smiled and wondered what Archbishop Stagniak thought when he saw Fr. Riley coming through the door. He was a formidable man, well over six feet tall with powerful shoulders and an athletic bearing. He had been first string offensive tackle for Michigan State University before entering the seminary, and he still looked like a football player. But above the massiveness of his body, he carried Old Ireland in his face, blue-eyed and freckled with close-cropped sandy hair that, if given a chance to grow, would have curled around his ears.

"Yes," Fr. Riley continued. "There were five of us priests he called in. All the local traditionalists. That went over real big in the diocese."

"I can imagine."

"They can't figure out why he's doing it. The *Catholic Examiner* says the Pope's putting pressure on him, and that he's giving in because he wants to be on the Curia. There's all kinds of speculation. The only thing they don't say is that maybe the Archbishop believes in what he's doing, that he wants tradition restored because things were changed which never should have been changed; and for the love of God, he wants to do what's right. No, they'd rather conjure up all sorts of ulterior motives."

"Because that's how they behave themselves," said Catherine sharply.

"I'm afraid you're right." It wasn't something he liked to admit, even to himself. "So, anyway, the New Mass and all the

20

reforms are over in Detroit. We don't really know what the rest of the clergy is going to do. I'm bracing for a widespread back-lash.

"Anyway, that's the background of how your mother-in-law came back. She heard about the announcement and knew she could come to the Old Mass with a clear conscience, since she was following the Pope. "

Catherine imagined her mother-in-law setting her chin, raising her head, and marching off to church. She smiled to think of it. "I am so glad," she said. "I can't tell you how worried I've been. It's unbelievable what's happening there. Almost too good to be true. After all these years! Have any other bishops joined with Archbishop Stagniak?"

"Only a few. So much for solidarity. But some may come around now that he's taken the first step. I understand Bishop Fournier of Orlando and Archbishop Webber of Providence are flying here in a few days for a meeting."

"What happens now?"

"When I met with the Archbishop, I told him that I would serve in whatever capacity he needed me. I was ready to give up Holy Martyrs if I had to, but he surprised me. He said he wanted me to stay where I was.

"Then he looked at me with this odd expression -- I thought he could see right through to my soul -- and he said, ' I understand that your school is doing well and that you have about three hundred families. Is that correct?" I answered, yes, think-ing to myself that he probably knew every last detail about how we were doing, but he didn't say any more about it. He's a good man, he is. So, to make a long story short, the Church is in bloom in Detroit, *Deo Gratias.*"

Catherine was quiet. It had been such a long struggle to keep the faith, to safeguard the tradition of the Holy Roman Catholic Church, fighting even against those in authority, bishops and cardinals, to stop the undermining and destruction of the Church established by Christ Himself for the salvation of souls.

And now here in America, in the New World not the Old, one courageous archbishop, pledging fealty to his holy pontiff, was planting the standard of the Faith and putting an end to the subversion of the Mystical Body of Christ.

Catherine's eyes were bright with a happiness she had not felt since Frank had died. "Oh, Father, I don't know what to say," she said. Her heart lifted in thanksgiving, and she felt a gentle peace wash over her. "It's such good news."

"That it is. Now the next part."

"The next part?"

"Yes, the part that concerns you. What would you say to moving back here?"

"That's certainly something I'd never thought about!"

"Well, think about it."

"Why would I move to Michigan?" she asked, comparing the flat and humid Midwest to the mountains in her mind.

"I would like you to be principal of the school." Fr. Riley smiled to himself, waiting for her reaction.

"What? Principal? For next year?"

"No, this year."

"But the school year's nearly over."

"I know. There's a good reason for that."

"You've taken me by surprise. I don't know what to think." Catherine paused, knowing how difficult it would be to leave Colorado. No, it was impossible. Her roots were in the West, and her memories of her life with Frank were tied up in the house he had built for her.

She played with the phone cord, wrapping it around her fingers, not knowing what to say. "I've never taught the younger ones. I'm used to college level teaching. And I've never been an administrator. I don't really think I would like sitting in an office, being out of the classroom."

"Could you get a Michigan certificate?"

"Probably."

"Good. We'd want you to teach as well."

22

"Oh. I see you haven't changed, Fr. Riley! What a task-master! Frank told me how you were in football practice."

"That's the only way to win. Now, what do you say?"

"May I have a day or two to think about it?"

"If you need it."

"Please. I'll get back with you on Friday. And, Father..."

"Yes."

"Thank you for considering me. I'm honored, but you've got me a bit confused. I've spent the last two months trying to get things in order and find a direction for my life, a focus, and I was pretty much settled into my new routine. This is certainly not anything I was expecting."

Fr. Riley chuckled. She could imagine his broad grin and crinkled blue eyes, and she smiled, too. "No, I guess not," he said. "I'll call you Friday about this same time."

"Thank you, Father. I'll let you know then."

"Fine, Catherine. God bless you."

They said good-bye and hung up. Catherine put down the phone and went into the kitchen to turn up the heat under the pot of soup simmering on the stove. The door that had seemed to shut in her face when Frank died opened a crack and the thin edge of light tempted her. She wondered what lay behind it. .

She ladled the vegetable soup into a deep bowl and laid a slice of cheese on a thick slab of the bread she had baked that morning. Bemused, she carried her steaming bowl over to the table, poured herself a small glass of wine, and whispered grace. She had brought a book to the table but she put it aside to mull over the ramifications of the unexpected call as she bit into the crusty bread.

Should she consider Fr. Riley's offer? She stirred her soup, cooling it, and its savory smell filled the little house on the mountainside. The clear day and a long walk into town had made her hungry and she was glad because she'd had no appetite for weeks. But what should she do about the school? She tried to lay it all out before her. She put aside the inducements to staying she was -- her friends, her neighbors, the lovely chapel where she and Frank had gone to Mass, and she looked hard at the stark other side of it.

She felt sad when she thought of the emptiness of the lives of so many of her colleagues, the bleakness of their discussions, their vapid ideas wafting though the lecture halls like thin smoke. And the students, Lord help the students, they seemed like a generation of foundlings, their souls patched and torn, their minds frozen in the cold grip of agnostic despair.

They were so different from her that she could scarcely understand them. They could question -- there was no doubt about that. It was their forte. Their idea of a stimulating class was not to be taught anything but to pummel her with questions one after another, staccato punches, not the least interested in the answer but thirsting for a knockout, driving her back into a corner, pushing to catch her in the ropes of ignorance or confusion.

Standing in front of them, she had often felt like a graduate student again, trying to defend her dissertation before the bearded scholars on her committee with their unkempt hair and hooded eyes, disdainful and remote.

For her students, there were no answers because they did not believe that there could be anything solid in the life of the mind, anything immutable. Knowledge, experience, existence itself were, for them, in a state of constant flux. No sooner was one step taken up the ladder of intellectual discovery than the previous rung was cut out from under them so that there could never be a steady footing and never any retracing of their steps.

Yet the climb must continue, for they believed with all the fervor of which a young heart is capable that the purpose of life lay in the quest, in the search, and not in the finding. They really didn't think that there was anything to find.

That was the curious part, Catherine thought. To them, truth was fluid, elusive, a teasing phantasm which danced before them, never to be embraced. They preferred the tired old onion metaphor which they all seemed to have heard in high school: you peel away the layers of the onion searching for its essence, its *onionness*, and what would you find? Nothing. The essence was in the peeling, the process. That was the sort of thing that passed for wisdom among them, the sort of idea which would make them nod their heads gravely.

Catherine could see the boys stroking their chins and the girls pushing their round metal glasses back up their nose and tucking their long straight hair behind their ears while they pondered the essential nothingness of things. It made her want to shake them.

She rose to put the kettle on to boil for tea. It was so frustrating sometimes, trying to teach those sophomores. What were they? Existentialists? Deconstructionists? No, their philosophy was not that well defined. It was inchaote, unfinished. They were merely shallow young critics tearing American culture apart, looking for flaws, passing judgment on the works of the writers of the past as though they, post-modern adolescents who had hardly begun to live and for the most part had not begun to think, had even an inkling of what they were doing.

Yet she couldn't blame them, not really. A peculiar torpor of the soul had spread through the world, and the students were badly affected. They were unwitting recipients of an education that bred attitudes of bored superiority and mocking condescension. She had long considered it her duty as a teacher to yank the cynicism from their minds before they were lulled into a walking sleep of reason and could no longer think. But, she had to admit, it was a losing battle.

Absentmindedly, she dunked a teabag into her willoware teapot, then took it out, dripping water on the ceramic counter. How different would it be, she wondered, teaching at Holy Martyrs? What would it be like not having to pretend she didn't notice the indifferentism and disbelief which stood as an impenetrable barrier between her and her students?

She couldn't even imagine it.

When Frank was alive, it was different. She could bear the discouragement because of him. Their life stood in stark contrast to the bleakness around her. She gave her heart to him; and with her, he could break through the reticence that made so many men strangers to their loved ones and to themselves. Theirs was a union of mind and soul unusual for the times.

When he came home between assignments, they would prop their feet up on the hunter green hassock between the two wing-back chairs in the living room. Warmed by a crackling fire in the stone fireplace and the delight of being together again, they would eat crackers and cheese, share a bottle of Chianti, and talk far into the night.

She loved him.

He was nine years older than she and his work had taken him all over Europe and Asia. He had been in Panama and Grenada and Kuwait during Desert Storm. He had covered the bombings of the cathedrals in Rheims and Seville, and he spent the six months before they were married in Croatia. His last assignment had been in the hills of Slovenia as the tiny country was torn on one side by a brutal neo-Communist uprising, the *Vox Populi*, and on the other by Muslims waging war for Allah, a *Jihad* in the Balkans.

Flying from one conflict spot to another, he had built a reputation as a journalist of integrity and candor. He was the kind of reporter who sought truth, and that was a rare quality at the end of the twentieth century. People read his work hungrily because they could trust him.

Over the years, he and Catherine grew more certain that the violent upheaval in the world, the wild storms and plunging temperatures, the roaring tidal waves and jarring earthquakes and, most of all, the unprecedented hatred everywhere were effects of the Great Apostasy foretold by Christ and the harbinger of the end times.

So they would talk, bolstering their courage, sorting it all out, looking at the world like a giant jigsaw puzzle laid out on the

26

coffee table, slowly putting the pieces in place, trying to understand, trying to prepare themselves for what they knew were terrors to come.

Yet Catherine never really felt that the violence would touch her, that the chaos that swirled about the world would ever engulf her personally. The spiralling breakdown of European civilization -- the destruction of so much that was beautiful and good, the worldwide riots and firebombs in the night, the frightful demands for revenge -- had seemed abstract to her, sitting in her cozy book-lined living room with its antique end tables and brass lamps, an old Oriental rug laid soft across the hardwood floor.

Frank had tried to warn her, to prepare her, but she refused to listen. No matter what happened in the world, he would be safe. Catherine thought he was invincible. He was competent and strong. He could confront whatever came his way. No, she had convinced herself, nothing would happen to Frank. She needed him.

Standing at the counter, Catherine forced herself back to the present before the tears came again and the aching emptiness. She tore off a paper towel to mop up the tea she had spilled, then walked back to the table for the dinner dishes. She stacked them in the sink and squirted them with detergent.

As the water ran over them filling the sink, she took Frank's green and white football mug down from the cupboard. She always used his cup when he was away on assignment, just as she slept on his side of the bed and buried her face in his pillow. He seemed closer that way, somehow, and now that he was gone and she would not see him until, God willing, they met again in Eternity, she fought to keep some small part of him with her. She set the mug on the counter and poured herself a cup of cinnamon tea.

Sitting at the table, she wrapped both hands around the heavy mug and, comforted by its warmth, slowly sipped the sweet spicy liquid. It was very quiet. The sun had sunk behind the western ridge and the distant sounds of traffic grew faint. The darkening night spread a thick blanket over the mountain like a mother tucking in her child.

CHAPTER

3

Deus, tu conversus vivificabis nos
Et plebs tua laetabitur in te

"**W**e'll be coming into Dearborn in about seven minutes, ma'am," Stan Tomaszewski said as he came back down the aisle. Catherine began to gather her things together, putting her unread book into her satchel and taking her coat down from the overhead rack.

She leaned back in her seat, waiting, and she felt a growing sense of anticipation that surprised her and made her realize that her love of adventure wasn't quite dead She watched out the window as the train passed the final neighborhoods of old frame houses and then roared behind the neat brick rows of stores on Michigan Avenue before pulling into the modern little station behind the Civic Center.

"You can pick up your baggage inside in a couple of minutes," said the conductor as she stepped off the train. He held out his hand to take her satchel as she came down the steps.

"Thank you."

"Say, miss, before you go. Is there one of them places where they say the Old Mass around here?" A wide smile spread across Catherine's face and her eyes danced.

"Yes," she answered. That's where I'm going. It's called Holy Martyrs. Are you familiar with the area?"

"Yup. My sister lives here."

"Well, it's in Dearborn."

"Whereabouts?"

"It's near Carlysle, I think."

29

"I'll find it."

"The pastor's name is Fr. Riley. I hope I'll see you there sometime."

"You can bet on it. What's your name, anyway, so's I can tell the priest when I call him?"

"Catherine Anderson."

"Glad to have met you, Mrs. Anderson. My name's Stan. Stan Tomaszewski. Wait'll I tell Stella."

"Good-bye, Mr. Tomaszewski. I'll see you later." Catherine started to walk away, but then stopped and waved to the silver haired conductor who returned the wave with a salute and slowly climbed back into the train.

"Catherine!" a woman's voice called to her. Catherine glanced toward the station, then ran up the steps.

"Mother!" She dropped her purse and satchel to the ground and held out her arms to the smiling lady with the onyx eyes who was hurrying toward her. Catherine was not tall, being just of medium height, but her mother-in-law barely came up to her chin.

"Oh, Catherine, it's so good of you to come!." There was a catch in her voice and she looked down quickly, blinking back tears. "I told Fr. Riley you would. When he said that he'd called and you were hesitant, I said, 'Give her a day or two, she'll come. She won't want to miss what's going on, not Catherine. She'll want to be a part of it.'"

Catherine laughed. "Thought you had it all figured out, didn't you?"

"Well, was I right?" Helen Anderson lifted her chin.

"Yes. Yes, you were."

"I knew it."

"It really wasn't a very difficult decision," Catherine said as she buttoned up her blue wool coat. "I thought of what I was doing at the college and then about what I could do at Holy Martyrs, and it just seemed that I should come, that I should teach here. The more I thought about it, the more I wanted to do it."

"I'm glad. It's nice having you here."

They walked together into the station to retrieve Catherine's luggage, and Mrs. Anderson bent down to pick up Catherine's bags.

"Now, Mother, don't do that. "

"I want to help."

"Well, then, take this," Catherine handed her the satchel and caught herself before she added, "It's not too heavy." Had she said that, Helen would have searched out the heaviest suitcase and insisted on carrying it. Mrs. Anderson shifted the padded strap and started toward the door with Catherine following in amusement. The older woman, still dark haired and with a quick graceful walk, reached the entrance and held the door open with her back as Catherine eased through it with her suitcases in tow.

"Is that all you brought?"

"I'm having some other things shipped after I get situated."

"What did you do about the house?" Helen asked as they walked toward the parking lot.

"I found a management company who would maintain it while I'm gone -- shovel the snow, make sure the pipes don't freeze, that sort of thing. I hope to go back in the summer for a couple of weeks."

"That would be nice," Helen nodded. "You wouldn't want to give it up completely."

"No. I really couldn't have. All my memories are there. In a way it seems like I can go back and relive them, step back in time for a little while and retrieve those days. It's probably silly, but I need solid things to touch and hold that reach back into the past."

"That's not silly at all. That's why souvenirs are so popular. Here's my car, the blue Lincoln," Mrs. Anderson said, pulling her keys out of her pocket. She opened the trunk and motioned for the suitcases. Catherine handed them to her one at a time, and her mother-in-law placed them neatly on the trunk floor and wedged the satchel in front of them, closing the door and slapping her hands of the lingering grime of winter.

They got into the car and fastened their seat belts. Mrs. Anderson took her driving glasses from a case clipped to the visor and slipped them on.

"I hate wearing these things. Dr. Smythe says I can't see well enough to drive without them," she complained as she started the car. "It seems to me that I can see perfectly well, but he said if I got in an accident and wasn't wearing them, I could get sued. So I guess I'd better wear them. At least I don't have cataracts. I still think he's wrong, though. He's young."

"It's probably better that you wear them. They look nice on you. "

Helen ignored the compliment. "Did you have lunch?"

"No, I just had some coffee on the train."

"Do you want to go to the club or to a restaurant?" Mrs. Anderson's favorite pastime was lunch at the Dearborn Country Club with her friends, followed by an afternoon of bridge. Catherine preferred coffee shops and she didn't play cards.

"I'd like to go to Leon's. Frank and I went there with some friends of his the last time we were in town. Would that be okay with you?"

"Leon's? Where's that?"

"Right down Michigan Avenue, toward Westborn."

"You want to eat there?"

"Yes, if you wouldn't mind too much." Catherine was sure that Mrs. Anderson minded very much indeed, but she couldn't face a country club lunch after her long trip. "I'm all wrinkled from the train and my hair is coming undone." She pulled at the long strands that were slipping out of the braid. "And I don't think denim and boots are all that suitable for the club, do you?"

Mrs. Anderson looked her over. "I guess you're right. You do look a bit dishevelled."

"Just off the range," Catherine said, poking her mother-in-law's arm affectionately. Mrs. Anderson clicked her tongue in maternal disapproval. It was, after all, a question of decorum, and Catherine was sometimes oblivious to the way things should be done. She was altogether too free and sometimes a bit careless. But at least this time she had the sense to realize that she wasn't properly dressed.

They pulled into the parking lot behind Leon's and parked the car. Catherine tried to smooth her hair while Mrs. Anderson took a mother-of-pearl compact from her purse and rechecked her makeup. She patted her nose with a little powder. "All set?" she asked.

"Yes."

Catherine held the door for Helen as they entered the restaurant which was bright and clean with a friendly hostess and a convivial atmosphere. Wide windows faced Michigan Avenue, and booths lined the walls. The rich smell of freshly brewed coffee and frying hamburger tantalized them as they waited for a seat.

Three young women at a center table surrounded by squirming toddlers in booster seats and high chairs caught Catherine's eye, and she looked at the children wistfully as the babies chortled and crushed their crackers on their trays. An exasperated mother tried to clean up the mess with a napkin, and the child started to scream, his face a brilliant red. Mrs. Anderson drew herself up straight as she followed the hostess to a booth by the window.

"Is this okay?" asked the hostess.

"Yes, this is fine," answered Mrs. Anderson, sliding gracefully into the booth. She put her purse on the bench at her side and picked up the large laminated menu. Catherine sat down across from her, struggling to remove her coat which was caught on the edge of the table. "What are you having?" asked Helen.

"Just a bagel and a fruit cup," answered Catherine.

"That's all?"

"It's Lent."

"Oh, that's right." Mrs. Anderson had been away from church so long that she had abandoned many of the customs and observances of her youth. When reminded of them, she began to feel guilty, even though for thirty years after the Second Vatican Council, it seemed that nobody cared about penance and sacrifice. It was only recently that Rome had begun to put an end to experimentation and "reform," and the thunderous voice of the strong new pope was echoing throughout the world.

"But you're exempt," Catherine said. "Remember?" Being over sixty, Mrs. Anderson was not obliged to fast but that didn't make her feel any better. She never appreciated being reminded of her age, especially if the reminder meant that there was something she couldn't do any longer. She bristled at the implication that she was old.

"I'll have what you're having."

Catherine smiled at her. The two women seemed so different, yet beneath the surface was a link of character that united them. It was more than the ties forged by the love of a mother for her dead son and a woman for her lost husband. There was a resoluteness about them, a thirst to do what was right, and a deep and steadfast courage. Neither one fainted at life.

"Anything to drink?" asked the sturdy middle-aged waitress who bustled from table to table.

"Tea, please," answered Mrs. Anderson.

"The same for me."

"Okay. I'll be right back with your drinks and take your order, ladies." She was back in a minute balancing a stainless steel teapot, two cups, and a plateful of white plastic half and half containers. She placed them deftly on the table and took their order, writing quickly, and hurrying off to the kitchen. Catherine blessed herself and said grace.

Mrs. Anderson wasn't used to seeing someone make the sign of the cross in public, and she dropped her eyes. "Did you have anything you wanted to do this afternoon, dear?" she asked as she stirred a little cream into her tea.

"No, not really, Mother. My head is still in kind of a whirl. I can't really believe I'm here."

Helen nodded. "It must seem quite strange. Starting all over again. And especially here where Frank grew up." Her firm mouth quivered slightly. Catherine looked at her mother-in-law across the table, meeting her eyes and holding them, feeling the older woman's pain. She reached for her hand and pressed it. Embarrassed, Helen withdrew her hand, and they drank their tea in silence.

The energetic waitress returned.

"Here you go, ladies, two bagels with cream cheese. All's we had was onion. Hope that's okay."

"My favorite," said Catherine.

"Be right back with the fruit. Sure that's all you want? Not much of a lunch. Hardly enough to keep up your strength, I'd say."

"It will be just fine, thank you," said Mrs. Anderson as she laid her napkin neatly across her lap.

Catherine giggled. "She's right. It is hardly enough to keep up your strength! Lent's tough."

Mrs. Anderson looked at her and sniffed. She disapproved of waitresses drawing attention to what one ate or didn't eat. She preferred that serving people be as unobtrusive as possible.

"Lighten up, Mom," Frank used to say. He was like Catherine, open and always interested in what people had to say. She supposed that was why he had become a journalist. Helen couldn't understand why he hadn't been more like his father. No one in the family had ever been a writer. He could have been an engineer, too, like Don, maybe even at Ford's, and he'd come home every night at six o'clock for dinner. He would have been safe.

She coughed to choke back the the sob that was welling in her throat. Catherine glanced up at her quickly. Helen took a small bite of her bagel and chewed it slowly, finally swallowing, while Catherine watched her questioningly.

"This is quite good, dear, don't you think?" Helen asked.

CHAPTER

4

Protector noster aspice, Deus
Et respice super servos tuos

"**I**'ve invited Fr. Riley over for dinner. I thought you'd want to see him," said Mrs. Anderson as they drove to her house in Dearborn Hills.

"Oh, yes, I do. "

"He's bringing a couple of people from the church whom he wanted you to meet, a Mr. and Mrs. Fortunata. Have you heard of them?"

"Yes, I know their daughter, Angelina. She's a good friend of mine. She lives in Colorado Springs and teaches at the community college there. We met at a seminar for English teachers several years ago. We try to get together whenever we can, which hasn't been too often lately."

"Is she married?"

"No, not yet."

"How old is she?"

"Angie's a few years younger than I am, twenty-seven or twenty-eight. She's been dating an Air Force captain who's stationed out there at Peterson. "

"Is it serious?"

"It could be."

Mrs. Anderson raised an eyebrow.

Catherine caught the question. "There are some problems."

"Oh?"

"First, she's not sure about the military life. She's a rather settled-in kind of person, and she's not really sure what it would

36

be like to be uprooted every few years. And he's definitely in the Air Force for the long haul. He lives to fly, I think. But she's scared, what with the world situation being like it is. It's so dangerous."

"She's wise to be cautious. She could be heading for some real heartbreak." Helen's hands tightened on the steering wheel.

Catherine looked out the side window as they drove west on Michigan toward Telegraph Road, the gray-brown wetness of early spring a blur before her. The two woman were silent, characters in a mournful drama that spanned the ages, women whose faces were marked and hearts torn by the loss of husbands and sons in the ferocity of war, wives and mothers whose tears laved the decades of their lives and who stood forever, one generation following another, as a testimony to the bitter consequences of rapacious pride and the unrepented sins of nations.

They knew what Angelina faced.

"What does he do in the Air Force?" Helen asked, breaking the silence.

"He flies X-182's."

"Oh, my. Aren't those the new fighter jets?"

Catherine nodded. "They first were flown in '97, I think."

Helen pulled to a stop at a red light and turned and faced her daughter-in-law while she waited for the signal. "What does this fellow say about our getting more involved in the war?"

"He thinks it's inevitable. It's impossible to maintain peace. The conflict is too diffuse. Between the radical Muslims and the *Vox Populi*..." Catherine's voice trailed off.

"Are those the Communists?" Helen didn't follow the news.

"Yes."

"I thought so."

"But they don't like to be called Communists."

"Whether they like it or not, that's what they are," Helen said. "Anyway, you were saying?"

"It's just that our troops are paralyzed by the rules laid

37

down by the U.N. -- humanitarian aid only while they shoot down our planes and bomb our hospitals and barracks --I mean, this has been going on for years, and it just makes our people ready targets.

"Remember how everyone said it would be another Vietnam if we got involved in the conflict? It's turning out that way. We've already lost over three thousand people. We're going to have to do one thing or the other -- declare war or come home. The Air Force is on alert again.

" Rick -- that's his name, Rick Woodward -- just got back from Germany in November, and we had gotten together a few times before Frank left himself. They understood the war better than I do and they knew the history behind all the factions in Eastern Europe and the Balkans. Myself, I had trouble keeping the countries straight. They change names and governments every time you turn around. Anyway, it was fascinating to hear them talk, but really frightening. Frank said General MacArthur had it right."

"General MacArthur? Douglas MacArthur? From World War II?"

"Yes. And Korea."

"He's the one who got in trouble with Truman, wasn't he?

"Yes. It was the same sort of thing. Men having to fight with their arms tied behind their backs. But the important thing was, apparently MacArthur said the problem was theological. That's what Frank meant. "

"What?" Mrs. Anderson was confused. She had been following the conversation up to that point. Now she was lost. Helen wasn't sure she would ever understand her daughter-in-law. Catherine was always saying something incomprehensible.

"When man abandons God, when first principles are ignored, when there is no adherence to the natural law, much less the divine law, war is inevitable. You can't have worldwide abortion and homosexuality, divorce, atheism, aggressive naturalism, and hope that people can get along by some sort of magical bonding.

There is no solution but a return to true morality and true faith. Frank always said that no peace is possible until there is a return to a Christian social order, until Christ is acknowledged as King over nations and peoples. And even then, there's still man's fallen nature to contend with."

"Oh." Mrs. Anderson wasn't sure what to say. She wasn't accustomed to thinking so deeply, but she was intrigued by Catherine's passionate explanation and would ask her about it more, later. Driving down Telegraph Road wasn't really a good time.

"Well, your friend will have to decide whether she's brave enough to marry somebody who's in the military."

"Yes." Catherine hesitated before saying anything further, then decided to go ahead. "But there's another problem, too, which is more serious as far as she's concerned."

"What's that?"

"He's not a practicing Catholic," she said as gently as she could to her mother-in-law who had stayed away from church herself for thirty years.

"That's not necessarily a hopeless situation," Helen said, drily.

"No, but it's different than it was with you."

"Stubborness doesn't differ that much from one person to another."

Helen turned into the driveway of her stately red brick colonial on South Highland and stopped to let Catherine out before she pulled the car into the garage behind the house. She opened the trunk latch and Catherine unloaded her luggage onto the driveway.

She stood waiting, looking at the well-kept front lawn with the crisp edging and the two-foot wide flower beds lining the sidewalk up to the front porch, the brown dirt punctuated by the waxy green blades of hyacinths pushing up through the thawing soil. It was warmer than it had been in Chicago, and Catherine looked up at the sky to let the breaking sun shine on her face.

Carefully trimmed box yews were in a neat row under the twin bow windows on either side of the front door, the living room on one side, the dining room on the other. A cardinal darted across the lawn to the blue spruce on the far side of the driveway, and a slow fat robin, colorless in comparison, poked its way across the grass. As Helen closed the garage door, Catherine picked up her luggage and walked toward the back of the house. She wanted to enter through the kitchen, like always.

They went in the back door and up the four steps into the big square kitchen. The room was bright and cheery. There was a garden window over the sink lined with small pots of basil and chives and mint. It was just like Catherine remembered. Nothing had changed. There was a window to the side hung with white eyelet curtains that Helen opened an inch.

"I want to smell the spring while I cook," she said.

The walls beneath and above the solid oak cabinets were papered in a small English print, and a heavy wood table with ladder back chairs graced the center of the room. Helen went to the closet to hang up her coat and put her purse on the shelf.

"Why don't you go upstairs and rest for awhile?" she asked.

"Thanks. I will. If you're sure you don't need me?"

"No, go on. You look exhausted."

"I am kind of tired. And I could use some freshening up. I feel like I've come across the country in a wagon train."

"Fine, dear," said Mrs. Anderson, not really listening. She was tying on her apron as she bustled across the room to the sink to wash her hands.

"Everything is laid out in the blue room."

The upstairs guest bedroom overlooking the backyard was where Catherine and Frank always stayed when they visited his parents. An antique cherry four poster bed with a hand crotcheted canopy dominated the room. Two identical brass and crystal lamps, shaded in fluted ivory linen, stood on the matching night tables. A reading chair with a needlepoint covered footstool was in the corner, a floor lamp on one side and a flourishing anchromeda on the other.

Catherine put her luggage down by the door and walked over to the double-hung windows along the back wall. She pulled back the wedgewood blue curtain and looked outside. An arborvitae hedge wrapped around the borders of the yard, turning it into a private retreat and providing a soothing stroke of green against the gray sky and brown grass.

She unbraided her hair and ran her fingers through it, loosening the long auburn waves and tossing them free. She glanced around the room. Thick towels and washcloths were stacked neatly on the Queen Anne bureau and a heavy cranberry colored terry cloth robe was hanging from a hook on the back of the bedroom door. Mrs. Anderson had set a vase full of hothouse daisies on the writing desk, and Catherine walked over to them and fingered the yellow and white petals.

Frank had always brought her daisies. They were her favorite.

CHAPTER

5

Dicite: Pusillanimes confortamini
Et nolite timere
Ecce Deus noster veniet et salvabit nos

Catherine came downstairs that evening wearing a pleated skirt and wool sweater over a white cotton blouse. She had exchanged her boots for leather pumps, and her hair was pulled back in a neat French twist, the heavy waves secured with tortoiseshell combs. She could hear Helen singing in the kitchen. She went to join her.

"Smells good."

"Does it? You can't really tell from in here. You have to go outside and come back in again to notice. I thought roast chicken would be nice. It's still a bit nippy out."

"Sounds great. May I peek?" Not waiting for an answer, Catherine opened the oven door on the three well-stuffed chickens, golden-brown and crackling in a roasting pan . "They look perfect. Anything I can do?"

"Do you want to peel the potatoes while I set the table?"

"Sure."

In the pale rose dining room, Mrs. Anderson draped white damask over the long mahogany table and set out her best china and crystal. She went to get the flatware out of the silver drawer, flicking a piece of lint off the top of the sideboard as she walked by.

"Helen, I'm home!" Don Anderson called as he came through the front door. Mrs. Anderson hurried to greet him, smoothing her apron and patting her hair. He bent down and kissed her cheek affectionately.   As they came into the kitchen, Catherine turned from the sink where she had just dropped the last of the potatoes into a pan of cold water.

"Catherine!"

He reached out to take both her hands and stood looking down at her. He had been pleased when Frank married the young woman from the West. Things were never dull when Catherine was around.

"When did you get here?"

"Just a couple of hours ago."

"Well , that's fine." He looked through the kitchen door into the dining room. "More company?"

"Yes, I called you earlier to let you know, but your secretary said you were going to be out at the plant all day. Fr. Riley is coming for dinner and he's bringing two other people from the church."

"Anybody we know?"

"No, but Catherine knows their daughter."

"Well, I'll leave you ladies to your preparations," he said as he ambled toward the door.

Don Anderson was uncomfortable in kitchens. Machines, tools, and engines were much more to his liking. He crossed the hall to the den, hung his jacket on the door knob, and took off his shoes. Helen had laid the *Detroit News* on the desk and he took it and settled into his red leather recliner, opening the paper to the sports page.

The doorbell rang as the walnut grandfather clock in the hallway chimed seven.   Mr. Anderson went to answer the door.

"Come in, come in. Good evening, Father." Don Anderrson had trouble calling the priest *Father*. He had known Thomas Aquinas Riley since he was seven years old, and he would always be *Tommy* to him, Frank's best friend from across the street. Besides, Don was not a Catholic; he had a trace of Presbyterian repugnance toward the title, which he tried to swallow because he didn't want to feel that way. He used to have a lot of respect for his wife's religion. During the early years of his marriage, he had sometimes wished he could have been born Catholic himself and wondered if he should look into it further.

But when the changes came -- the guitars and commotion and, most of all, the unrelenting silliness -- he was repelled by the banality and unseemliness of it. He thought it was more like a junior high school talent show than worship.

The mystery and sacredness, the majesty of the Mass, that had appealed to him were gone. He lost the attraction and put it out of his mind. Now things seemed to be changing again. He'd have to think about that.

"Hello, Mr. Anderson," the priest said, grasping Don's hand firmly. Frank's parents were like second parents to Fr. Riley. He and Frank had spent their childhood going back and forth between their two houses, camping out in each other's backyards and shooting baskets in the driveway. All through school, they had studied together, first at one kitchen table, then the other. He felt especially close to the Andersons now that his own mother and father had both died.

"I want you to meet some friends of mine," he said. "Vito and Teresa Fortunata."

Don Anderson extended his hand in greeting. "How do you do? Here, let me take your coats."

Teresa Fortunata, dressed in a checkered black dress with a starched white collar, her wiry gray hair parted in the middle and pulled back in a bun, returned the greeting with a wide Sicilian smile that spoke of lush vineyards and green meadows and warm salty air. She was quiet by nature but she always liked to meet new people and hear them talk. Her husband, on the other hand, was not looking forward to this evening with strangers.

Vito Fortunata was ill at ease. His blue serge suitcoat was tight across his shoulders, and he had already loosened his tie. Vito's forehead was damp, and he wiped the back of his hand across it. Teresa looked at him sympathetically. She could tell what he was thinking, but she wasn't worried. He would enjoy himself once he relaxed a little. People liked him. There was no man on God's earth like Vito Fortunata, she thought. He had worked hard all his life and only missed work once when Nick, their middle son, was in the hospital with a ruptured appendix, and they thought he was going to die. Teresa moved closer to him and slipped her arm under his. Her gold mother's ring with five birthstones, one for each child, caught the light from the chandelier. Vito patted her hand.

As Don was ushering his guests into the living room, Catherine came flying through the door.

"Fr. Riley!" she came toward him holding out her hand, delighted to see him, her green eyes merry.

"Catherine." He took her hand and clasped it firmly, releasing it to introduce her to the Fortunatas.

"I'm so happy to meet you both," she said. "I almost feel like I know you already. Angie has told me so much about you."

Teresa inspected her daughter's friend and was satisfied. She nodded at her. "Angelina talks about you all the time. Says you're a teacher, too."

"Yes, another English teacher," said Catherine. "Would you like to come back into the kitchen with us? My mother-in-law is stuck at the stove."

"Sure." There was nothing Teresa would have liked better. She wasn't much one for living rooms. She followed Catherine down the hall.

Don Anderson turned to Vito, "Are you a Pistons fan?" Vito looked at his host, surprised. That wasn't what he expected. He was afraid they would be sitting around discussing golf scores or the stock market and Vito didn't play either one. The tension left his face and he relaxed.

"Yeah, I try to catch the games. They got a pretty good offense this year finally. Thought they'd never get it together."

45

"Once they got rid of that showboat Gonzales..."

"Yeah, that was the key. That new coach, Harris, worked out real good too. Pulled it together."

"They're a team again. You can't get anywhere if you just have a bunch of individuals out there grandstanding. Say, Father, would you mind..." Don looked back at the priest. "I've got the tape of the Chicago game. One of the guys at work taped it. We can watch some of it while the girls are finishing up the dinner. We'll stay out of their way."

"Go right ahead. I heard about the tight finish," answered the former athlete as he and Vito followed their host through the French doors into the den.

Helen Anderson turned as Catherine and Teresa came into the kitchen. "Oh, hello, I'll be just a second," she said, scooping the stuffing from the chickens. She quickly covered the large bowl with aluminum foil and put it into the oven to keep warm, then walked foward to greet Teresa.

"Mother, this is Teresa Fortunata, Angelina's mother. Mrs. Fortunata, my mother-in-law, Helen Anderson."

"Glad to meet you, Mrs. Anderson."

"Please call me Helen."

Teresa glanced around the well-appointed kitchen. "Is there anything I can do?" she asked. Mrs. Anderson was about to say that she had everything under control, but she caught her guest's hopeful smile and reconsidered.

"Yes, another pair of hands are always welcome. Catherine, would you hand Teresa an apron, please?" Catherine went to the drawer for the apron, and Mrs. Fortunata happily pulled it over her head and tied it in the back around her plump waist.

"There. All set. Now, what do you want me to do?"

"Would you stir the gravy? I don't think it's thick enough, either."

Teresa picked up the whisk lying by the side of the stove and ran it through the golden brown gravy. "It could be a little thicker."

Mrs. Anderson was carving the chickens, and she pointed with the knife.

"The flour's in that cannister." Teresa picked up the measuring cup on the counter and expertly mixed some flour and water, stirring the mixture into the bubbling gravy until it was smooth and thick. Catherine was pouring the wine. The three spoke little as they worked, caught in that peculiar tension that women feel as they attend to the last details of a company dinner. Mrs. Anderson dried her hands on a paper towel and hung up her apron. "Let's call the men."

"In nomine Patris et Filii et Spiritus Sancti..." intoned Fr. Riley as they stood behind their chairs in the dining room for the blessing. Candles in the wall sconces, on the sideboard, and in tall brass candleholders on the table were burning and cast a shimmering light on their faces. The table was heavy with food -- platters of chicken and bowls of potatoes, stuffing and steaming beans. Hot crescent rolls, the smell of yeast lingering, were in two baskets, wrapped in linen napkins.

It was a pleasant evening with talk of families and jobs and spring gardens. Vito Fortunata was a former auto worker, who had retired after thirty years at Chevrolet; and he and Don had a good natured debate about the relative merits of General Motors and Ford cars.

"What do you do now since your retirement, Vito?" asked Helen .

"Father's been keeping me busy the last five years. I've been an amateur carpenter all my life. I like working with wood, making things..." He held his big square hands up in front of him as though he were holding a smooth piece of wood. There was the grace of an artisan in the gesture.

"He made my new kitchen cabinets," Teresa said proudly to Helen.

"Yeah, that was some job. She was hanging over my shoulder the whole time. Worst boss I ever had."

"Oh, you. Come on!" Teresa elbowed him. "Don't lie."

"Anyhow, Father's got me working at the school. The building's getting pretty old and it was kind of run down. There were lots of things that needed fixing."

Vito lifted his coffee cup and tilted back slightly in his chair, his shirt buttons straining at the middle. "Now, Father, here, he's a good boss, cuts you some slack." He smiled broadly and his white teeth gleamed against his olive skin.

"That's because I know I can always get Teresa after you if I have to," answered Fr. Riley. Teresa enjoyed the gentle teasing as she sipped her wine.

"You'll like it at Holy Martyrs," Vito said to Catherine. "Those kids are real nice. Father's got 'em all whipped into shape."

"They're pretty well behaved. The teachers are doing a good job. But there's still plenty of mischief in them and some rough edges."

"That's 'cause they're kids," said Vito.

Fr. Riley shrugged his shoulders. It was more than that. He was concerned about a brittle attitude, a hardness of heart, that he sometimes sensed in some of the older students, and he wondered what to do about it. That was one of the reasons he had wanted Catherine to come to Dearborn. He hoped she could get through to them. She was kind, but she wouldn't put up with any shenanigans. He relaxed a little as he thought about it.

But the thing was, there were other problems that worried him. Problems that had very serious ramifications for the school and the church. He was handling them alone. He hadn't told anyone downtown yet, at the Chancery, because there were people there he didn't trust. People who hated him. He leaned forward slightly, his left elbow on the table, and cupped his chin in his hand, thinking, his thumb and fingers pressed against his jaw to ease the tension.

"How many students are there, Father?" asked Helen.

Fr. Riley was startled out of his troubled thoughts, and he sat back up abruptly, dropping his arm to his lap.

"We have ninety-seven. A good start. When we first opened, we had seventeen, six from one family."

"How long have you been open now, Father?" asked Don.

"This is our fourth year."

"How many teachers?" Catherine wanted to know.

"Five. Two for the elementary -- Judy Long and Barbara Clark. It gets a little hectic, sometimes, but they keep it under control. Then there are three high school teachers -- Mr. Corwin teaches science and math. He's an engineer like you, Mr. Anderson -- retired from Boeing out in California. Miss Stevens -- she just graduated last year from Christendom College -- teaches history, geography, and art. I handle religion and Latin, and Catherine, here, will take over the English classes as well as being principal. She'll be running the show."

Catherine blushed and dropped her eyes.

"Who has been teaching English?" asked Helen.

"A Mrs. Carruthers. That's a long story."

"What happened?" Mrs. Anderson was curious.

"I had to let her go in February."

"Why?"

Fr. Riley wished the subject hadn't come up. He chose his words carefully. "Well, she seemed to be a pretty good teacher at first. She was enthusiastic and seemed very knowledgeable. But she had a way of undermining the discipline of the school that was disturbing. She would collude with the students against the rest of the teachers. It was kind of odd. A very difficult situation."

Fr. Riley laid down his fork. They were all turned to him, waiting for him to go on. He really didn't want to talk about it.

"It got to the point where everyone could sense an undercurrent of resentment, rebellion even, and it took me awhile to figure out where it was coming from. A couple of teachers came to me -- separately, actually, and unknown to each other -- and laid out what was going on. I felt rather a fool for not having noticed.   So, belatedly, I started watching and listening."

Patricia Carruthers was a fifty-three year old grandmother from Beverly Hills with thirty years of teaching in parochial schools, married to a dentist, she had said. She told Fr. Riley that she wanted to come to Holy Martyrs from Bishop Foley because she wanted to teach in a traditional school. She held a master's degree in English literature from Marygrove and came well recommended.

At first, Fr. Riley thought she was a good teacher. But things were not what they seemed. She was a clever manipulator. And worse.   Fr. Riley took a deep breath. The muscles in his stomach tightened.   There was more, but he couldn't talk about it openly. He would have to tell Catherine later. As principal, there were things she would need to know. He wondered what she would think.

"So, to make a long story short, I let her go and then I called Catherine."

"What would you have done if she hadn't come?" asked Mrs. Anderson.

"The thought never entered my mind. I entrusted the whole thing to Our Lady. She never lets me down. And I didn't think Catherine would, either. " He tried to keep his voice light.

"No," answered Don Anderson, "she wouldn't. We're glad you called her. It's nice to have our girl here."

"Thanks, Dad," said Catherine softly.   "It's good to be here."

"Now, I got something for you to do, Catherine," said Vito, nestling his coffee cup in the palm of his hand. "You get on that phone and call Angie and tell her to come, too."

"There's nothing I would like better, Mr. Fortunata. Do you think it would work?" she asked with mock seriousness.

"Not so long as that fly-boy is out there," he answered.

"Angelina called this morning," Teresa said quietly.

"You didn't tell me."

"You were working. I was going to tell you later."

"What'd she say?"

"She said Rick..."

"The flyboy," interrupted Vito.

"...was being sent back overseas. He leaves next week for Belgium. She was pretty upset."

"She should be," said her father.

"Yes," said Don, "it's bad over there. Gets worse every day. We're heading for World War III, that's for sure."

"Yeah," said Vito. "You're right. Did you hear what they're doing in Italy?" Vito asked.

"No, what?" Catherine answered.

"Well, you know they've been in that depression the last three years and the drought last summer didn't help anything. So they declared some kind of emergency and they're starting to confiscate church property."

"What?" Helen looked at him in surprise.

"Yes, it's true," Father Riley said gravely.

Vito ran his fingers through his hair. "Yeah, I found out from my cousin. He's some kind of councilman in Palermo. He said the government's getting the people all worked up." Vito thrust his chest forward, put his hand over his heart, and imitated the *Vox Populi* politicians.

"'This country can no longer tolerate the massing of treasure and the hoarding of resources which belong to the people,'" he said pompously. "'The people have a right to eat and to enjoy the fruits of their forefathers' labors.'" Teresa stifled a laugh, and Vito picked up a roll, buttering it while he talked.

"What it boils down to is, they're raiding the churches and taking whatever gold and stuff is left and putting it in the national treasury. 'Course the people never see any benefit from the robbery, just the fat cats, like always."

"What is the Church doing about it?" Helen asked.

"Unfortunately, there is not too much they can do, " answered Fr. Riley soberly. "They arrest anyone who protests."

51

"Arrest them for what?" asked Don.

"Treason."

"Treason!" Catherine was shocked.

"Yes, for obstructing the will of the people. And the penalty for that, of course, is death."

"Oh, dear God," said Helen.

"Has anyone been arrested?" asked Catherine.

"Yes." Father Riley tightened his jaw. "Fr. John Boccatello," a classmate of mine from the seminary. And Bishop Stephano Andreoni of Milan. They have been confined without recourse to counsel."

"How can they justify that?" asked Don Anderson.

"They don't even try," answered the priest. "It's a revolution and they know the people are behind them."

"How can that be?" asked Helen.

"They're hungry and looking for somebody to blame," said Fr. Riley somberly. "Holy Mother Church is it. They want to destroy Her."

Like always, he thought, recalling St. Augustine. Two cities in this world. Two universal societies -- the City of God and the City of the Devil -- with boundaries never to be joined, locked in perpetual opposition, moving toward the climactic final battle when the City of God would shout in majestic triumph, evil vanquished forever. When? he wondered. Just how close are we? And he pondered in his mind the prophecies of the time of tribulation, the time of sorrows.

The rest of the dinner passed quickly. They spoke little, unable to shake the sense of impending violence and upheaval. It had all been brought so much closer. An icy foreboding gripped them. Frank's death. Rick's orders to Europe. The arrest of Fr. Riley's former classmate and friend. The bishop in handcuffs and shackles like St. Peter in chains. The world rocked on its axis. And they knew that the quiet days and pleasant duties, the civility they had taken for granted, were ending.

The European terror had crept into the dining room

The hall clock struck ten as the women finished clearing the table. Don Anderson went to the closet for his guests' coats.

"Say, Don," said Vito as he held his wife's brown tweed coat behind her, "How about coming out to breakfast with us after Mass Sunday?"

Helen caught her breath. The Fortunatas assumed Don was a Catholic. Nothing had been said during dinner to indicate otherwise. But Don hadn't been to a Sunday Mass since that day in the sixties when they brought in the table and the guitar playing nuns in miniskirts. Helen tried to catch her husband's eye but he had turned toward Vito.

"Now that sounds like a good idea," Don said affably. Catherine had come up next to Helen and they looked at each other, eyebrows raised.

"Good. After the ten o'clock? Then maybe Father here can join us. What do you say, Father? Are you free?"

"I'd like to come, Vito, but we're going to be having a visiting priest from the archdiocese. I don't know when he's coming."

"Bring him, too," said Theresa.

"Thanks, both of you. Let me check and see just what's going on. I'll let you know."

"Fine. Sounds good."

Vito turned to Don and shook his hand with the firm grip of a man who has worked with his hands all his life. "Thanks for inviting us. That was some dinner, Helen. We enjoyed it." He bowed his head slightly toward her, and she returned the gesture with a slight nod.

"You're very welcome," she said graciously. "I'm so glad that you could come." She turned to Teresa. "We'll have to get together more often."

Teresa smiled her wide warm smile. "Yes, that'd be nice." She buttoned her coat. "Well, we'll see you Sunday. Thanks again."

Fr. Riley waited for a moment as the Fortunatas went out the door. "They're good people," he said.

"Yes," said Catherine.

"I like them," said Don.

"I thought you would. Thank you both. It was a nice evening. Mrs. Anderson, you're as good a cook as my mother was. That was a *tour de force.*"

Mrs. Anderson's cheeks reddened. "Oh, it was just chicken. Good night, Father."

"Good night. God bless you all. See you Sunday, Mr. Anderson," he called back with a challenge in his voice as he walked toward the car.

CHAPTER

6

Exsurge, Domine
Adjuva nos, et libera nos

It was a sunny Thursday morning, and the yellow forsythia bloomed by the back door. The thick smell of soft earth and wet grass rose from the ground. Helen and Catherine came down the steps, missals in hand. Catherine had draped her mantilla over her shoulders like a scarf and she waited while Helen pulled the car out of the garage. She was looking forward to her first day at Holy Martyrs and was surprised that she was so excited. She felt alive and eager to get to work. Standing by the driveway, she looked up at the gray sky turning blue as the sun began to rise like a burnished coin over the trees and houses.

She could hardly wait to get to school.

The drive to the church was slow, the roads clogged with carloads of people hurrying to work. Catherine watched them as they darted in and out of traffic, pulling close to the cars ahead, honking their horns loudly and slamming on their brakes.

So much intensity, she thought. So much aggression. It seemed that the country had turned into nothing more than a giant economic machine, grinding out profit and loss statements. Companies closing down, moving out, casting the workers in the streets. Unremitting anxiety in the workplace. And the people drove themselves harder and harder to assuage their insecurity, their fear, desperate to keep their place above the red line.

What has happened to America? she wondered as a black sports car pulled abruptly in front of them, cutting them off.

Helen braked hard to avoid hitting it.

"Did you see that?" she exclaimed, her hands shaking on the steering wheel.

They arrived at Holy Martyrs. Catherine lifted her mantilla over her head as she got out of the car and looked over at the school. It was a solid one storey red brick building. The east windows shone in the morning sun. Everything was neat. The foundation beds. The little yard leading to the concrete parking lot. The playing field on the far side of the grounds. All in order. The wind picked up slightly and Catherine caught the edges of her mantilla as it slid off her head. Behind her, Helen reached up and pulled it back up over her hair.

They entered the quiet church. The children had not yet come in. The sanctuary lamp was lit over the altar signalling the presence of the Blessed Sacrament, and the morning sun streamed through the stained glass windows, casting a kaleidoscope of color on the floor between the pews. White-gold flames from the votive candles flickered in front of the side altars and shone on the marble faces of Mary and St. Joseph in the alcoves above.

A small altar boy in black cassock and white surplice came through the sacristy door bringing the cruets of water and wine. He placed them carefully on the credence table, genuflected, and swiftly, quietly, left again, returning in a moment's time to light the candles. Catherine came up the center aisle and looked at the life-sized crucifix hanging above the altar. My God, I love You , she whispered, as her eyes fell to the gilded tabernacle below the image of God Crucified.

"*Dominus meus et deus meus,*" she prayed, dropping her right knee to the floor, bowing her head, and making the sign of the cross. She rose and entered the pew, leaving room for Helen, who rested one hand on the wooden back for balance, genflected, then slipped into the pew and knelt beside Catherine . Their shoulders straight and unmoving and their hands folded, they prepared themselves for the ancient mysteries.

They would walk the road to Calvary and kneel once more at the foot of the Cross, their hearts joined with the hearts of all who walked this road before, reaching back in time to Golgotha, and to the heart of the Blessed Mother.

Two boys in navy blue pants and white shirts straightened their ties and opened the double doors at the back of the church. They stood like sentries as the lines of uniformed students filed in noiselessly. They stood waiting until they heard a sharp handclap behind them, then bent their knee before the Divine Saviour present on the altar. In their pews, they knelt without squirming as they waited for Mass to begin.

The first and second graders opened their illustrated Mass books and quietly looked at the pictures. Behind them, the older students marked the pages of their missals with ribbons. The teachers took their places at the ends of the pews, the last students sliding over to make room. Several more parishioners dotted the seats at the back. There was not a sound in the church.

A bell rang from outside the sanctuary door and the two altar boys came in, their faces scrubbed and hair neat, palms pressed together and fingers pointing to heaven. The second boy dipped his fingers into the holy water fount and reached out his hand to touch the tips of the priest's fingers, offering him the holy water, then blessed himself.

Clad in the purple vestments of Lent, Fr. Riley went to the foot of the altar and handed his biretta to the server. The young boy put it down then came back to kneel beside the priest. Bowing, Fr. Riley made the sign of the cross, then joined his hands before his breast.

"*Introibo ad altare Dei.*"

"*Ad Deum qui laetificat juventutem meam,*" answered the acolytes.

The Holy Sacrifice had begun.

After Mass Helen stopped to talk with a small group of women outside the church, and Catherine walked over to the school. She went in the side door and walked down the long hall to the office where she waited for Fr. Riley.

"Good morning, Catherine," he said as she rose when he came through the door. "Please..." He motioned for her to sit behind her new desk. Fr. Riley took the visitor's chair. "Well, this is it. Do you think you'll be ready to start tomorrow?"

"Yes, that's no problem."

"Good." He opened a file folder and laid it on the desk. "Let's go over some of the administrative details, and then we can go down to the teacher's lounge so you can have a cup of coffee and meet some of the others."

"Sounds good."

They spent the next hour reviewing the school curriculum, enrollment, and schedules. Fr. Riley gave her the keys to the school and a stack of lists that Mrs. Janis, the secretary, had prepared. Catherine scanned the inventory of school supplies, books, and reference materials, jotting notes in the margins, as Fr. Riley outlined the school day for her. Closing his folder, he looked at his watch.

"That's enough paperwork for now, I think." Catherine stacked the papers into a neat pile and slid them into an empty folder lying on the desk. Fr. Riley buzzed the secretary on the intercom.

"Mrs. Janis. "

"Yes, Father."

"Could you and Miss Stevens come down to the teachers' lounge? And would you ask Annie Whittaker to watch her class for her when she leaves?"

"Yes, Father. But Mrs. Wasniak is here right now going over the plans for the reception after the concert. We're just finishing up. We should be done in about twenty minutes."

"That will be fine."

58

Fr. Riley and Catherine walked along the quiet corridor to the teacher's lounge. Catherine peeked into the classrooms as they passed them. The desks were in straight rows, and there were walnut bookshelves beneath the windows which ran the length of each room. The Venetian blinds were open and pulled up halfway. Purple bordered bulletin boards were filled with school papers. Over each blackboard was a carved wooden crucifix; and in the corner of each room on a little wall shelf was a small plaster statue of the Blessed Virgin Mary.

As they passed one of the rooms in the high school wing, Catherine saw a tall gangly boy rise to recite. He stopped speaking to stare as she and the priest walked by the open door. His look made her uncomfortable, and she was glad when they had passed the room..

The small teacher's lounge was at the end of the hall. A red checked vinyl table cloth covered an eight foot banquet table in the center. An electric coffeepot perked gently, and the nutty aroma filled the room and wafted down the hall.

"Shall I pour the coffee, Father?"

"Yes, please," he answered. Catherine walked over to the counter, and Fr. Riley pulled out the folding metal chairs.

There was a vase of Shasta daisies by the coffeepot. She was startled to see them there. She lifted a drooping petal with her index finger. Daisies. Just like at the Andersons'. It made her feel like Frank was near, letting her know by the flowers that he was watching over her. She knew she was being silly, but she shivered as she poured the coffee, trying not to spill it. Her hands shook a little as she carried the cups to the table.

"What do you think?" he asked.

"Everything seems fine," she said, passing the sugar bowl to him. "I'm anxious to look through it more this evening. The curriculum looks good. Well balanced."

"Yes..." He paused. "Catherine, I need to go over some things with you."

Catherine looked at him. He seemed tense, tired. The

59

cheerful expression he usually wore had collapsed around his mouth and eyes. She had never noticed the lines in his forehead before or the pallor of his skin. He had always seemed so young and vigorous.

"Some things have come to light since I called you and asked you to come. I probably should have let you know right away, but things were pretty unsettled, and I wasn't sure. So." He looked down at his hands.

"What is it, Father?" Catherine asked.

"There's something going on, and I don't like it. But I don't really know what it is. How's that for an explanation?"

"In the school?"

"Yes. Remember the teacher I was telling you about? Mrs. Carruthers?"

"The one you had to let go."

"That's the one. Married to the dentist. Taught at Bishop Foley." He rubbed his forehead. "This is going to sound pretty farfetched..."

"Tell me. Nothing surprises me any more."

"Her name wasn't Mrs. Carruthers, and she wasn't married, and she never taught at Bishop Foley. The references she brought were fake."

Catherine was puzzled. "Didn't you check them?"

"Yes. I called. Everything seemed fine."

"Now you're confusing me."

"She was sent here. It was a set-up."

Catherine drew in her breath.

"I'd prefer that no one else know about this yet. Like I said, I'm not sure what it's all about." He looked out the window. "She was a nun."

"A nun? What in the world...?"

"From the education office downtown. Administrative assistant to the director of parish schools. Sister Agnes Hopaluk."

"Why?"

"Same reason as always. They want to destroy the

Church."

"But Archbishop Stagniak..."

"Archbishop Stagniak doesn't have many friends."

"So she was sent here to undermine what you're doing."

"Exactly."

"And then that would prove that what you're trying to do is impossible."

"Right."

"And it would prove that Tradition is unworkable, dead, and they would force the Archbishop to back down."

Fr. Riley relaxed. He had been concerned that he was over-reacting and that his emotions were getting the better of him. But Catherine was reaching the same conclusions that he had.

"How did you ever find out?"

"A few days ago, the day before you got here, in fact, Mrs. Whittaker came to see me. She has a grand-daughter in the school. Annie. Well, anyway, she came to my office and pounded on the door. She was pretty agitated. At first I thought there was an emergency, that someone was dying. I couldn't believe what she told me.

Mrs. Whittaker's face was flushed, and small beads of perspiration glistened on her forehead. She tucked a stray strand of hair behind her ear and came nervously into the office.

"Father Riley, I have to talk to you," she said.

"Hello, Mrs. Whittaker. How are you?"

"Not good, Father. Not good. Things are weird." She sat down and put her purse on her lap holding the strap with both hands, pulling it along her palms. She jiggled her feet and the purse bobbed up and down on her legs.

Fr. Riley sat quietly waiting for her to tell him what was the matter.

She stopped pulling on her purse strap and began to finger the button on her coat. "Do you want to know what happened?"

she asked finally.

"Yes. What happened?"

"Remember a couple of weeks ago when I was sick I told you Mary Ann was coming?"

Mary Ann was her youngest daughter, a nun in Columbus, Ohio. She didn't come often. Mrs. Whittaker's old-fashioned beliefs infuriated her, and she stayed away as much as she could. Sister Mary Ann was the pastoral administrator at St. Andrew's Worship and Community Center.

The church had been featured in *Architectural Digest* in 1999 and had won the Franklin Hodges Centennial Award for innovative design. Mary Ann had overseen the construction. The building was a cavernous structure of coarse white concrete and glass; and gaping skylights cut a circular pattern through the shake shingled roof.

The walls of St. Andrew's rocked with loud music and extemporaneous prayer; and the priest, who preferred to be called the minister of the eucharist, came once a week to celebrate the communal meal and share his thoughts on peace and love and the brotherhood of all men. He roamed the aisles during the "Kiss of Peace," laughing, hugging , and building community among the People of God.

When Mrs. Whittaker suffered a gall bladder attack and had to be hospitalized, Mary Ann reluctantly tore herself away from St. Andrew's and stayed in Dearborn until her mother was discharged from Providence Hospital. When Mary Ann picked her up, Mrs. Whittaker wanted to stop at the church on the way home.

Mrs. Whittaker paused in her story to unbutton her coat. "So, Father, when I said I wanted to make a visit, she says in this real cold way, 'Oh, all right. I'll wait in the car.' But I said, 'Come on in, it won't kill you.'

"Well you should have seen her face! You'd think I was torturing her. Anyway we went in so I could light a candle and she waited at the back. There were a couple of students in there and then one of the teachers came in to get them. I was all by myself. But, I didn't stay too long, you know..."

"No."

"I didn't want to get her upset. But, what's to get upset about? Anyway, we went back out to the car, and she about roared out of that parking lot.

"I was pretty nervous; I'd never seen her drive like that. 'Mary Ann!' I said. 'What are you doing? Slow down!'

"She stopped real hard at the corner and turned and glared at me. Oh, Father..." Mrs. Whittaker was starting to cry. She pulled a crumpled handkerchief out of her pocket and dabbed her eyes.

"Are you all right?"

"Yes. Oh, Father, you should have seen the look in her eyes. It was awful. Like hate. My own little girl. I couldn't figure out what was going on. I mean, I know she hates the Old Mass and everything and thinks I'm a fanatic, but I didn't think she hated *me*." She covered her face with her hands.

"I'm sure she doesn't hate you, Mrs. Whittaker. What do you suppose upset her?"

"I don't know. All she said was, 'What's Agnes doing there? How'd your brainwashers get to her?' I didn't know what she was talking about.

"'Agnes? Who's Agnes?' I said.

"'Sr. Agnes Hopaluk. We taught together in Livonia. I thought she was working at the chancery. This is too much. If you people can get to her, you can get to anybody.'

"'What in the world are you talking about?' I asked. 'I don't know any Sr. Agnes.'

"'Well, funny you don't know her,' she said, 'since she teaches at your school.'

"I was really confused trying to figure out what she meant. Then I remembered that Mrs. Carruthers had come in while we were there. 'You mean that teacher who came in the church?' I asked.

"'Yeah.' she said, real nasty like.

"'That's no Sister Agnes.' I said. ' That's Mrs. Carruthers. She's married to a dentist and has five grandchildren. Maybe she looks like your friend.'

"Well Mary Ann just stared at me like I was lying and didn't say anything else all the way home. When we got there she carried my bag in and said, 'I think it's best if I leave now.'

"I was so upset. I didn't even ask her to stay. I just said good-bye and thank you and all that and went into the house. I haven't heard from her since."

Mrs. Whittaker had slumped back in her seat and Fr. Riley spoke to her in a low voice for a long time.

"So that's how I found out," said Fr. Riley as he finished telling Catherine the story.

"Did you tell Mrs. Whittaker that her daughter was right?"

"No. I haven't told anyone. I just did some detective work." He was quiet, wondering what to say. It was one of the strangest things that had happened to him since his ordination. Fr. Riley knew it would be a long time before he would be comfortable in his own parish again. He had become wary, and he didn't like it. Catherine rose and went over to the counter to get the coffee pot. She came back to the table and refilled Fr. Riley's cup.

"What kind of detective work?" she asked, brushing her hair back from her forehead.

"The first thing I did was call the Michigan Dental Association."

"And?"

"They never heard of a Dr. Bernard Carruthers but they suggested that I call the office of licensing and regulation in Lansing."

"And there's no such dentist in Michigan..." Catherine said, waiting for confirmation.

64

"Right."

"But the references. Who was listed?"

"The principal of Bishop Foley. The archdiocesan education office. Marygrove. I checked with them all by phone, and they gave me glowing reports. Obviously, whoever answered the phone was in on this."

"But I still don't see how you found out the references were fake, then." Catherine was puzzled.

"First I called the chancery and asked to speak to Sr. Agnes Hopaluk. They told me she was on special assignment. And then by chance I happened to remember that the aunt of one of our students teaches at Bishop Foley. So I got her name and called her."

"And she never heard of Mrs. Carruthers."

"You guessed it. And neither had the principal."

Catherine put both elbows on the table and rested her chin on her hands. A bell sounded and she could hear doors opening and students walking down the hallway to change classes. They moved quietly, not talking; and soon another bell rang and doors opened and shut again. Fr. Riley sat listening and looking at his empty coffee cup.

Catherine broke the silence. "Well, at least she's gone now. She failed."

"Yes. I think, though, that this was just round one. There are too many people in high places who hate what we're doing."

"But look at what you're accomplishing!."

"Doesn't matter. There's a tight little group that's been grabbing power for forty years, and just when they figured they had done it, that the old religion was dead, the Holy Father makes his great move. They're running out of time and they're desperate."

Fr. Riley rested the tips of his fingers on the edge of the table. "No, they're not about to give up without a fight, no matter what the Pope says or the Archbishop. They think they can wait it out, that they have the numbers. "

65

"Can they?" asked Catherine.

"Ultimately, no. They will have to comply soon or the Holy Father will excommunicate them. He's not afraid of that. He'll give them a chance to come around; and if they don't, well, they can go peddle their heresy somewhere else. The problem for us now is, that the battle's not over. We'll have to see what happens. I've learned from this last fiasco. I'll be more careful now."

"It makes you wonder what was going on behind the scenes. I mean, who sent Sr. Agnes here? And what did she do after she left?

Fr. Riley started to answer, but their conversation was interirupted by a knock at the window of the partially opened door.

"Come in," the priest said.

Evelyn Janis pushed the door wide and came in. The school secretary was a childless woman in her late fifties, and the cares of the years pulled at her broad face. A deep line between her eyebrows and closely set eyes gave her a look of suspiciousness and distrust.

Every night at nine o'clock, she set her hair with pink foam rollers and covered them with a puffy blue slumber cap. In the morning, she combed the tight curls into a bubble and sprayed it with lacquer until it sat on her head like a stiff brown nest. She rarely smiled. She was too busy for pleasantries; and besides that, she did not generally feel particularly friendly. She was a woman motivated by duty and not enthusiasms.

Mrs. Janis was accompanied by Carrie Stevens, the art and history teacher who doubled as the school choir director. Carrie slid in the door behind Mrs. Janis and closed it behind her, leaning back against it as she waited for the secretary to come into the room. Miss Stevens was petite and blue eyed, with deep dimples, a pink mouth, and short blond curly hair . She looked like a high school student herself, a cheerleader, and Catherine wondered if the other teachers were jealous of her.

Fr. Riley stood and introduced them. "I'll leave you ladies

66

to get acquainted," he said. "Mrs. Janis, when you're through here, would you ask Mr. Corwin to meet me in Dr. Anderson's office? Then, Catherine, meet us back there in, say, twenty minutes or so."

"Fine."

"You can find your way back, all right?"

"If I get lost, I'll call for Mrs. Janis."

"Hmmph. Seems to be what everybody does around here. Calls for Mrs. Janis."

"Don't be a grump, Mrs. Janis, you know we all depend on you," Carrie said coming over to the table toward Catherine. "Hi," she said, holding out her small hand. "I'm so glad to meet you. We've been waiting for you. Father told us he's too busy now to run the school so he was sending for you, said he was getting us a new boss. You're a lot younger than I thought. I expected somebody austere and gray. You don't even look like a principal. You'll have to pull your hair back in a bun and get some ugly glasses and a sour expression."

Catherine smiled at the young teacher who had pulled out a chair and sat down. Mrs. Janis remained standing, her arms folded, her fingers tapping a silent rhythm.

"I'm glad to meet you, Dr. Anderson," Mrs. Janis said. "We heard you left college teaching to come here."

"Yes," answered Catherine. "I was an asociate professor at Rocky Mountain College."

"Where was that?" asked Mrs. Janis.

"Colorado."

"Oh, how could you leave Colorado? It's so beautiful," gushed Carrie, barely giving Catherine time to get the word out of her mouth. "I just love it. We used to go skiing in Summit County. My dad and brothers had to hit Palavaccini every winter while my mom and I went to Copper. Were you ever there?"

"Yes. I lived in Dillon."

"That's right down the road! Anyway, my mom and I wouldn't go with them to Arapahoe. I mean, that's taking your life in your hands. You just keep waiting for disaster. They' ve got signs everywhere: Danger. Avalanche Area. With a skull and crossbones and huge black letters. Not for me. But anyway, it's beautiful, isn't it? Lots of blue sky and sunshine. Not gray like here."

The words tripped over each other when she talked, her emotions close to the surface. There was a girlish charm about her which was engaging, but it made Catherine feel old, as though the girl in her had died with Frank.

"This'll be a change for you," remarked Mrs. Janis drily.

"I'm looking forward to it."

Catherine thought about what it would mean and how different it would be . She had often felt like she'd been living a double life when she was teaching at the college, like her inside and outside didn't match, and she was split in half. It had made her feel disloyal, as though she were hiding her religion, and she struggled to keep her faith intact as she breathed the dry stale air of the college.

The world had shoved Christ into a dark closet, and no one dared open the door in public, she thought. The empty pantomine of modern life played on. But to teach in a Catholic school! To work in a place where religion held first place, where God was adored and the saints imitated. The students and teachers sharing the same Faith, working toward the same goal, all on a pilgrimage to Heaven.

Her thoughts raced ahead. She tried to imagine them all, finally, at the end of their lives, at the Judgment, and -- dare one think it? -- the Redeemer smiling at them, one by one as they came, and bidding them enter. She felt a thrill of anticipation and joy.

And Frank would be there waiting for her.

She turned her mind to the task at hand. To work with others with a common purpose, to build on the foundation of religion, of truth. What couldn't they do? What couldn't they accomplish? She was on fire with purpose and determination. She hoped she was equal to the task, that she wouldn't fail. Failure was too horrible to contemplate. She imagined Christ looking at her, showing the way He had appointed for her, and she knew she must do well.

For love of Him.

"The students are pretty well behaved," said Mrs. Janis, interrupting her thoughts. "But there are some problems. Always some problems. Most of the parents cooperate, but there's some..."

"I'd say that's fairly typical," said Catherine matter-of-factly. She didn't like Mrs. Janis' complaints and decided that she was not going to allow that sort of thing to take root when she was around. She tended to take student problems in stride and expected a certain amount of tension in teaching.

Man's tendency to laziness and misbehavior, the stain of Adam's sin on the human race, did not disappear because the students were in a Catholic school. Or because the secretary wanted them to be perfect.

"Well, they're your problems now. I don't have time to get involved with them. I'm too busy. "

"Mrs. Janis worries a lot," said Carrie. "But we really couldn't function without her." Carrie looked up at Mrs. Janis with respect, seeing through the crusty exterior, the fussiness. The older woman's face softened as she caught the expression in Carrie's eyes.

Catherine watched them and wondered if she had judged Mrs. Janis too harshly. She was ashamed of herself for her lack of charity, but she was still irritated by the negative attitude. It put a damper on other people's happiness. But perhaps the woman wasn't as brittle as she sounded, Catherine thought, trying to be fair.

"Now, come on, Mrs. Janis," continued Carrie, "don't scare Dr. Anderson. You know things go pretty smoothly around here most of the time."

"Hmmph. What good is most of the time? It's the times they don't that I worry about."

"Nothing you can do about that, Mrs. Janis," said Carrie. "It's just like Father always says -- 'This is earth, remember, ladies... not heaven.' By the way, did you see the rough draft of the concert programs I put in your mailbox yesterday?"

"Yes. I typed up the copy this morning. Mr. Fortunata took it to the printer when he went out to the lumberyard this morning."

"See?" Carrie said to Catherine. "What'd I tell you? If you need anything done yesterday, ask Mrs. Janis."

Mrs. Janis shrugged her shoulders again.

"When is the concert?" asked Catherine.

"Not until May. We're just getting started with the pre-parations.

"What sort of concert is it?"

"We have the all-school chorus, the high school ensemble and the children's choir from the elementary grades. Bernadette O'Keefe will play the piano. There'll be a couple of soloists. Brandon O'Keefe -- that's Bernadette's brother -- is singing the *Ave Maria*. You should hear him! He sounds like an angel."

"Some angel," muttered Mrs. Janis. "More like the devil in disguise."

"Mrs. Janis!" exclaimed Carrie. "He's a nice boy. A little mischievous sometimes, that's all."

"A little! That boy drives me to distraction. Every week he has detention. And who has to supervise that? Guess. And does he ever sit still? No. I pity his poor mother."

"Anyway, you must hear him, Dr. Anderson."

"I'd like that."

"Can you come by for practice tomorrow after school?"

"Yes, I think so. Unless Father has something else he needs me to do."

"We'll be in the music room.

They talked for a while about the school and the other

70

teachers.   Mrs. Janis picked up Fr. Riley's coffee cup and reached for Catherine's. Catherine put out her hand to stop her. "I'll get it, Mrs. Janis. You needn't bother."

"I'm up anyway. Let me take it." Catherine withdrew her hand and Mrs. Janis went to the sink and turned on the water.

CHAPTER

7

Deduc me. Domine, in via tua
Et ingrediar in veritate tua

Catherine returned to her office and found Fr. Riley, lost in thought, sitting in the visitor's chair, bent over the desk and busily writing on yellow legal paper. He didn't hear her come in behind him through the open door.

"I'm back, Father," she said. He looked up startled.

"Oh, good. I was just writing a letter to Archbishop Stagniak on the Mrs. Carruthers situation. He wanted me to report as much as I knew."

"He must have been shocked when you told him."

"No, he wasn't. Disappointed, but not surprised. I'll be just a minute. Mr. Corwin should be along shortly." He turned back to his papers.

Catherine walked to the other side of the desk and looked around the office. Besides the desk and two upholstered visitors' chairs, there were three oak file cabinets along the wall. A crucifix hung above the door, and there was a picture of the Little Flower to the side. The room was papered in a pale yellow linen weave, making the walls look dappled with sunshine. Pots of ivy and philodendron hung in wicker baskets by the windows over the bookcase.

A keyboard and monitor were on a small computer table beside the desk. Catherine sat down and peered at it, relieved that it was one she knew how to use. A laser printer and reams of paper were on a little rolling cart along the wall.

Catherine swivelled her chair so that she could see out the

window.   She didn't want Fr. Riley to think she was sitting there
staring at him while he wrote his letter.   She saw Vito pull up in
his panel truck and start unloading some wood.   Two high school
boys hurried over to help him.   She watched them for awhile,
then turned back around and pulled the intercom toward her to
see if she could figure out how it worked.

"There, I'm finished," said Fr. Riley.   "Can you look on
that Roladex and give me the Fed Ex number?" Catherine twirled
the card file for the number and gave it to him.   He marked it in
the margin.   "I'll type this up myself and overnight it to the
Archbishop."   He tore the yellow pages from the pad and folded
them, putting them in his pocket.

There was a knock at the door.   A small man, who looked
to be about sixty, stuck his head in the door tentatively.

"Did you want to see me, Father?"

"Yes, Mr. Corwin. Come in. I want you to meet our new
principal, Dr. Anderson."   Mr. Corwin eased through the door, so
quietly that the air around him scarcely moved.   He glanced at
Catherine shyly, then looked down.

"Glad to meet you, Doctor Anderson," she thought he
said. Catherine smiled at him, but he didn't see it. He was still
looking at the floor, his eyes fixed on his brown wing-tipped
shoes.

"Please sit down, Mr. Corwin, so we can get acquainted,"
said Catherine.   Fr. Riley rose and motioned for Mr. Corwin to
take his chair.

"I'll be right back," the priest said, nodding in the direction of the parking lot.   "I'm going to run out and give Vito
and the boys a hand hauling that wood in."

Catherine turned and looked back out the window. The pile
of planks that Vito was unloading was growing higher and more
precarious.   The two boys were lugging a long heavy board
through the front door which they had forgotten to prop open.
They were trying to keep it from closing with their backs as they
came through and were having a great deal of trouble.

Fr. Riley slid through the space behind the boys and held the door for them. When they were in, he bent down by the porch and took some bricks that were hidden behind the shrubs for this very purpose and stacked them against the open door. With the smooth grace of long years of football and track, he sprinted over to help Vito who was struggling to lift a six foot square of plywood off the roof of the panel truck.

In the office, Mr. Corwin had finally looked up and was struck by the animated interest and patience on Catherine's face. She had propped her elbows on the desk and her chin rested above her folded hands. She didn't seem to mind being quiet. Too many times people expected you to say something before you had anything to say.

Catherine reached for a book that had fallen on the floor and slipped it into the bookcase behind her, then turned back toward him. Mr. Corwin sat quietly in the chair, his hands resting on his knees.

He had been afraid she was going to be like that other woman -- what was her name? Carruthers. He grimaced as he remembered her. He wasn't looking forward to another encounter like that. Mr. Corwin was a mild man and he didn't usually talk much; he always preferred to listen. He learned a lot that way, but sometimes what he learned, he wished he didn't know. Usually he took people the way they were -- he didn't like to make waves and couldn't remember ever having a real enemy -- but ...

His teeth tightened. *That woman.* There were some things he had learned that he had been meaning to talk to Fr. Riley about just before she left. He wasn't sure whether he should still bring them up or not. He'd have to consider whether it would be helpful or just cause problems. But at least in the meantime, this new principal wasn't the same type. He started to lose his shyness.

"I'm glad to meet you, Dr. Anderson. I hope you like it here."

"Thank you," she said. "I've heard a lot about you. You

74

used to be an engineer, didn't you?"

"Yes. Nuclear. I retired two years ago."

"My father-in-law is an engineer. Mechanical, I think." Mr. Corwin relaxed. She was easy to talk to. She asked him about his classes; and by the time they started to talk about physics, his favorite subject, his self consciousness had disappeared. They had been talking for about fifteen minutes when Fr. Riley came back, brushing the sawdust off his cassock.

Mr. Corwin stood up and reached across the desk to shake Catherine's hand. "It was nice talking to you, Dr. Anderson." He started to leave, then turned back. "I think we're lucky that you're here," he said quickly, then nodded at Fr. Riley and hurried soundlessly out the door.

"Looks like you made quite an impression on him," said Fr. Riley. "He usually doesn't talk outside his classroom."

Catherine smiled. "He was interesting," she said. "And I never found science all that fascinating, to say the least. Maybe if I'd had a teacher like Mr. Corwin, I would have liked it better. Too many materialists spoiled it for me.

"You know, I think if a teacher really loves his subject, it comes alive for the student. There's some kind of wonderful thing that happens, a particular kind of charity that belongs to a student and teacher." She sighed. "But then, of course, the converse is also true. No love. No learning."

Fr. Riley sat down and rubbed his chin thoughtfully. He liked her attitude, the way she had of drawing out the strengths and talents of other people. He thought she would make a good principal. He had been troubled more than he wanted to admit by the problems with Mrs. Carruthers. There had been days when he feared he would have to close the school. But now, *Deo Gratias,* things were going along well.

He pulled the intercom over to his side of the desk and sent for the two elementary school teachers, Judy Long and Barbara Clark, to come to the office as soon as they were free.

Mrs. Long got there first.

75

"Hello, Father, Hello..." she nodded to Catherine. "You won't need me long, will y'all? I left Mary Margaret Haneghan in charge, but you never know what goes on when you leave the room." She stood in the doorway, a matronly thirty-five year old woman whose husband was a Dearborn police lieutenant and whose three children were students in the school.

Her voice still carried more than a trace of Tennessee. Judy had met Lt. Long when he was in the Navy and stationed in Millington, just outside of Memphis. Thirteen years before, she had come north to marry him, but she had never become a Yankee. She had a Southern soul.

Fr. Riley smiled at her in greeting as she came into the room toward Catherine's desk. "I just wanted you to meet Dr. Anderson." He made the introductions, and they were all starting to talk when Mary Margaret came running down the hall and through the door.

"Mrs. Long! Mrs. Long!" Judy Long looked at Catherine with an expression of "What did I tell you?"

"What is it, Mary Margaret?"

"Billy's got a bloody nose."

"Excuse me," Judy said and hurried down the hall. Mary Margaret turned to follow her.

"Wait, Mary Margaret," said Fr. Riley, stopping her. Mrs. Long will take care of it. I want you to meet our new principal... Dr. Anderson... Mary Margaret Hanaghan."

Catherine looked at the plump little girl in pigtails who stood shaking in the doorway. Fr. Riley nodded his head at Catherine for her to handle it. Her first school crisis. At least it was a minor one.

"What happened, Mary Margaret?" Catherine asked.

"Tommy was collecting papers and Billy's foot was in the aisle and..."

"And what, Mary Margaret?"

"Well Tommy fell down and he said Billy tripped him on

purpose, so he slugged him in the nose." Catherine nearly laughed, but she caught herself in time and looked as stern as she could manage.

"Send Tommy to me."

Mary Margaret started to sniffle. "Oh, I'm so sorry, Dr. Anderson. I tried to make them be good."

"It's all right Mary Margaret. It wasn't your fault. Here, take a tissue and wipe your eyes. You wouldn't want them to know you'd been crying," she whispered confidentially.

"Thank you, Dr. Anderson. Mary Margaret dried her eyes and started to leave, but then she turned and slipped over behind the desk and wrapped her arms around Catherine's neck and burying her tear-stained face in her shoulder. Catherine touched her hair lightly and Mary Margaret looked up at her. "You're pretty," she said and hurried out of the room.

Tommy Flanagan came in, his head down, hiding the freckles that dusted his face. Fr. Riley stayed in the background.

"Hello, Tommy. I'm Dr. Anderson."

"Good morning, ma'am."

"What happened?"

"I was picking up the homework papers like Mrs. Long said and Billy tripped me."

"And what did you do then?"

"I punched him. Dr. Anderson, *he did it on purpose!*"

"How do you know that, Tommy?"

"Because...well, just because, that's why."

"If you don't know for certain, you should have assumed it was an accident."

"Yes, ma'am."

"And you owe Billy an apology."

"Gosh, Dr. Anderson, do I have to?"

"Yes, Tommy."

"But, Dr. Anderson, guys..."

"You will do it, Tommy, and then you will stay in for recess for a week and I will give you some work to do. Today you will wash the elementary school blackboards and report to me when you're finished."

"Yes, ma'am. But, Dr. Anderson..."

"Yes, Tommy?"

"What if he did do it on purpose?" Tommy looked at her beseechingly, his blue eyes pleading.

"I'll talk to him, Tommy. If he did it on purpose, then he'll have a punishment, too. But first, sir, you must apologize."

"Yes, ma'am." Tommy drew himself up straight. He'd never been called *sir* before. He felt better already. Catherine buzzed the second grade classroom. "Mrs. Long, would you send Billy down when his nose stops bleeding?"

"He's fine now. He'll be right there."

Billy Pitlowski, a pugnacious seven year old with a blond crew cut and blood on his rumpled white shirt was there in a minute. Catherine greeted him and motioned him into the room.

"How is your nose, Billy?" asked Catherine.

"Fine, now," he answered, glaring at Tommy.

"Billy, what happened?"

"Tommy was collecting the papers like he always does. He's teacher's pet. She always chooses him. So, he came down my aisle and I had my paper ready, but I needed to stretch."

"You needed to stretch?"

"Yes, ma'am. My legs were getting real tired. So I needed to stretch."

"But you knew Tommy was coming down your aisle."

"Yes, ma'am. But I didn't trip him on purpose."

"But if somebody were walking by just when somebody else decided to stretch his tired legs, wouldn't there be a chance that the first somebody would fall?"

Billy thought for a minute, wiping his face with his sleeve.

"I guess."

"Then you should have known Tommy could trip if you stretched just then? Isn't that right?"

"Yes, ma'am."

78

"Then I think you both owe each other an apology. And Billy, you will also remain indoors at recess for a week. "

"Yes, ma'am," they answered together. Tommy reached out his hand to Billy, "Sorry, Bill."

Billy took it and shook it firmly. "Sorry, Tom."

"Good," said Catherine, satisfied. Now, I expect you both to behave like Christian gentlemen from now on. Is that clear?"

"Yes, Dr. Anderson," they said and walked back to class together, starting to feel a little like the Christian gentlemen she expected them to be. Barbara Clark passed them in the hall.

"Good morning, Miss Clark," they said together.

"Good morning, boys. Did you just come from Dr. Anderson's office?"

"Yes, ma'am." They wanted to get away before she asked them any more questions. Teachers were always asking questions.

"Not in trouble, are you guys?"

Billy and Tommy looked at each other. "Not any more, I guess," said Tommy.

"We were," said Billy."But it's okay now."

"Glad to hear it," Miss Clark said. "You boys be good now."

"Yes, ma'am,"they answered and hurried back to class.

In the office, Fr. Riley looked at Catherine with approval. "Good job," he said.

"Thanks," she answered. "It's a little new."

"You've got the right touch, though."

Catherine was embarrassed.

"Really," he said. "That's the way I'd like things handled around here." He looked off in the distance, thinking of Mrs. Carruthers and the turmoil she had caused, relieved that that chapter in the life at Holy Martyrs was finished.

Barbara Clark knocked at the open door and Fr. Riley motioned her in and introduced her to Catherine.

"Did you get those two fellows straightened out?" she asked.

"For the time being, I think. You know how boys are," answered Catherine. Barbara agreed. She liked her answer. Boys and girls were different and had to be treated differently. For herself, she'd rather teach boys. They were more direct. Girls were always getting their feelings hurt. But she didn't have a choice. She had them both and would have to do the best she could. Teaching wasn't easy.

"So you have the upper elementary grades?" asked Catherine.

"Yes. Five through eight."

"That's quite an assignment."

"You're right about that." Thank God they got somebody in here who knows what it's like, she thought.

"How do you manage it?"

"Organization, I guess, and my mother saying, 'What are you complaining about? When I taught in parochial schools we had forty kids in our classes and nobody thought anything of it. You young people are spoiled.'"

Catherine laughed. "A little dose of maternal pressure does wonders for motivation, doesn't it?"

Barbara Clark laughed with her. "You bet. I mean, how could I fail, I only have twenty-three students! A computer could do it. Speaking of which, I'd better get back. They have a word processing class next, and I don't want them turning on the machines when I'm not there. Who knows what might happen." She said good-bye to Catherine and to Fr. Riley who was busying himself with the copy machine in the corner and left.

"Well, what do you think?" he asked as he closed the lid of the machine and walked over to the door. He stood watiting for her answer.

"I think I'm glad to be here," said Catherine.

"Good. Come on. I'll take you on a tour of the building."

80

The school had long tiled hallways and wide expanses of windows in each room. Vito had refinished all the woodwork and classroom doors and the floors were polished. Religious art hung on the walls...The Holy Family, St. Cecilia, St. Francis of Asissi. There was a huge print of Da Vinci's Last Supper in the cafeteria...

During the seventies and eighties when many churches were being closed and everything sold, a group of people, the Fortunatas, Mr. and Mrs. Janis, the Wasniaks, and the Whittakers, had bought up as many things as they could -- statues, vestments, books, paintings -- and stored them all in Vito's basement. Holy Martyrs was the beneficiary of their foresight.

In the corner of each hallway was a life-sized statue -- St. Anne in the elementary school wing, St. Anthony near the choir room, the Blessed Virgin in the main hall. At the entrance to the school was St. Sebastian, standing straight and unflinching on a pedestal, his arms shackled behind him, the arrows of his martyrdom jutting from his chest and back.

The priest and the principal entered each classroom and as they came through the door, the students rose at once. "Good morning, Father," they said with the characteristic inflection of Catholic school students, in voices like chant, "Good morning, Dr. Anderson."

The classes were small, and the students seemed well mannered and cheerful. Having made the rounds, she and Fr. Riley returned to her new office.

"So that's the school. How do you like it?"

"I think it's wonderful. I'm anxious to be part of it."

"Good. Mrs. Carruthers didn't scare you off?"

"No."

"Keep your eyes open, though. If it happened once..."

"It'll probably happen again..."

"Glad to see you're as optimistic as I am."

" I wonder what that woman's up to now."

"Back to being Sr. Agnes, I'd guess."

He told her about the high school English classes that she would be assuming and went over to the bookcase and took four thick anthologies from the top shelf. "Here are the textbooks. You'll probably want to supplement them, which is fine, just let me have a booklist." He trusted her judgment, but he was ultimately responsible for everything taught in the school, and he was taking no chances. "Basic anthologies of English and American authors. Look them over and let me know if there are any problems."

Catherine took the books from him and laid the stack on the desk. Lifting the top one, she ran her fingers over its smooth binding and opened it carefully, leafing through the pages.

"Any questions?"

"None right now. I need to think about all this. I'm sure I'll have a long list for you tomorrow."

"Fine. But if anything comes up this evening, let me know."

"Thank you, Father, but I'm sure it wouldn't be anything that couldn't wait until the morning."

She thought he was going to leave, but he hesitated a moment. Catherine pulled out her chair and sat down, then waited with her hands folded on the desk.

"A couple of things happened before you came back from the teacher's lounge," he said. "First, remember that visiting priest I mentioned at dinner last night?" Catherine nodded. "Well, it seems he's been sent to observe."

Catherine looked questioningly at the priest. "Observe?" she repeated, feeling cautious.

Fr. Riley's face was grim. "Yes. Bishop Washinsky is sending him."

"Doesn't sound good, does it?"

"No."

"Does the Archbishop know?"

"I don't know. Probably not." He rubbed the back of his

82

neck. "Ostensibly, he's coming to learn. I doubt he's ever even seen the Latin Mass. But I don't know why the Bishop would send him here. I just got the phone call that he's coming, no explanations, no chance to ask any questions. It's a little odd. I thought the Archbishop had set something up at the seminaries for these young priests. He told me about it himself."

"What do you think?"

"I don't know what to think. You could say that it's a good idea. Let him see what we're all about. Let him get a taste of it. But on the other hand..."

"There was Sr. Agnes."

"Yes. It makes me somewhat apprehensive."

"Did you talk to the Archbishop?"

"No. I don't want to jump over Bishop Washinsky's head . I think I'll just have to wait and see." He picked up a pen and rolled it in his hands.

"At least you're doing what you're supposed to, what the Archbishop wants. It's not a case of being in rebellion or something that they'd want to monitor you."

"No. But I'm not looking forward to it."

"When is he coming?"

"Sometime next week. He was supposed to come today, but there was a delay." He tapped the yellow pad that was still lying on the desk.

"You said two things happened," she reminded him.

"Oh, yes. I forgot. Preoccupied again. Do you know a Stan ... let's see, what was his name? I've got it somewhere. Tomaszewski? That's it. Stan Tomaszewski."

Catherine broke into a wide smile. "So he called you? He said he would."

"How do you know him?"

"He was the conductor on the train coming here."

"The conductor?" Fr. Riley grinned.

"Yes. He saw me saying my rosary and he asked me if I were 'one of those Catholics.' When I said I was, he wanted to know where. So I told him."

Fr. Riley looked over at her. There was no denying that Catherine seemed to touch people's hearts, but he hadn't expected to see evidence of it so often. Mr. Corwin...Billy and Tommy... She would have made a good missionary, he thought. But then, maybe that's what she was. It was a rare gift she had, that way of reflecting the beauty and love of her faith.

Fr. Riley laid down his pen. "He and his wife are coming up from Chicago, and they'll be here Sunday for Mass."

"That's great. I'll have to look for them afterwards," Catherine said, then remembered the breakfast that they had arranged with the Fortunatas. She wondered if she should ask Vito if he'd mind a couple more people coming along.

Fr. Riley left for lunch at the rectory and Catherine spent the rest of the day working at her desk. Before she knew it, the three o'clock closing bell had sounded. She stood by her office door as the children passed through the halls and hurried out the door, breaking their quiet lines into lively groups of four or five in the parking lot, their laughter and squeals carrying back into the building.

Catherine walked to the school entrance and stood for a few minutes watching them cross the parking lot and begin their walk home. Once they were out of sight, she opened the door and headed down the sidewalk to the front entrance of the church.

She was all alone. She dipped her fingers in the holy water font, blessed herself, and walked up the center aisle all the way to the communion rail where she knelt down and buried her face in her hands. One of the side windows was open slightly and it was cool, but she didn't notice. She pulled her rosary from her pocket and began the joyful mysteries, losing herself in contemplation.

Fr. Riley came in through the sacristy door to check the church before leaving on a sick call and seeing her, he withdrew quietly. Catherine didn't hear him come or go. She finished her rosary and went to sit in the front pew to think about the events of the day and seek God's help in her new work.

She was pleased with how things had gone and hoped she would do well in her new position, but she was a little afraid. How she wished she could talk to Frank! She longed to hear the reassurance in his voice, his confidence in her.

Everyone was kind and helpful, but it wasn't the same. The Andersons and Fr. Riley were dear to her, but she felt so alone, like an observer going through the motions. There was a veil between her and the others.

Well, she thought, maybe that will change. I can't expect anything else. Not yet. But she wondered if she would ever really feel at home at Holy Martyrs. Sighing, she dropped her head into her hands and made an act of faith.

She took a dollar out of her purse and walked over to the side altar to light a candle. Kneeling before the serene face of the Blessed Virgin, she said the *Memorare*, then went back to the front pew and sat down.

It wasn't just her feelings that she was concerned about. She was disturbed by what had happened with Sister Agnes and wondered what she would have done if she had encountered the nun in disguise. Would she have known? And why was it happening, anyway?

Catherine had been so happy when the Pope had reinstituted the true Mass and firm doctrine, rejoicing with the remnant of Christendom when he began to cleanse the Church of disobedience and error, of apostates and heretics. She chided herself for being naive, but somehow she had felt that, well, now everything would be all right, that the fight was over.

Against all reason, really, she had thought that the bishops would immediately unite with the Holy Father and set themselves to the task of restoring their Catholic heritage. She had not understood the enormity of the undertaking nor the strength of the resistance, a resistance that shook all levels of the Church. A ruthlessness had been set loose that knew no boundaries.

She would have to be careful.

Billy Pitlowski was walking home along McKinley Street, taking his time. There had been five boys to start with -- Tommy Flanagan, the two Long brothers, and Micky Shaunessey -- but Billy's house was farthest from school, and he was left to walk the last block alone. He had found a very nice rock, quartz, he thought, remembering his science class. He cupped it in his hand, feeling the ridges with his thumb, then held it up close to his face, watching the stone glint where the sun struck it. When he turned it and held it in the shadows, it was a dull flat gray.

It was perfect, just right for kicking. He tossed it in front of him on the sidewalk and took the first kick. Four squares. He had to concentrate. It wasn't any good kicking it far if it went into the grass. But four squares was sissy stuff. He ran up to the rock and kicked again. Five. He was getting better. He started to get warm and so he pulled off his sweater and jacket and stuffed them in his bookbag.

Mrs. Obertynski was sweeping her sidewalk. She had started with the porch and had moved down the front walk, banishing the winter debris with broad sweeping strokes, the broom thin as a switch against her heavy arms. She watched Billy come down the street. She recognized the Holy Martyrs uniform.

"I'm not too sure about that school," she had told Mrs. Adams next door just the other day. "I knew some people who sent their kids there. You wouldn't believe it -- so much regimentation. Too strict, in my view. It's not natural. And homework! Every night. One hour, two hours. They don't think anything of it. And did you know they make those kids go to church *every day*? I wouldn't send my kids there if the Archbishop paid the tuition."

"They don't know how to raise children," answered Mrs. Adams. "They're kind of old fashioned."

"Old fashioned?" Mrs. Obertynski .interrupted, "That's

not the half of it. Sounds like a cult to me, the way they all flock around that priest of theirs. Next thing you know, they'll be blowing themselves up or drinking poison. Or worse."

Brad Cranshaw, the postman, said they were a threat to the community, and something should be done. It was a shame. A real shame. She gave the walk a vigorous sweep and then stood back to let Billy pass. She held the broom high to the right and was just coming down to the concrete when she stopped abruptly. *There was blood on that boy's shirt*. She would have to see about that. She stood in his path.

"Stop right there, young man," Mrs. Obertynski said.

"Good afternoon, ma'am," answered Billy, trying to be polite, but more than a little annoyed that his momentum had been broken. He was up to seven squares. Now he'd probably have to start all over again.

"Is that blood on your shirt?"

Billy looked down. There were just a couple of stains. He'd forgotten all about it. He pulled his shirt away from his chest and looked down. It wasn't too bad, he thought. It was dry now.

"I asked you a question."

"Yes, ma'am."

"What's your name?"

"Billy Pitlowski."

"How did that happen?" She pointed at his shirt.

"Oh, it's nothing," answered Billy. A little blood never hurt a guy, he thought. Of course his mother probably wouldn't like it. He grew a little nervous thinking about that.

"What happened?" repeated the portly Mrs. Obertynski.

"Somebody punched me," answered Billy, taking aim with his foot.

"Who hit you?"

"Just somebody," he answered.

Mrs. Obertynski grabbed his arm. "When an adult asks you a question, you're supposed to answer," she said angrily.

Billy slipped out of her grasp. He still didn't answer her because he didn't know if what she said was true. He knew there were certain times when you didn't have to do what adults said -- like you weren't supposed to get in a car with strangers or take candy from them. He wasn't sure about answering their questions. He'd have to ask Fr. Riley about that. In the meantime, he'd stay on the safe side.

"I don't think Dr. Anderson wants me to say," he said.

"Who?"

"Dr. Anderson. The principal." It didn't seem like she would want him to tell. The fight was school stuff, and he didn't know this lady. Besides, he wasn't going to rat on Tommy. They already shook on it. He bent down to pick up his rock and slipped it into his pocket. He'd wait until he got past her house to start up again.

"Good bye, ma'am," Billy said. He was trying to remember his manners.

Mrs. Obertynski said nothing. She stood there, her stance wide and her solid frame filling the sidewalk. She was breathing hard. She tightened her grip on the broom and watched him go Billy didn't see her hurry into her house. He was positioning his rock.

CHAPTER

8

Parasti in conspetu meo mensam
Adversus eos qui tribulant me

Friday passed in a flurry of activity as Easter approached. There were only two weeks left. Mrs. Janis bustled through the halls, making sure everything was clean that needed cleaning, badgering Vito to straighten his workroom, checking that the bulletin boards had been stripped. She hurried back to her office to see about the flowers. Had she remembered to order the white carnations? The Altar Society wanted them for the Altar of Repose on Holy Thursday along with the lilies. She wasn't sure. She dialed the florist.

Down the main hall and around the corner, Catherine sat at her desk and busied herself with administrative duties all morning. She became so engrossed that she almost missed lunch. Looking up at the clock, she was startled that it was after twelve. She grabbed the small brown paper bag containing her peanut butter sandwich and apple and hurried over to the teachers' lounge .

The other teachers were assembled. Their lunches were spread out on the long table and the coffee was just starting to perk. Mrs. Janis had not arrived yet. She was waiting for Mrs. Hanaghan to pick up Danny for a dental appointment. Mr. Corwin looked up as Catherine came through the door and started to rise, but she motioned for him to remain seated and took her place at the table.

"Hi, everybody," she said as she pulled her sandwich out of the bag. "How's it going today?"

"Not too bad," said Miss Clark. "No problems, everybody had their homework done for once. I couldn't believe it."

"That's got to be a first," said Carrie.

"And the sun's shining," interjected Mrs. Long.

"For a change," said Mrs. Janis walking through the door.

They were eating their lunches when Fr. Riley came in for his midday visit to the school.

"I'll be hearing confessions today as usual at two o'clock," he said. "Mrs. Long, could you have the third graders come over at 1:45?"

"Yes, Father, I'll have them over there for y'all."

"Good. And Mr. Corwin, I'll need a couple of the chemistry students to come over to the rectory. We've inherited a chem lab from St. Albert's, and I'll need some boys to carry the boxes over. Right after lunch, okay? I won't keep them long. See which ones wouldn't mind putting in a couple of hours setting it up. We can do it in the morning before Mass or in the afternoon -- whichever suits their schedules better. Tell them to check with their mothers and give me a call to let me know." He turned to Carrie. "Mr. Fortunata says he'll have the stage finished next week. So you won't have to worry about having a place to perform."

Since the gymnasium where the concert was going to be held did not have a stage, Fr. Riley talked Vito into building one, and he had gotten the Altar Society to sew red velvet draperies for it.

Teresa, Madeline Wasniak, and Gertrude Whittaker had brought their sewing machines and notions baskets over to the school on Monday. They set up tables at the far end of the gym, away from the lumber and saws, where they could work. They'd been busy cutting and stitching all week, hanging the long swatches of rich fabric over clotheslines that they had strung along the length of the back wall.

"How's the music coming?" Fr, Riley asked.

"Very well, Father," Carrie answered. "I've invited Dr.

Anderson over to hear them today after school. She said she could come if you didn't have any other work for her to do. Do you?"

"Nope, not a thing."

"Can you come over then?" asked Carrie.

"Yes," answered Catherine. "I'm anxious to hear them. Especially Brandon."

"Hmmph," said Mrs. Janis.

It was nearly three thirty when Catherine locked her office and walked down the high school wing to the music room. As she turned the corner, she heard the pure sweet sound of the children's choir singing the beautiful strains of *O Sanctissima*. She moved her lips slightly, singing softly to herself and felt her soul lift and expand with joy. This was where she was meant to be; this was the consolation the Good Lord was offering her in her sorrow.

Someday her broken heart would heal.

After Mass on Sunday, the Andersons, the Fortunatas, and the newly arrived Tomaszewskis gathered outside the church. Just as Catherine had thought, Vito had been eager to invite Stan and Stella to join them. They introduced themselves and chatted amiably while they waited for Fr. Riley. Vito was telling the history of Holy Martyrs, and Catherine listened attentively. There was a lot she hadn't known.

Don Anderson stood a little back from the group. He had fixed a pleasant smile on his face, but he was far away, lost in thought. Something had happened to him during the Mass, and he was trying to figure it out. He had been struck by the solemnity of the liturgy, the peacefulness. He had not followed along in the missal that Helen had brought for him -- he wouldn't have known how to use it anyway. He was content to watch. He stood when the others stood and knelt when they knelt, trying to fit in.

But then, suddenly, he was gripped by a feeling he didn't understand. His heart started to pound, and sweat broke out on his forehead. He took a deep breath, but the feeling wouldn't go away. What was it? It wasn't fear, not exactly. It was different, a wondrous thing. Something he never felt before. He searched for the word. Awe. That was it. There was no other word for it. He wondered what was happening. He clasped his hands behind him and rocked back on his heels, thinking.

It was Passion Sunday, he remembered hearing Fr. Riley say. Everything was draped in purple. The life-sized marble forms along the side of the church and at the back were covered. So was the crucifix above the altar. He felt the heaviness, the solemnity. There was total silence. He had knelt watching, curious, as the priest stood facing the altar, whispering prayers Don couldn't hear, and then bells rang. Triple bells that rippled like the music of angels.

Fr. Riley knelt, then rose, and Don watched as he held a flat white disk high above his head with both hands. Don wondered what it was and what Fr. Riley was doing. Around him, people softly struck their breast once and then looked up, faces solemn, and made the sign of the cross. The priest knelt again. Why? What were they doing? Don wondered. What was going on? Fr. Riley lifted a golden chalice, and the people responded the same way. Silence. Silence. All around an almost superhuman stillness.

Don had not prayed for years and didn't really know how. But now he felt like praying. He felt like calling out to God, reaching for Him. An inexpressible longing seized him

His heart felt like a wax candle, burning and melting, and he laid the palm of his hand against his chest. Tears came to his eyes, and he bent his head low. Helen had glanced over at him, concerned for a moment that he was ill, but seeing that he was all right, she returned to her prayer book.

"Isn't that right, Don?" Vito was asking, pulling Mr. Anderson back to the present.

"What's that? Oh, sorry. I didn't hear you."

"I said we're lucky to be here."

Don was still struggling with the feelings that had swept over him during Mass. "Right," he agreed. "That's right, Vito."

Helen looked at him curiously. He was certainly behaving strangely. She hoped he wasn't having a stroke.

"Here comes Father Riley," said Vito. "Father! Looks like you've got a couple new fish here." Fr. Riley strode quickly over to the group, extending his hand to Stan.

"Welcome, welcome," he said. "I understand you met our principal on the train."

"Yup, she's the one that reeled us in," he said. He remembered the priests of his childhood saying that they always hoped to get some big fish in Advent and Lent. Well, they caught a couple of doozies today, he guessed. He gestured toward Mrs. Tomaszewski. "This here's Stella, my wife, Father."

"I'm glad to meet you, Mrs. Tomaszewski," said Fr. Riley. He turned to Vito, "Well, where are we heading?" he asked.

"I made reservations at the Dearborn Inn," said Vito, who had thought that the style and atmosphere of the historic inn by Greenfield Village suited the Andersons. He thought it was classy like Mrs. Anderson.

"Oh, that sounds nice!" exclaimed Helen. She turned to the Tomaszewskis. "How long will you be in town?"

"Until Easter," said Stella. "Stan's taking his last vacation before he retires next month. His sister lives here, so we're staying with her. You have a nice church here, Father," she said wistfully. She looked over at Catherine. "You should have seen Stan that day he met you. He was so excited. It's been hard for us, you know, all the changes over the years. We're not that kind of people. We like the old ways, like when we were kids. We thought it was gone forever," she sighed.

93

"You and everybody else," said Vito. "It wasn't that they didn't try to kill it, that's for sure."

The women moved closer to Stella. Teresa took her arm. "That's how we all felt when we first came back," she said. "Makes you want to cry."

Don was startled by her words. He was puzzled. So he wasn't alone in feeling like he did. They felt it, too, and they'd been Catholics all their lives. Something was definitely going on. He mulled it over in his engineer's mind, taking each event and looking at it, turning it, examining it.

"Shall we take off?" asked Fr. Riley.

"Fine with us," said Stan, taking his wife's elbow as she steeped down the curb into the parking lot. They drove in procession, winding their way through the neighborhoods of neat little bungalows built just after World War II to Outer Drive, up Monroe, and over to Oakwood to the Dearborn Inn.

There were only two weeks left of Lent and the air was beginning to warm. People were outside. A gentle breeze blew and Don cracked the window slightly. As they drove along the old streets of Dearborn, Catherine gazed out the side window as the neighborhoods unrolled, block after block.

Some children were playig on the merry-go-round at Elmhurst Park and a few others rode their bicycles under the arched branches of the budding trees. Across the street, two young women walked together along the sidewalk pushing strollers, their babies bundled in thick blankets. Catherine watched them as the Lincoln drove by, turning her head until they had gone too far and she couldn't see them anymore.

Within a half hour, they were sitting in the Early American Room at the Dearborn Inn, their plates heaped with sweet Virginia ham, fried eggs, and hash brown potatoes. Vito reached over the table to the basket of warm buttermilk biscuits and removed the homespun napkin laid over them.

94

"Well, what did you think, Stan?" asked Vito.

"Just like we remembered," said Stan.

"From thirty years ago," added Stella.

"The Promised Land," said Vito. "We're like the Hebrews wandering in the desert. They had us by ten years though."

"I really don't think I could have stood another ten years," said Stella softly.

"No, it got to where we couldn't take one more day." Stan made crisscross cuts across his thick slice of ham..

"Tell him about that priest last Easter."

"Oh, yeah, that one was a real killer," said Stan.

"We got up and walked out..."

"Yeah, in front of everybody." He laid down his knife and speared a square of ham with his fork. "My mother must've rolled over in her grave. This guy -- excuse me, Father, but that's what he was -- gets up there and says that Christ didn't rise from the dead. It was just some spiritual thing. He said Catholics have misunderstood the meaning of the Gospel." He bit the ham off his fork and made a face. "Sure, we misunderstood it."

"Yeah," said Vito. "For two thousand years. Pretty stupid."

Fr. Riley clenched his teeth.

Stan broke the yoke of his egg and dipped a piece of toast in it while he talked. "So he's going to enlighten us now that we're *mature in the faith.* 'See,' he says, 'here's what really happened,' and he got this weird look on his face..."

"...Like we're a bunch of kindergarteners who believe in the Tooth Fairy and he's going to break it to us gently..." interrupted Stella.

Stan nodded. "Anyhow, he says when the people saw Our Lord after He rose, you know, in the Garden and all those other places -- well, they didn't see *Him*, they saw Jesus *in each other.* Just like we have to see the Christ in each other. That's the real meaning of Easter. Like that's supposed to be better? Right. A real jerk."

95

Stan flicked his shoulder like there was something sitting on it that he was trying to dislodge.

Teresa watched Catherine shudder and laid her hand briefly on her arm.

Vito pushed away his plate. "Yeah, well, did you ever have one of those nuns come in to give the sermon?" he asked.

"You mean the *homily*?" Stan answered.

"Yeah. I forget all their new words."

"We had some of them. How about you?"

"We had one that was something else," said Vito. "I swear she was a witch."

Don looked up at him from his potatoes, his fork stopped in midair.

"I mean it.   She was talking about the wisdom of the Goddess, and then she starts waving this thing like a magic wand or something. Pointing to the four corners of the earth, she said. I guess nobody ever told her the world was round. Anyway, she starts prancing around the sanctuary, moaning and groaning."

He imitated her waving arm movements. " Then she goes, *'We are blessing. We are earth. We are power.'* It was the weirdest thing I ever saw."

Stan nodded. "I know what you mean. Our kids had one of those in religion class at St. Dominic's. Drove me nuts. And do you think the priest would do anything about it? Nah. Not a chance. Not only that, but he liked having dancing girls in the sanctuary. Every special occasion -- Christmas, Easter, Pentecost, you name it -- we'd have these girls in leotards and some kind of gauzy things come traipsing up the aisle like a bunch of stupid butterflies or something and then they'd sway around the table while one of them sat on the floor and played a zither. It was unreal."

Fr. Riley's neck burned under his Roman collar. "That sort of thing was all too common, I'm sorry to say. " He forced himself to be calm. "I really don't have words strong enough to condemn it. Things should get better now." He wished he could believe what he was saying, but he had the gnawing feeling that things were going to get worse, much worse, before they got better.

Around the world, the wounded modernists rebelled against the restoration the pope had begun. They wanted no part of it. They screamed at what they called the *Dinosaur Takeover* of the Church. Only a few were faithful. There were reports of angry flare-ups and near riots, and thousands of armed protestors had stormed the Vatican on Wednesday. Three Swiss guards had been killed before order was restored.

In the major dioceses of America and throughout Western Europe, marches were being organized to force the bishops to defy the pope and keep things the way they had been since the Second Vatican Council. Syndicated cartoons of Innocent XIV tying rebels to the rack circulated everywere. Those bishops who dared attempt to follow the papal order were given the same treatment in the press. The mockery and defiance spread daily.

Fr. Riley wondered why things had been relatively quiet in Detroit. There hadn't been any mass demonstrations when Archbishop Stagniak ordered the churches to comply with the Pope's command. It put him on guard. He didn't trust the calm; and the incident with Mrs. Carruthers --Sr. Agnes, rather -- confirmed his suspicions. He knew it was just beginning. He laid his knife and fork across his empty plate and turned his attention back to the conversation.

"Makes you fighting mad," said Vito.

"And you couldn't do a thing," said Stan. "Just sit there and swallow it. Obedience. We were all good at that."

Catherine was silent.

"But we can do something now, can't we Stella?" he said turning to his wife.

"Yes. Finally," she answered and smiled at him.

"What are you going to do?" asked Helen.

"We're moving here."

"All right, man!" said Vito. "But what about your job?"

97

"I only got three weeks left before I retire."

"Are you coming here right away, then?" asked Helen.

Stan poured himself some more coffee. "Yup. Soon's we can sell the house."

"What about your children?" asked Teresa.

"What about them?" answered Stan. "They're all grown up."

"Won't it be hard to leave them?"

Stella shrugged. "What can you do? They have their own lives to live. They don't care the way we do. " She closed her eyes for a second and sighed. "We did the best we could. They're spread out all over the country anyway. So. We want to come here, be where things are the way they're supposed to be. Who knows? Maybe they'll come around someday."

Teresa was quiet. It was the same, then, for them as for her. The kids went for the new ways. Nick, Marty, Rose. Only Angelina had the faith, and she was in Colorado. She shook off the thoughts about her children and sipped her coffee and ate her toast, listening to the others.

The conversation turned to moving companies and real estate agencies, and Vito told Stan about a house down the street from him that was for sale, walking distance from the church.

The breakfast was finished, but the men and women around the table continued to talk, and as they did, by the grace of God, the bonds of charity grew strong among them.

98

CHAPTER

9

Sancte Michael Archangele
Defende nos in prælio

Catherine arrived at Holy Martyrs early on Monday. She wanted a chance to prepare herself before her first real week as principal began. Her books were piled in front of her, but she couldn't sit still. She played with her wedding ring, straightened the file folders, then got up and sharpened a handful of pencils. Wood dust fell on the bookcase, and she brushed the shavings into a tissue and threw it away.

Back at her desk, she tapped her fingers on the blotter, then pulled the class lists from her drawer and looked over them. She decided that learning names would be a good place to start. She scanned the pages. There were several families whose names were repeated. That would make it easier, she thought.

She spread the papers out on her desk. Let's see now, she thought -- Five Flanagans ...five! ... and she'd met one of them, Tommy... two Whittakers, four Pitlowskis... that was Billy's family... three Hanaghans ...ah, Mary Margaret...two Wasniaks in the seventh grade. Twins? Then there were Mrs. Long's three. What grade were they in? She ran her finger down the list but was interrupted by a knock at her door.

"Come in," she said, looking up. A young man in his late twenties came into her office. Slender and of medium height, he was dressed in unpressed khaki pants and a turquoise sweater over an open collared white shirt. He wore huaraches with no socks. The bearded visitor had a Spanish look, black haired, and the left side of his mouth turned down at the corner. Heavy lids hung over his black eyes. Something about him bothered Catherine, but she couldn't put her finger on it. Maybe it was his expression, but she didn't want to look directly at him to try to figure it out. She wondered who he was. He made her skin crawl.

"May I help you?" she asked smoothly, keeping her voice even.

"Dr. Anderson?"

"Yes, and you are..."

"Stefan Rodriguez."

"Hello, Mr. Rodriguez. What can I do for you?"

"Stefan, please," he said, looking straight into her eyes. Bold, she thought. He stepped closer to her desk and she felt more and more uneasy. She considered standing up, but decided to stay where she was. She didn't recall the name Rodriguez on the class lists, so he must not be a parent. Who was he then, and what was he doing here?

"I am looking for Fr. Riley," he said.

Fr. Riley was in the sacristy vesting for Mass, but Catherine didn't want to tell that to Stefan Rodriguez. She didn't know who he was, and he stared at her in a way that made her nervous.

"If you'll have a seat, sir, I'll see if I can find him for you." Rodriguez sat down, looking around, invading the room with his eyes. Catherine was growing more and more edgy. She buzzed Mrs. Janis on the intercom. No answer. Great, she thought. She's already gone over to the church. She looked over the little card of names and numbers taped on the side of the phone, wondering if any rang in the sacristy. She found it. Number 7. She hit the button harder than necessary.

"Holy Martyrs Sacristy," a boy answered.

Success. Must be one of the altar boys, she thought.

"This is Dr. Anderson. To whom am I speaking, please?"

"Good morning, Dr. Anderson. I'm Robert O'Keefe." *Ah, one of the O'Keefes. Brendan's brother. And .Barbara, no, Bernadette's...*

100

"Are you serving this morning, Robert?"

"Yes, ma'am."

"Is Fr. Riley there?"

"Yes, ma'am. Just a moment please."

Fr. Riley came to the phone. "Yes," he said, sounding hurried.

"It's Catherine, Father. I'm sorry to bother you so soon before Mass."

"No problem, Catherine. What is it?"

"There's a gentleman here looking for you, and I thought, rather than sending him over, I should let you know."

"Good," he said, pleased with her prudence. There was no telling who the fellow was, and he would just as soon not have strangers in his sacristy. Too many irreplaceable things were kept there. "Did he tell you his name?"

"Mr. Rodriguez."

"Mister?"

"Yes, Father."

"What's he look like? What's he wearing? No, wait, obviously you can't say. Hang on, Catherine, keep him there. I'll be right over." He hung up leaving Catherine holding the phone, her hands trembling. Not two minutes later, his starched white surplice billowing over his cassock, Fr. Riley came bursting through the door. Rodriguez made no movement to stand. He sat leaning back in the chair, his legs stretched out into the room, crossed at the ankles.

"What is the meaning of this?" Fr. Riley demanded.

"Whatever do you mean, Father? Meaning of what? I was told you were apprised of my coming."

"You know very well what I mean, *Father* Rodriguez. A-round here you will wear clericals."

Catherine gasped. *A priest...* This was the visiting priest. *Terrific.* First Mrs. Carruthers and now this black-bearded priest with no socks.

"I do not wear a cassock unless I am performing a liturgical

101

function, and I do not own one of those ridiculous black suits. Surely you are aware that the Second Vatican Council mandated our being more accessible to the people. We are one in the priesthood of Christ."

"Surely you are aware, Father," Fr. Riley emphasized the title, "that, speaking of mandates, the pope has recently commanded a return to the venerable traditions of the Catholic Church, and wearing a collar is certainly one of them."

Fr. Rodriguez smirked. "Bishop Washinsky assured me that would not be necessary. I am here for informational purposes."

"You are sadly mistaken if you think that you are going to hang around here dressed like a layman for informational or any other purposes."

"I think you will find, Father, that it is *you* who are mis-- taken." He rose ceremoniously. "Now that I have made your acquaintance, I shall go to the rectory for my breakfast."

"Have you said your Mass?"

"Daily Mass is not required, nor do I say private Masses. It is necessary that a quorum of the faithful be present for the sacred meal."

Fr. Riley started to argue but decided against it. He would have to handle this with the bishop.

"As you wish. But you are not to appear here again in lay clothes. I will have the appropriate things sent over to you."

Fr. Rodriguez shrugged, then turned and looked at Catherine. She was aware of an unpleasant feeling along her arms like old nightmares of crawling insects. Her throat thickened, and she held her breath until Fr. Rodriguez got up and walked out. Fr. Riley glared at his back.

"We'll talk later, " he said to her. "It's nearly eight."

Catherine nodded, unable to speak. She straightened out the papers on her desk and put them back in the drawer, then grabbed her missal and her chapel veil and hurried over to the church where she took her place behind the rows of students.

It was hard to concentrate, and the Mass had ended before

she was able to calm herself, begging St. Michael the Archangel, defender of Christ's Church, to protect them all.

Catherine did not see Fr. Rodriguez again the rest of the day. She visited each classroom in the morning. She had closed her notebook and was walking to the door to leave the senior history class when she felt as though someone's eyes were boring through her back. She looked around the room and recognized the boy who had stared at her as she passed through the hall her first day at the school.

He sat forward, his shoulders stooped as though he were carrying a heavy burden. Longish hair of a dull brown color fell limply around his ears and brushed over his collar in the back. His shirt sleeves were too short and exposed his wrists, making his hands look disproportionately large. Hunched over his desk, he played with his pen between his fingers.

Catherine caught him looking at her, but he didn't drop his eyes. A strange look, intense and compelling. It made her uncomfortable. There was no teenage curiosity in it and certainly no friendliness, but a kind of cold scrutiny, a hardness. Now what's that all about? she wondered. She motioned to Carrie to come out into the hall.

"I just have a question," said Catherine, as Carrie shut the door behind her. "Who is that tall boy in the middle row?"

"That's Laso Matov."

"Any problems with him?"

Carrie hesitated. "Well, not really. It's hard to say... I don't know. Nothing you could really say is a problem, but..."

Catherine waited, but Carrie didn't say anything further. She tried to draw her out, "More an attitude thing?" she asked.

"I guess you could say that. Fr. Riley said something about it last week. He's got hard eyes. Sometimes I think I'm imagining it, but it seems like he's looking at me funny. I *must* be imagining it because he's never disrespectful, and he turns his work in on time and everything. He's very bright. Especially in science. He always gets first honors. But..." Carrie had run out of words.

"I don't think you were imagining it," said Catherine. "I noticed it, too. Let me know if there's any problem," Catherine said as she started to leave, then hesitated for a moment. "Carrie, is Laso an altar boy?"

"No. Not any more. He used to be, though. Fr. Riley was really disappointed when he quit. I guess he was one of the best ones Father ever had. Really devout and everything." Carrie paused. "And you know what else?"

"What?"

"I don't know if I should say. Maybe I shouldn't have noticed."

"Noticed what?"

"He never goes to confession when the school goes."

"No?"

"No. And he never goes to Communion, either."

Catherine was surprised. She'd have to mention it to Fr. Riley. And that look was unsettling.

Fr. Riley did not make his usual brief visit to the teachers' lunch room at noon, and no one mentioned having seen Fr. Rodriguez, so Catherine didn't bring it up either. Lunch passed pleasantly; and despite the morning's anxiety, she was glad she had come to Holy Martyrs. Rocky Mountain College was far from her mind.

After lunch she taught the high school students, and it wasn't until she was back in her office after the closing bell had rung that she realized that Laso had not been in English class. She tried to remember which grade he was in. She pulled her class list out. There he was. A senior. So he should have been in the Survey of Literature class. Now where was he and what was going on?   She buzzed the secretary's office.

"Yes?"

"Mrs. Janis.   It's Catherine Anderson."

"Yes, Dr. Anderson."

"Could you check if Laso Matov had an excused absence this afternoon?"

"I don't have to check.   I already know.   Some lady called earlier, said she was Laso's aunt.   But she didn't have an accent or anything, and Laso's family hasn't been over here all that long. Laso and his father just got here last year.

"His uncles came over in '95 to escape the war, so it seems to me she should talk like the rest of them.   Of course, maybe she's American.   An aunt by marriage or something.   Her voice sounded familiar, but I couldn't place it.   Anyway, she said she had to come get Laso for an appointment.

"I wanted to ask what kind of an appointment, but I figured it wasn't my business, even though I think the school should know. 'Where's his father?' I asked. She said he was at work, and that's why she was calling. So I said fine, what time? After I hung up, I thought I'd better ask Fr. Riley if he could go.   I didn't think about asking you.   I'm not used to you being here yet.   I'm sorry."

"That was fine, Mrs. Janis.   I've only been here a couple of days.   You were right to go to Father."

Evelyn Janis relaxed.   She didn't want to antagonize the new principal.   "So I told him what happened and he said, 'Let him go,' But I was suspicious.   Looking for an excuse to skip school, that's what I thought.   Got somebody to call in for him and skipped out."

Catherine didn't think that was likely after what Carrie had told her about his being an honor student.   Still, it was curious. She thanked Mrs. Janis and hung up the phone.   She went back to her paperwork, waiting to see if Fr. Riley wanted to see her.   She didn't know just when he meant when he said, "We'll talk later."

Mrs. Anderson was going to pick her up at four thirty.   At

105

four fifteen, Fr. Riley had still not come by. Catherine was geting anxious to talk to him, especially after the episode with Laso. Add that stare to Fr. Rogriguez' visit, and it was enough to make anyone nervous, she thought, lifting and winding a strand of hair at the back of her head that had fallen loose from her French twist. She removed one of her combs and jabbed it back into place, then walked around her desk to get her coat from the hook behind the door. She would just have to wait to find out what was going on.

But waiting drove her crazy. She opened the bottom drawer of the file cabinet for her purse, then closed it and relocked the drawer. Loading her books and papers into her briefcase, she paused and took a deep breath, then decided to go over to the church for a few minutes.

She laid her lace mantilla over her head, tying the ends under her chin so it wouldn't fly off in the wind that whistled through the windows and hit against the roof. She had about fifteen minutes. Helen was coming to pick her up after her bridge game at Dearborn Country Club, and she wanted to stop at Jacobson's on the way home.

There was a dress she was thinking about for Easter, and she wanted Catherine to see it before she bought it. Catherine locked her office door and walked over to the church. The high gray clouds were starting to thicken and drop, and the afternoon grew dark.

In the church, all the windows were shut and the air was close and heavy. The votive candles flickered. Catherine slipped into a back pew. At the front, in the sanctuary, Fr. Riley knelt on the thin red carpet. His face was raised to the crucifix and his shoulders were straight, lifting and dropping slightly as he breathed, his black cassock falling behind him in smooth folds over his feet. Catherine said her prayers, then went outside to wait for Mrs. Anderson.

Fr. Riley did not move.

CHAPTER

10

Eripe me de inimicis meis, Domine,
Ad te Confugi

Catherine went outside just as the Lincoln was pulling into the parking lot. She waved and started to run toward the car, then remembered her new position and slowed to a quick walk. Mrs. Anderson clicked the unlock button, and Catherine slid onto the front seat, the automatic seat belt closing around her.

"Hi," she said. "Perfect timing."

"How was your day?"

"Different."

"Do you have time to stop at Jake's?" asked Helen.

"Sure do," answered Catherine, relieved that Helen had changed the subject. She didn't want to tell her about Fr. Rodriguez. "I'd like to see that dress. How was your bridge game?"

"Oh, it was fine. But, you know, I really don't think it's as much fun as it used to be."

"No? Why is that?"

"Oh, I don't know," said Helen as she drove uptown. "Maybe I'm just getting old. It seems, well, I don't know. Kind of boring."

Catherine looked over at her mother-in-law and smiled. She understood what was happening. In the cultural devastation of the eighties and nineties after Frank had grown up and left home, Helen tried to fill the emptiness of her days with lunch and bridge and shopping. But it wasn't enough. There was a hunger in her soul which she longed to satisfy.

"Teresa called me this morning. She invited me to join the Altar Society. She's the president. "

"Will you?"

"I think so. I'd like to help out. And I'd like to meet some of the other women. Teresa said about twenty of them come regularly. Some can't because they work and some have babies at home, so it's hard for them. But I think I might like to go."

"When do they meet?"

"Thursday afternoons."

"Isn't that a bridge day?"

Helen was silent for a minute. "Not anymore," she said. She'd have to call Sally Green tonight and tell her she would need a new partner. She drove north on Military toward Michigan Avenue. "Would you mind stopping at Pier One first?" she asked. "They have white linen napkins on sale, and I need some new ones for Easter."

Catherine didn't object, so Helen turned left into into the parking lot. Most of the spaces were full, and she had to park close to Michigan Avenue in front of Dunkin' Donuts.

"It's just a little walk," Catherine said, as Helen scanned the lot for a closer place. "It'll do us good."

She got out of the car and looked over at the Catholic church across the street. As she started to turn to walk to the store with Helen, a flash of turquoise caught her eye. It couldn't be. She squinted to see better. Coming down the sidewalk from the Sacred Heart Community Center were three people -- two men and a stocky, gray-haired woman.

The woman, who looked to be about fifty years old, was wearing an ill-fitting pant suit and beige crepe-soled shoes and was struggling with a heavy brown briefcase. She was in front of the man in turqouise, and Catherine couldn't get a good look at him, but then the woman stopped to put the briefcase down for a moment. The man came around her, leaving her to manage her burden alone.

There was no mistaking the black hair and khaki pants. *Fr.*

Rodriguez! What was he doing over here? And, no, it couldn't couldn't be... She looked again at the taller one.

He was younger than she had thought, a boy, not a man. He had come up next to Fr. Rodriguez, and she could see him better now. Tall, round shouldered, a navy blue windbreaker zipped tight up to his neck, she recognized him. *Laso.* At that moment as if by a signal, he looked over at her.

Did he see me? she wondered, moving quickly to the other side of the car where Helen stood waiting. She was afraid he did. She felt the same hard stare driving into her that she had experienced twice before. She shivered and wanted to grab Helen's arm, but she restrained herself and thrust her hands into the pockets of her coat. Helen looked at her.

"Is something wrong, dear?" she asked.

"No. I just thought I saw someone I knew."

"Well, you look like you've seen a ghost. You're all white. Maybe we shouldn't go shopping."

"No, really, I'm fine. Come on. Let's go get those napkins."

They were out of the store in ten minutes, and the threesome was gone.

"Shall we walk to Jacobson's or do you want to drive over?" asked Helen.

"Let's walk."

They walked the block to the department store and rode the escalator to the second floor, where Helen walked straight to designer section. A tall slim saleswoman, dressed in a sleek charcoal suit with white trim and Christian Dior glasses hanging from a gold chain around her neck, approached her.

"May I help you?" she asked.

Helen described the dress to her and the woman listened, peering down her nose.

"Ah, yes. I know which one you mean. Size?"

"Six."

The woman went into the back and came out carrying a

dotted Swiss muslin of navy blue with a full skirt and gathered waist. The long thin sleeves were cuffed in white and a delicate cutwork collar circled the high neckline. Dainty pearl buttons ran down the length of the dress. The saleswoman held the hanger in one hand and draped the dress out in front of her, the bottom of the skirt falling over her other arm.

"Yes, that's it," said Helen. She turned to Catherine. "What do you think?"

"It's perfect. Do you need to try it on?"

"No, I did already. It fits fine. I'll take it."

While Helen waited to sign the charge slip, Catherine wandered over to a wall rack to look through the dresses hanging there. They were a blur before her eyes. All she could see was Fr. Rodriguez sitting in her office that morning when Fr. Riley had come in, and she remembered the expression on his face, how his mouth curled into his beard and his eyes had glinted in the fluorescent light. It was not a pleasant memory. And the thought of Laso and his riveting stares played on her mind.

She wondered who the woman was. Must be the aunt, she thought or ... no...surely not... An idea was starting to form and she wanted to reject it as she did most stories of intrigue and collusion. Catherine trusted people, and she liked to look on the bright side of things. In spite of all that had happened, she wanted to believe that the world was a more benign place than it was. She was mindlessly sliding the dresses along the rack when Helen came over to her. I'll have to talk to Fr. Riley tomorrow, Catherine decided as she stepped back from the display.

"Did you want to try anything on?"

"No, I was just looking."

"Do you have something for Easter?"

"Yes, I have the silk dress Frank brought me last year from Belgium."

The reference to Frank unsettled Helen. The pain which was always close to the surface broke through, and she caught her breath. This would be the first holiday without Frank, and she didn't want to face it. She had to move quickly, distract herself, before she started to think about the past, about her little boy at Eastertime. That was the hardest time now, when memories of his childhood loomed before her eyes. She pulled her spring coat around her and with clicking heels hurried toward the escalator.

Agnes slammed the door and settled heavily into the seat.

"Did she recognize you?" asked Fr. Rodriguez as he started the car.

"I think so," answered Laso. "Who would have thought that she would see me? I'm going to be in trouble now."

"I knew we shouldn't have come together," said Sr. Agnes angrily. "Someone was bound to see us."

"You're both getting paranoid. Relax," said the priest. "It was just an innocent meeting of friends."

"You keep forgetting, Stefan, that Fr. Riley was on to me."

"You don't know that for certain."

"No. But I'm sure he knew."

"What exactly did he say when he dismissed you?" The tight control that Fr. Rodriguez was imposing on himself was starting to crack, and his voice was cold.

"He said I had an attitude problem."

"Those were his words -- attitude problem? Doesn't sound like Riley."

"No. You know how pompous he is." She grimaced, her thick gray lips pressed together. "A real holier-than-thou type."

"Yeah, I know. They're all like that. Traditionalists." He spat out the words. "Bunch of right wing bigots."

Laso sat in the back seat, hunched down, his neck hidden in the collar of his jacket and his hands jammed into his pockets. He looked at the back of the seat, expressionless, his eyes glazed over.

"So what exactly did he say?"

"He was real sanctimonious. He said that he felt that I had

some difficulty accepting the traditional ways of the school and that *perhaps*-- as though he gave me any choice--I would be happier somewhere else, where they might be more *sympathetic* to my educational philosophy."

"And that was it?"

"More or less. He asked if I wanted to talk about it, if I had any questions, you know all that stuff about, 'I'm so concerned....Can I help you through this...blah blah blah.' Made me sick. Like those people *care*. They're so wrapped up in the past they can't even see where History is taking us. Neanderthals."

"Now they have the Pope on their side," muttered Laso.

"That's not a big problem," said the priest. "The bishops aren't going along with him. Collegiality is too big an issue. He can't exercise any authority without consensus. And I don't think he's going to get that. But that's all he said?"

"Pretty much."

"Then what makes you think he knows?"

"I don't know. The way he looked. Something about him. Too much in control or something. Too calm."

"They're always like that. Self righteous bunch of..." He clamped his mouth shut, bitting off the profanity. "Doesn't mean anything."

Agnes shrugged. Fr. Rodriguez headed east on Michigan Avenue to Detroit. They were going to Greektown to have dinner with a group of priests from California.

Fr. Rodriguez parked his car down the street from Old St. Mary's, and the three of them walked the half block to the New Hellas Cafe. The street was quiet, and they were surpised there was no line at the restaurant. They requested a large table in the back and sat down to wait for the others.

"They should be here any minute," said Sr. Agnes, looking at her heavy stainless steel watch.

"Waiter!" said Fr. Rodriguez impatiently. A dark eyed adolescent in a clean white apron came over to the table.

"Yes, sir," he said. "What can I get for you?"

"Coffee for us and Coke for the boy."

Laso bristled. He was perfectly capable of ordering for himself and he didn't like to be referred to as a boy. He nursed his irritation as he looked at the menu.

"We're waiting for some friends, then we'll order our dinner. But bring us some flaming cheese now."

"The waiter nodded and slipped back to the kitchen.

"Now, look, Laso, said Sr. Agnes."Now that I'm not at Holy Martyrs, you're all we've got left. So don't mess things up."

Laso's face reddened. "Look yourself," he wanted to say, "you are the one who got thrown out of the school. Not me." He kept quiet, though, and sipped his coke. He thought they had better treat him right or he would quit. He didn't like their company any more. They seemed to be angry all the time, and it was contagious. If it weren't for the money that he needed to send back home, he'd just as soon call it quits right then.

But his mother was lying paralyzed in a hospital in Ljub-ljana, and she was not recovering as well as they had hoped. He and his father had come to Detroit from Slovenia to try to raise money to bring her to Ann Arbor for surgery, but they still didn't have enough. They had learned that it cost a lot to live in America even though they were staying with relatives, and Laso had seized this chance to earn some money. He didn't think he was doing anything wrong at first, but lately, he'd wondered.

"Your job, Laso," said Fr. Rodriguez, holding a piece of melted cheese on a fork to cool, "is to report what this Anderson woman does. Stay focused. We want her watched. She could be a real problem."

"Yeah, you watch her," said Agnes. "It wasn't so bad back when Riley was trying to run the school. He couldn't be there as much, so it was easier to do what we needed to do. But now she's going to be around all the time, and we're not going to be able to get our people in. Except for you, of course, Stefan..." She gazed at him and fluttered her thin gray eyelashes. Stefan, revolted, turned away.

"We want a weekly report," said the priest. "I'll be tied up with Riley most of the time. Pretending to learn the old ways. I intend to be a slow learner. Anyway, watch her...what she's doing....what she's changing around....what her routine is. That sort of thing. Now, what have you observed so far?"

Laso didn't want to say. He had been watching her as they had told him to. He had told himself that she was an enemy, someone to be feared, because that's what Fr. Rodriguez and his friends had told him. But he could no longer ignore what he had seen for himself. He had pasted a sullen expression on his face because he was afraid that his real feelings would start to show. The truth of it was, he liked Dr. Anderson. She was pretty and intelligent and she carried herself like, well, like his mother did. Graceful. With a dignity you didn't see that often. "A lady... like a princess," his grandmother would say.

"I asked you a question," said Fr. Rodriguez pointedly.

Laso raised the glass of Coke to his lips. He drank deliberately.

"We don't have all night," said Agnes.

"I can't have much to say when you pulled me out of her classes," said Laso.

Agnes rolled her eyes. "Any changes in the school routine?"

"None so far. I'll let you know."

"See that you do. And keep your mouth shut, remember." The nun riveted her eyes into his, commanding his assent. Three men approached the table.

"Rodriguez?"

"Jaime! Good to see you, man!" said Fr. Rodriguez, jumping up to embrace the newcomer. They slapped each other on the back and sat down.

"It's been awhile, Stefan. How're things?"

"Not good at all, as you've heard." He raised his arm. "Waiter!" The young boy hurried back to the table. "Four beers. Draft." He turned back to the man called Jaime.

"What about me, Stefan?" whined Agnes.

"What about you?"

"Maybe I wanted a beer, too."

"Did you?"

"No, but you could have asked." Fr. Rodriguez looked at her disgustedly. She was getting on his nerves.

Jaime turned the coversation back to Archbishop Stagniak. "Stagniak of all people. I thought he was a Teilhardian."

"Nah, not him. He's one of those lock-step guys."

"We almost fell over when he made that announcement. Restoring tradition! Following the pope! What's the deal? Alzheimer's?"

Fr. Rodriguez shrugged. "Who knows? All I know is we're stuck with it. We're doing what we can, though. How's it going in San Diego?

"Good. Fine. No opposition there. We got it locked up, I think. The bishop would be a fool to change things now."

"What about obedience and the infallibility thing?"

"What about it? Nobody believes that stuff anymore. You know anyone who does? Besides Riley and Stagniak, that is?"

Fr. Rodriguez shrugged.

"Look, Stefan. I want you to meet Dan Gregson and Jeff Van Meter. They're on the priests' council with me, and they've got some experience with the sort of thing you're doing."

Fr. Rodriguez looked them over. Maybe he could trust them, maybe not. He'd be careful. "Nice to meet you," he said. He nodded toward his companions. "Sr. Agnes Hopaluk and Laso Matov."

"Seminarian?" asked Fr. Jaime Rivera.

"Not yet," Stefan answered. "He's got a job to do first." He narrowed his eyes and looked across the table at Laso, then turned back to Rivera, assuming an expression of benign affability. "He was thinking about it...that's how I met him. Washinsky made me Director of Vocations last year."

The waiter interrupted them to take their orders and Laso took the opportunity to study the men. Fr. Rivera was short and dark, and he pulled himself close to the the table and leaned on his arms. Fr. Van Meter's pink-rimmed eyes were fringed with pale lashes, and his hair was sparse. Although he couldn't have been thirty, his hairline had receded halfway back his head. Laso didn't like the expression on their faces. They all looked like that, he thought: Fr. Rodriguez, Sr. Agnes, these three from California. There was a coldness in their eyes, a ruthlessness.

Laso finished his Coke and motioned to the waiter that he needed another one, while Fr. Gregson tried to decide what he wanted to eat. He shoved his empty beer glass over to the waiter.

"Bring me another one of these," he said without looking up. His stomach hung over his belt and his knit shirt had ridden up baring a strip of soft pink flesh. Laso cringed as the priest scanned the menu and smacked his lips.

"I'll be right back with your drinks," said the waiter, "and give you a little more time to decide." He hurried away. Fr. Gregson slapped the menu shut and folded his hands on the edge of the table, pushing his chair back slightly so he'd have more room to breathe.

"So you want to go to the seminary?" he asked, puffing.

Laso nodded. It was true. He had considered it. A year ago, he had wanted it very much. He had called the Vocations Office when he had first come to America. He was lonely and worried about his mother. He thought that maybe God would be pleased with a sacrifice. If he gave his life to God by being a priest, maybe God would help his mother.

He was only sixteen at the time. They had told him to wait awhile, finish his education, and then come back, but Fr. Rodriguez' ears had picked up when he heard where Laso went to school. An idea formed in his mind. He knew that they were playing around with the old ways at Holy Martyrs even before the Pope's October Surprise. He went to Bishop Washinsky with the information, and the plan developed.

For his part, though, Laso was becoming uncomfortable. He liked Fr. Riley, and he wasn't unhappy at the school. He was homesick. He missed his village and his friends, and he was worried about his mother. But he wasn't sure he wanted to be a spy, because that's what he was, he realized. He'd gone along, doing what they said, thinking he was working for the Church. Coming from a country under martial law, he found it easy to do what he was told. But now he wasn't sure.

The waiter set the drink refills on the table. "Thanks," Laso said and slid the glass over to his place. He was hot, and he drained his second Coke, trying to cool off. He put down the empty glass and picked up the frosted glass of ice water, pressing it against his wrist. He looked around the table.

The waiter had come back again and was handing the bread baskets over their shoulders. Everyone was ignoring Laso now. They'd gotten the information they wanted, and he no longer interested them. He relaxed and put down the glass. Reaching for the bread, he cut a slice, then tore it into four pieces and slowly buttered the sections, so he wouldn't have to look up again. He laid three of the pieces on the bread plate and nibbled at the fourth.

Fr. Gregson took the loaf of bread from the wooden board in front of Laso and tore off the crust. He shoved it into his mouth and washed it down with noisy gulps of beer. Fr, Van Meter reached reached across the table and forked the last piece of melted cheese congealing on the plate. He bit it in half. Holding the fork with the other half in the air, he turned to Fr. Rodriguez.

"Have you started the information campaign?" he asked. A piece of cheese stuck to his front tooth, and he picked at it with his fingernail.

"No," answered Rodriguez. "We're still in the beginning stages. We had a little setback." He pointed his thumb at Agnes.

"What happened?"

"Riley got wise somehow. "

"Did he fire you?" asked Jaime Rivera.

"You could call it that," she shrugged. "Now we've got this kid working for us."

Laso had to force himself not to look at her. His expression would have betrayed him. He was starting to compare Sr. Agnes with Dr. Anderson, and he was beginning to fear that he had somehow wound up on the wrong side of things. People had been nice to him at the seminary at first, and they treated him like he was important. He was lonely and not thinking clearly.

Fr. Rodriguez and Bishop Washinsky had seemed to take a personal interest in him. They had called him in for long talks, and he felt that they were confiding in him. His adolescent head had swelled, and his young heart had warmed to the men showing him such kindness.

They told him that people were trying to destroy everything they had worked for all their lives, that there were bad men, bigots and fascists, who were trying to impose their ideas on everybody else and hold back the renewal, the great flowering of the Church, the culmination of the quest of the People of God: The Omega Point. They painted pictures of stark oppression and crushing obedience and convinced Laso that people like Fr. Riley were charismatic cultists, trying to control people's minds for their own purposes. They could not be trusted. Laso was told to disregard his own impressions, that the zealots were good at deception.

And Laso had believed them.

Fr. Rodriguez had treated him like a brother. He took him to dinner and ball games and talked to him like his ideas mattered. Laso had felt his resentment of his school and its rules deepening. He was close to rebellion, but Fr. Rodriguez cautioned him against it, saying they needed him to stay where he was and not make trouble. And so Laso had gone along with it, finding himself hating school, hating his teachers, hating the complicated ceremonies of the Mass. He was changing. Changing and accepting the changes in himself, thinking they were necessary, that he was *growing*, as Fr. Rodriguez explained to him.

Until this week. Until he realized that he respected Fr. Riley, that he liked him. How could anyone say Fr. Riley was dangerous? And then he saw Dr. Anderson and heard her laugh. He couldn't understand why Sr. Agnes and Fr. Rodriguez had been in such a fury when they heard she was coming.

They said she would destroy his individuality and independence; but thinking about her, he couldn't see how. When she came, he had watched her, staring at her to the point that she was starting to notice it, and the more he watched her, the more he liked her.

He was confused and didn't trust his own reactions but now, this evening, as he watched these men, these *priests*, at the table and listened to their talk, how could he trust *them*? They reminded him of the Communists back home who were always plotting an uprising since they had fallen from power a decade before. The waiter brought the platters of souvlaki and rice and Laso tried to sort out his thoughts.

Sr. Agnes excused herself and left the table.

Helen had drawn the blinds and turned on the lights as darkness wrapped itself around the house. The three Andersons were sitting at the kitchen table eating dinner. Don was contentedly cutting his pork chop and telling about the design for a new type of fuel system that he was working on when the phone rang. "Some salesman, probably," he said, as Helen rose to answer it.

"Hello... Yes... Just a moment please." She held the phone out toward Catherine. "It's for you."

Catherine looked at her questioningly. Helen shook her head and held the receiver against her chest to blot out the the sound. "I don't know who it is. It's a woman."

"Ms. Anderson?" hissed the voice as Catherine raised the receiver to her ear.

119

"Yes, this is Catherine Anderson." She hated to be called Ms.

"If I were you, lady, I'd go back to cowboy country where you belong."

"I beg your pardon?" Catherine asked coldly. Her stomach tightened. She swallowed, debating whether to slam the phone down or listen to what the caller had to say. She decided to listen.

"You heard me. We don't want you around here. We don't need troublemakers like you. You're in our way. You'd better leave before you get hurt. If you stay here, you'll regret it."

Catherine's temper started to flare. "Now, just a minute, madam..."

The phone clicked in her ear.

Helen and Don were watching Catherine, their faces worried. Pressing her hand against her forehead, she hung up the phone and leaned against the wall. Helen stood up and went over to her, putting her arm around her waist.

"What is it, dear?" she asked. "What's wrong?"

Don held out the chair for her and Catherine sat back down. "That was the strangest phone call." She repeated the conversation.

"Now who in the world would be calling you and saying such things?" asked Helen indignantly. She started stacking the dishes.

"Looks like our girl stepped on somebody's toes," said Don.

"Do you think it was a wrong number, dear?" Helen bent over to pick up a fork she had dropped.

"No," answered Catherine. "It was for me." The woman knew her name and the reference to Colorado was unmistakable. She wondered if she should tell the Andersons about what had happened at school. She hadn't wanted them to worry, but the decision had been taken from her.

But what could she say? She really didn't know that much herself. She assumed the call was related to Fr. Rodriguez' visit and somehow with the little group she had seen coming out of the Community Center, but she wasn't sure. She didn't think she had done anything to alienate the priest or Laso either, for that matter. And she didn't even know who the woman was she had seen or if it was the same one who had just called.

"Please don't worry," Catherine said. "I guess this is just the sort of thing we should expect when we're trying to do what we're doing. The devil's not real happy with us, you know." She tried to keep her voice light, but it wasn't easy. Her folded hands trembled in her lap.

"Well, Catherine, it looks to me like maybe you've got some of those fellows Vito and Stan were talking about yesterday lurking around somewhere, and they obviously don't want you here. They could be dangerous. You'd better be careful." Don paused. He'd spent a lot of time thinking in the past twenty-four hours. He turned to his wife.

"You know, Helen, all these years, I didn't understand why you weren't going to church when you always had before. Then you started going again, and I didn't understand that either. I admit, I thought it was a big fuss over nothing."

He straightened his tie. He had never talked about religion with Helen, and he was unsure of himself. He didn't like to feel so vulnerable, but he pushed himself to continue. He had to, for Catherine's sake as well as Helen's.

"I was wrong," he said. " It matters a lot. You don't get calls like that if it's not important. The stakes are pretty high, I guess, and it looks like the other side's afraid to lose."

Helen was looking at her husband intently. Her cheeks flushed and tears welled in her eyes. He had never known how hard it had been for her when the changes came. She had never tried to explain to him what she was going through because she

121

was afraid he wouldn't understand.   But she was ashamed of herself now for having had so little confidence in him.   She looked down at her hands lying folded on the table, and Don reached across and laid his hand over them..

"I wasn't much help to you those years," he said.

She shook her head at him. "You were fine," she said. "You've always been a help to me. I just thought you..."

"That I wouldn't understand?"

"Yes," she whispered.

"Well, now, old girl, you know, I probably wouldn't have. But maybe I do now." He looked over at Catherine across the table. "Maybe I can help you both now."

Catherine smiled at him feebly.

"Don't let those people get under your skin," said Don. "They're just trying to intimidate you, whoever they are. They'd like to see you gone. Must mean you're doing something right."

"Yes," said Helen. "But it's awfully frightening."

"I don't know if I'm frightened or angry," said Catherine. "The nerve!"

"That's better," said Don. "Don't let them scare you. Just keep your eyes open."

Catherine nodded. She was puzzled. It was hard for her to understand deliberate ill will. She could understand people getting angry and shouting at each other or getting their feelings hurt and saying hateful things that they later regretted. But she could not understand cold-blooded malice. It made her cringe.

"Why don't you two go on into the den?" said Helen. "I'll just wash these dishes up real fast and join you in a minute."

"Let me help you, Mother."

"No, you go along. Relax a little." Helen waved them out the kitchen door and turned to the sink, squirting the liquid soap and holding her hands under the hot running water. She felt better. She wouldn't use the dishwasher. She'd rub and polish the glasses until the light shimmered in her palm like a handful of crystal beads. The warm water was soothing, and there was no machine clatter to disturb the evening any further. It gave her a quiet time to think.

She was worried about the phone call and frightened for Catherine. She couldn't bear it if something happened to her. Not after Frank. She shuddered to think about it. For years she had longed for a daughter, but she hadn't been able to bear any more children. Catherine was the daughter of her heart.

Looking out the window over the sink at the moon rising above the trees, she considered the mysterious workings of God. He had answered her prayers, but not in the way she expected. She plunged her arms into the hot soapy water and attacked the pots and pans with a Brillo pad.

Helen finished washing and drying the dishes and stacked the plates in the cupboard, then brushed the place mats and put them in the drawer under the counter. As she walked to the closet to get the broom, she wondered whether she should call Fr. Riley and tell him about the telephone call. She debated with herself as she swept the floor. It wouldn't hurt to let him know, she decided, and she rested the broom against the wall and picked up the phone.

CHAPTER

11

Animas pauperum salvas faciet.

Don and Catherine crossed the hall to the den. The lamps were lit, casting a warm glow on the wood panelled walls. Don picked up the newspaper from the seat of his recliner, sat down and raised the footrest. He turned to the business section to check the stock market, scanning the columns, but the numbers didn't register, and he turned the page back to the editorial section.

There was nothing interesting there, either, so he laid the open paper across his lap and leaned back, folding his hands on his flat stomach and closing his eyes. Catherine glanced over at him from the table in the corner where she sat working on her lesson plans. She turned back to her books and papers and started to write.

"You know, Catherine..." Don said, startling her. She thought he was asleep. She looked up.

"Yes, Dad?"

"Well, I've been thinking...I mean...do you have a couple of minutes?"

"All kinds of time," she answered. She wondered what he wanted to talk about. From the look on his face, it had to be something serious, which puzzled her, because he had never been interested in philosophical conversations. He was nothing like Frank in that regard, Catherine thought. He rarely talked about politics, much less anything deeper. His thoughts were usually centered on engineering, golf, and Helen Justine Anderson .

He rose from his chair and came over to the club table where Catherine was working. Pulling out the chair across from

124

her, he sat down, not saying anything. He pulled at his ear and looked up at the ceiling. Catherine closed her book.

"Well," he said. "I got to wondering about things..." He was quiet again.

Catherine waited.

" I didn't want to bother Mother with it. I mean, I didn't want her to think I was some kind of an ignoramus or something, but..." He loosened his collar.

"What were you wondering about, Dad?"

"You know, I don't know that much about your religion. I kind of thought all religions were, you know, alike."

"Yes..."

"But they're not."

"No."

"Well, why does everybody say they are, then?" he said with exasperation. "They say it and you just accept it as true. You never think about it." Don looked up at the ceiling and traced the molding with his eyes. "Then one day you start to think about it, and you realize it's not true. You've been fooled all your life. Makes you feel kind of. stupid."

He walked over to the gas fireplace and adjusted the flame, then stood with his back to the fire. He looked down at the floor and smoothed the hearth rug with his foot.

"I mean, I thought there were lots of ways to get to heaven. You know, you have to be good, play by the rules, not hurt anybody, and that's all there was to it. You didn't really...I don't know how to say this...you didn't really have any connection, you know, with, well, with..." he coughed.

"With God?"

He nodded. "Yeah... With God..." It was hard to say it. He scratched his head, then smoothed his hair. "You know, you said your prayers at night when you were little and then you mostly forgot about it when you got older. You sort of think it's for women and kids and people like Fr. Riley. Even Frank. I was kind of surprised that he took to religion like he did. I didn't

expect it. I sure never thought it had that much to do with me."
Don came back to the table and sat down.

"But something changed your mind?"

"Yeah...I'm a little bothered by it. It makes me feel kind of funny."

"Mixed up?"

"Yeah, you know, like you don't recognize your own thoughts anymore."

He leaned forward and closed his eyes. Catherine didn't know what to say, so she sat quietly, watching her father-in-law. The mantle clock chimed, and Don waited until it stopped.

"I first started thinking about it when Frank died..." His voice caught in his throat, and he dropped his head. The house was quiet and Catherine waited. Don rubbed his eyes, then laid his thin fingers on the table, pressing them into the wood.

"I try not to think about my boy ..."

An image of Frank when he was five years old flashed through Don's mind. He was learning to ride a bicycle and Don was running beside him in case he lost his balance. All his life he had tried to protect him. But in the end ...

In the end, he had failed.

Don shut his eyes, then tried to speak.

"I try to pretend sometimes that he's just off on assignment somewhere, that he'll be back. But at night...I remember all the little things and ...Oh, God, it hurts so much..." He covered his face and his shoulders shook with silent sobbing.

"I know," whispered Catherine as tears burned her eyes. "I know, Dad."

Don pulled a handkerchief out of his pocket and wiped his eyes. "Yes...well..." He drew his breath in tightly and sat up straight.   "Anyway, that's when I started to think about it." He cleared his throat and continued, "And then we had that dinner last week, and I listened to all of you talk, and it was kind of different, you know. Not like at the club or Kiwanis or anything. It was sort of like you all -- you and Mother and Fr. Riley, and somehow, Frank, too -- were part of something... Something bigger than yourselves. He stopped short, afraid he was making a fool of himself. "Does that sound dumb?"

"No," said Catherine softly. "Not dumb at all." She knew what he meant. "Because we are, you see."

"What?"

"Part of something bigger than ourselves."

"Oh. You mean the Church?"

"Yes. But it's different than what you mean by church. It's not just a group of people getting together on Sunday."

"No? Well, what is it then?" Don asked, puzzled, the lines in his forehead deepening "It's different, that's for sure," he said, rubbing his chin.

Catherine was wondering how to answer his questions when there was a knock at the front door. She heard Helen talking to someone, but they didn't come into the den. Don was looking at his hands while he waited for Catherine to explain what she meant. He didn't seem to notice that they had company.

"You see, Dad," she continued gently. "There aren't all kinds of ways to get to Heaven. There's only one."

He scratched his forehead. "That's what I was starting to think."

"You were right."

"Things started adding up that way and I got confused."

"It hits you kind of hard at first when you begin to see it," she said softly. "But that's the truth. There is only one way, One True Church. One path. And all the people on the road are part of something bigger than themselves."

She paused and took a deep breath, daunted for a moment by the magnitude of what she was trying to say. How could she ever explain it? Don looked across at Catherine; and when she smiled back at him, her eyes were liquid, shining like pools of deep green water in the firelight.

"It's supernatural," she said, her voice even and steady, as though she were reading a text from the *Summa*. But as she

127

spoke, her emotions surged and pressed against the words, the power of her faith propelling them forward breathlessly. "It's a union of our souls with Christ." she said. "A real union, not just symbolic.   That's why we can hope for Heaven... not because of ourselves, but because of Him..."

She wished she could say it better, wished she could put into words the majesty and wonder of it.   "Our Lord founded the Church for us so that through it, in it, we could save our souls." Her voice became urgent, sweeping over Don like a wave of grace, carrying him on the crest. She saw his eyes move as though he were watching something unfold in his mind.

"And, Dad, that's the only way. It's the whole purpose of our life, to find the truth and embrace it, to live in the love of God and be with Him forever."

Don listened thoughtfully. "And so you think you'll see Frank again someday, too?"

"Yes."

"I'd like that. I could accept his death better, I think, if I could believe that someday, I'd see my boy again..." Don's eyes filled with tears.

"You've taken the first step, Dad. "Death is not so fearsome when you know the separation is only temporary."

"Not forever then..."

"No."

"And there's certain things you have to believe and certain things you have to do? Or else you don't make it..."

"Yes."

" I remember a long time ago some people used to say stuff like that, guys I knew in school and the service. I used to think they were nuts." He saw her drop her eyes, and he could have bitten his tongue.

"It's still true, Dad," Catherine said, brushing her hair back from her forehead.

"But there are a lot of people in the Catholic Church who

128

don't believe that, right? Otherwise, you'd hear it more."

"I'm afraid you're right. There's been a real revolution over the past forty years, and everything was up for grabs. There was nothing sacred anymore, nothing they didn't want to change."

"Who?"

"People in the highest places. Those with authority."

"But why?"

"I don't know, Dad. Our Lord warned us about these times. It's in the Gospel. The wars and earthquakes and upheaval, the false prophets. Anyway, they changed some very important, ancient things. Things that Catholics had always been told could never be changed, like the Mass. And doctrine." She paused. "Am I explaining this all right?"

"I'm following you. It makes sense. So that's why Mother stopped going to church, and that's why that woman wants you to leave..."

"Yes. The Pope is putting a stop to the confusion, and he's determined to restore all the beautiful things we thought we had lost forever. And that's making a lot of people very angry. "

"I see what you mean. This is a lot to think about." He watched the fire. "There's one other thing I want to know," he said finally.

"What's that?"

"What happens during Mass when those bells ring and the priest holds up that round white thing?"

"Ah, Dad, that's the Mystery of Faith." Catherine leaned toward Don, her emerald eyes glowing. "It's the Body of Christ, Living and True ...under the appearance of Bread. And the Chalice contains His Blood. It's God Himself come down from Heaven at the call of the priest to offer Himself for us."

Don nodded, thinking. That explained why there was that stillness, that hush, and the strong heavy feeling that pushed and prodded him. God was in the church. And everybody there that day knew it except for him. But now he had so many other questions.

He'd have to think about it some more.

Helen came into the den followed by Fr. Riley, who had driven right over after she called him. Don and Catherine rose to greet him.

"I thought Father should know about that strange call," said Helen, explaining why he was there.

"You're right," said Don. "Come on, Mother, we can go into the living room so they can talk."

"No, stay," said Fr. Riley. "Catherine may need you to know what's going on. If that's all right with you, Catherine?"

"Yes, it's fine. I just didn't want to worry them."

"They heard the phone call."

"Yes," said Catherine. "But there's more."

Helen looked at her, alarmed. "Nothing threatening, Mother...just strange. I was planning to tell Father about it tomorrow."

"Well you can tell us all now."

"Okay, Catherine, let's hear it," Fr. Riley said as they sat down at the table where Catherine had been working. Catherine stacked her books and papers to make room for him and Helen. Fr. Riley was worried. He tried to keep his anxiety out of his voice, but he wasn't succeeding very well. Catherine, the school, the children, could be in danger. He would have to notify the bishop and wondered whether he should go directly to Archbishop Stagniak. He decided that that was probably what he would do. He was afraid that any message he sent through the channels might get circumvented.

Catherine told him about the telephone conversation.

"It's curious that it was a woman," said Fr. Riley. "Can you describe her voice?"

"She sounded strident, clipped. Midwestern accent. Not distinctive." Catherine paused, realizing that she was sounding like an English teacher.

"Any guesses?"

"I don't want to guess."

"That means you have a suspicion."

"Yes."

"It's probably the same as mine."

"Sister Agnes?"

"Yes," answered Fr. Riley.

"Then let me tell you the rest. Is Sister Agnes short and boxy looking with unattractively styled brown hair?"

"Yes."

"And does she have thick features and a mannish walk?"

"I think you could say that. How did you know?" Catherine told him about seeing Fr. Rodriguez, Laso, and the unidentified woman that afternoon

"Laso was with them?"

"Yes. He wasn't in class this afternoon. I asked Mrs. Janis about it , and she said he had an appointment and left early."

Fr. Riley looked perplexed. "Now why in the world would Laso be mixed up in this? I'll have to talk to him tomorrow."

Mrs. Anderson was thinking back over the afternoon and understood why Catherine had looked so funny in the parking lot.

"Do you have any idea what's going on?" asked Catherine.

"Not really," answered Fr. Riley. "I guess we'll just have to be patient."

"Do you think we should call the police?" asked Helen nervously.

"What could they do?" asked Catherine. "There's no law against bothersome phone calls. I don't even think there's a law against threatening ones. They'd just have to wait until there was some action."

"I suppose you're right," admitted Helen. "But, still..."

Don reached over and patted her hand. "It'll be all right, Mother, " he said.

CHAPTER

12

Parce, Domine,
Parce populo tuo

Laso got to school early Tuesday morning. He was helping Robert O'Keefe set up the chemistry lab. Rob was washing test tubes and hanging them to dry in their racks. Laso had opened a box and was lining up the jars of chemicals on the counter. Hydrochloric acid...copper sulfate...nitric acid....charcoal...magnesium carbonate... nickel chloride...glycerol.

He separated them and dusted them off, taping the loose labels back on and putting them in alphabetical order on shelves in a white metal cabinet on the back wall. He pulled another box out from under the counter and did the same thing. Rob finished the test tubes.

"Now what?" he asked.

"There's a box of beakers over by the door," said Laso. "They need to be washed, too. They're pretty dusty."

Laso watched him lay down his towel and walk to the front of the room for the box of beakers. Looking over his shoulder to make sure Rob hadn't turned around, Laso took two of the jars and put them in his book bag, then turned his attention back to the loose labels.

"Hey, Laz," Rob called, making Laso jump. "Some of these are broken."

"Wrap the broken ones up in some newspaper and put them in that wastebasket by the desk. I'll take it out so the little ones don't get into it and cut themselves." They finished cleaning up as the Mass bell rang.

Laso sat distractedly through the Mass, unable to follow along. He said a few prayers for his mother, rubbing his long slender fingers together and scratching his face. He sat back to let the others in his row out for communion, slid back on the kneeler, hanging his head over the pew in front of him, his hands on the top of his head, pressing into his scalp. Catherine knelt in the pew behind him and watched him with growing concern. She stepped out of her pew and joined the slow procession to the communion rail.

Since they hadn't had breakfast, the students filed into the cafeteria after Mass for milk and graham crackers. Mrs. Long and Miss Clark stood at the door as they came in, keeping order. Mr. Corwin hurried down to the science lab to check on the work Laso and Rob had done that morning, and Mrs. Janis fretted over the mail.

Catherine went to her office and was folding her mantilla when Fr. Rodriguez knocked on the door. He had refused to wear the clerical suit and collar Fr. Riley had provided for him. He was casually dressed again, in olive green pants and a tan sweater. She sighed, wishing he would go away.

"Yes, Fr. Rodriguez, what can I do for you?" Catherine, who always rose when a priest entered the room, remained seated.

"I wish you'd call me Stefan," he said, his voice smooth and slippery like oil.

"That's hardly appropriate."

"Depends on your point of view."

Fr. Rodriguez sat down without waiting for an invitation and stretched his arms forward bending his joined fingers back, then stretched his neck from side to side. "Too much weightlifting," he said by way of explanation. "Makes you stiff."

Catherine was acutely uncomfortable and sat still, not saying anything. He looked at her and wondered how vibrant young women could get involved in stale old customs and dry, empty formalities. His hooded eyes rested on her wide gold wedding ring. Married, too. He wondered what kind of a man would put up with all the nonsense around Holy Martyrs. It didn't make any sense to him. History was moving forward, the pace ever quickening, and he was on the cutting edge and nobody, but nobody, was going to stop it. Not this woman with her silky voice and bright eyes, not Riley, not the Pope himself. He'd see to that.

Catherine pulled some papers from her desk drawer. If he weren't going to tell her what he wanted, she certainly wasn't going to sit there doing nothing. He watched her, sensing her nervousness, amused at her proper little ways. Typical English teacher. She was a relic, all right, maybe as bad as Riley. He laid his arms on his lap and leaned back, looking at her, a smile playing on his lips. She couldn't stand it any longer.

"Was there something you wanted to see me about, Father?"

"I thought we should get acquainted." He looked directly in her eyes and she turned away immediately, an unpleasant chill running along her arms and up her neck.

"Really, Father," she said, "If you have nothing you want to see me about, I must ask you to leave. I have a great deal of work to do."

He made no move to leave, and she wondered what she should do and how long he intended to stay. She thought of excuses she could give to leave herself, but she was afraid he wouldn't go, and she wasn't about to leave him alone in her office. He stood up and walked behind her desk, brushing close to her as he went over to the window, leaning on the sill and looking out at the playing field. Catherine clenched her teeth.

"Nice set up you've got here," he said. "But it's a lot of space for so few students. I imagine the bishop will want to bring some more in from areas that have no schools. How would you like that?"

"That's up to the Bishop," she said coldly. "We're here to teach."

He came back around the desk and sat back down. "Right. And just what are you teaching? You're raising a bunch of robots

134

here who can't think for themselves."

"That's ridiculous," Catherine retorted, biting her lip so she wouldn't lash out at him with the anger she was feeling. Her face reddened and her eyes blazed.

"No? Then what's it all about, then? Line up, do this, do that, be quiet. I even heard one of the dolts you call a teacher say, 'You will keep silence in here.' Now you tell me who talks like that anymore?"

"May I remind you, Father, that we have the approval of the Archbishop for what we are doing here?"

"Right. The Archbishop." He curled his upper lip contemptuously. "He and the pope are two of a kind."

"Yes," said Catherine. "And thank God for that. Now, really, I must get back to work. I'm sure Fr. Riley would be happy to discuss these things with you. "

"I'll talk to him later. But there is something I was going to mention to you."

"Oh?"

"Yes. Laso said he thought you saw us yesterday."

Catherine was startled that he would bring it up. "Yes, I did. I didn't know you knew Laso."

"I suppose I should explain. I met Laso last year when he came to the Seminary. I was Director of Vocations for the archdiocese and we struck up a friendship."

"Laso came to the seminary?"

"Yeah, checking out his vocation, as you people call it. Another anachronism. I told the Bishop that *Director of Ministries* would be a better title for what I did, but he didn't want to get a lot of people upset so we left it the way it was."

Catherine didn't know what to think. She thought of Laso's not going to communion, and she remembered that she hadn't mentioned that to Fr. Riley yet. She'd have to do that today. And now, this was surprising, that he had thought he might want to be a priest. The two things didn't add up. Something was wrong. She tried to pay attention to what Fr. Rodriguez was

135

saying.

"So anyway, that's how I knew him. You know about his mother?"

"No, only that she's paralyzed," said Catherine. "What about her?"

Fr. Rodriguez told her about what had happened to Laso's mother when the fighting penetrated their village and how Laso had come to America with his father the previous year.

"So then when I was assigned to come here, I thought I'd give Laso a call. Maybe have him tell me a little about the school so I'd know what to expect. You should be able to understand that."

Catherine nodded. She was still thinking about Laso. She wanted to talk to him, get to know him. Maybe she could help him somehow. She thought of how he stared at her and how uncomfortable he made her. But behind that, she saw a young boy who missed his mother, brought to a new country thousands of miles from home. And she thought of the war going on in Europe and how worried Laso must be. She made up her mind to talk to him after class.

"So that's the story. We went out to lunch and then went over to the Sacred Heart Community Center for a little get-to-gether. I know a couple of people there."

"There was a woman with you as well."

"Oh, that's right. That was another friend of mine, Sr. Agnes. She's from downtown."

And what was she doing with you? Catherine wanted to ask, but she kept quiet. Fr. Rodriguez' story was full of holes. In the future, I would ask that you not remove students from class for whatever reason," she said firmly. "You could have met with him after school."

"I didn't think an afternoon would hurt. Everybody likes to play hookey once in a while. Didn't you?"

"No," she answered. "I did not. And even if a student

were to want to skip school, it's certainly not something you should encourage. In this case, it wasn't Laso who wanted to miss class anyway. It was you who wanted him to."

Fr. Rodriguez shrugged his shoulders. She annoyed him. He wondered how she could be such a prig. These people were all alike, he thought. When he had come to the office this morning, he thought that maybe he might gain an ally in the new principal. He saw how mistaken he had been. The woman was a stone wall. He'd have to take another approach.

He stood up.

"Well, I guess I'd better go. Tommy Boy is probably looking for me. I was supposed to be at the rectory for breakfast."

Laso was walking down the deserted hallway to the cafeteria. He was late. He'd been helping Mr. Corwin in the chem lab, and they'd gotten into a discussion about a new theory being proposed by Dr. Walter Thompson out of MIT which could revolutionize the scientific world and put an end to the bizarre speculative physics which had been dominating the universities.

It was fascinating, Mr. Corwin had said, a return to Newtonian physics but in a new and startling way. Laso was lost in thought, his sharp mind focused on the intricacies of the new theory. He didn't hear Fr. Rodriguez come up behind him.

"Did you get the stuff?" he demanded. Laso turned and faced him.

"Yes, I have it," said Laso, his accent thickening as it always did when he was tense. "But I do not understand why you need it."

"Just a little experiment I'm doing."

Laso stalled, reflecting. "I don't know. I have been thinking. I do not think I should give it to you."

"Why not?"

"Well, first of all, it is stealing."

"No, it's not. Everything in this school belongs to the

137

archdiocese and I was sent here by the Bishop. So it's not stealing. It's communal property."

Laso started walking toward the cafeteria, his books under his arm. "You may say so, Father. I am not so sure."

"Let me take responsibility for that. I'm a priest. I'm telling you it's not stealing. It's not a sin to take what's already yours."

"What need do you have of it?"

"I already told you. I'm working on something."

Laso set his chin and the boyishness in his face disappeared. "I think you had better get what you need someplace else. I am not giving it to you."

Fr. Rodriguez stepped in front of him, blocking his path, and grabbing his shirt. "Listen, punk, you'll do what you're told. Obedience, remember?"

"Not this time, Father." Laso straightened his shoulders. He had a lot to think about. Things had been turned upside down in his mind for too long, and he needed some time. He wished he could talk to his mother. She had a way of making things seem clear without saying much. He tightened his grip on his books.

"You don't want to make me mad," threatened Fr. Rodriguez and he reached up with both hands and shoved Laso against the wall, bringing his fist up to his face.

"Your anger is your own concern, not mine," said Laso stiffly, fighting for self control. He forced himself not to strike back.

Fr. Rodriguez was becoming increasingly agitated. Only the sight of Miss Clark coming out of her classroom and into the hallway deterred him from giving full expression to his rage. He did not like to be thwarted. Laso shouldered his way past the priest and headed quickly toward the teacher. She was carrying two packing boxes, and her books were balanced on top of them.

"Good afternoon, Miss Clark," Laso said. "Let me get those for you." He put his own books down on the floor and took the packages from her. She reached down for his books.

"I'll carry these," she said. "A good trade, I'd say. Thank you, Laso. You came just at the right time."

And so did you, thought Laso, relieved. "You're welcome, Miss Clark. Where do you want these?"

"In the teachers' lounge." She started up the hall, and Laso was walking behind her when Fr. Rodriguez stopped him, gripping his arm and squeezing his thumb deep into the thin layer of muscle, reaching a nerve. Laso stifled a cry of pain and nearly dropped the boxes.

"Just a minute, Laso," Fr. Rodriguez demanded. "Where is that stuff?"

"In my locker. But you're not getting it. Now, if you please," he said ceremoniously as he shook his arm free. "I have work to do." He walked past Fr. Rodriguez toward the teachers' lounge. Miss Clark was standing and holding the door open for him. He set the boxes down against the wall.

The teachers were talking and eating their lunches and didn't pay any attention to him, except for Dr. Anderson who happened to glance at him and was struck by the expression in his eyes. Laso met her gaze; and for the first time since she had come to Holy Martyrs, he did not stare at her. His look was troubled, and her heart reached out to him.

"Thank you, Laso," said Miss Clark, dismissing him. He nodded and started to leave, but Catherine touched his arm as he went by.

"Could you stop by my office after school, Laso?" she asked. She wanted to say as little as possible in front of the other teachers, and Laso didn't ask for an explanation.

"Yes, Dr. Anderson, but I have to help Mr. Corwin at four."

"I'll only keep you a few minutes. I'll see you then." He nodded again and left for the cafeteria.

"Poor boy," said Mrs. Long, her Southern drawl stretching the vowels. "Misses his mama, I'll bet."

"Oh, for heaven's sake," said Judy Clark. "He's not a baby!"

139

"Just the same, it must be hard for him. He's alone a lot. The whole family works all the time, his father, his aunt and uncle, his older cousins. They don't get home until after eleven, and they're gone before he gets up. The only time he sees them is when he goes over to the store on Friday and Saturday to work. And then they keep him there until one or two in the morning."

"He can handle it," said Miss Clark.

"The boy's a genius," said Mr. Corwin simply, as though that would alleviate any loneliness he would feel.

"Really?" asked Catherine.

"Yes. He took the AP tests for college last year and placed out of a year of college calculus. His ACT scores were really high too."

"36 in science," said Mrs. Janis who kept the student records. And 35 on the math, 787 on the quantitative SAT. "

"He could get a scholarship anywhere in the country," said Mr. Corwin.

"Is he going to stay here?" asked Catherine.

Miss Clark shrugged. "Who knows? Would you want to go back? I wouldn't. What a mess! All that burning and looting. I'm sure sorry now I never got to Europe before the war started. I hear you wouldn't even recognize it now. So much has been destroyed."

"Those poor people," said Mrs. Long. "I can't imagine living like that."

"Well, we might get a taste of it ourselves," said Mr. Corwin. "The president's mobilizing troops in Greece and they're sending more of the Air Force to Belgium. now and Italy." Catherine looked up quickly, thinking of Rick and Angie, and pushed her hair back from her forehead.

"They're planning air strikes against the *Vox Populi* if they don't back off by next week, " continued Mr. Corwin. "Red shirts. I was talking to some Air Force people the other day, and they think we've got to bomb them, wipe out their strongholds before they take over Europe completely. Once we start doing that, we're in it for the long haul."

Mrs. Long shook her head. "I can't follow this. I can't even figure out who's on which side."

"That's the problem. This isn't like any war anyone has ever fought before," Mr. Corwin said quietly. "There are Communist revolutions coming up within all the new democracies. So while we wouldn't necessarily have anything against the governments of those countries, we have to stop the uprisings within them. It seems Communism isn't as dead as everybody thought."

"Makes you think of the Fatima message, doesn't it?" said Carrie Stevens. "Russia will spread its errors throughout the world..."

"Sure does," said Barbara Clark.

"Did you hear the news this morning?" asked Mrs. Janis.

"No, what?" asked Carrie.

"There's a report that the Pope is going to reveal the Third Secret on Good Friday."

Most people had never heard of the Third Secret, and those who had had forgotten it long ago. When the Blessed Mother appeared to the shepherd children at Fatima in October of 1917, one week before the Communist Revolution, she had entrusted three secrets to them.

The first two had been told, but not the third, which was to be revealed in 1960. The Catholic world had waited for the request of their Queen to be obeyed, but it never was. Locked somewhere deep in the archives of the Vatican, the secret lay in wait until the time of its fulfillment.

"Where'd you hear that?" asked Mr. Corwin.

"On the radio driving in this morning," said Mrs. Janis. "Do you think it's true?"

"Who knows?" said Mr. Corwin.

"I think it is," said Carrie emphatically.

"Well, if anyone is going to do it, it'd be this Pope," said

Evelyn Janis. "What's it say about him on the list?"

"What list?" asked Judy.

"The list of the popes. The prophecies."

"St. Malachy's list?" asked Catherine.

Mrs. Janis nodded.

"The Glory of the Olive."

"I wonder what that means," said Barbara.

"I heard that his father owned an olive orchard, and he used to play among the trees as a child with his brothers and his cousins; and that when he was a teenager contemplating the religious life, he'd spend days and nights in prayer out there all alone," Catherine answered.

"That doesn't tell us anything about Fatima. I thought maybe…"

"No, it doesn't. But it fits him and these times, which means there's only one pope left after Innocent XIV --if the list is exhaustive, that is. And do you remember which day he issued the *Restoration of All Things?*" Catherine's eyes grew distant.

"When?" asked Barbara Clark.

"October 13, the anniversary of the Miracle of the Sun."

"No kidding. I didn't put the two together."

"Most people didn't," said Catherine.

A bell rang, interrupting them. The children were going outside for a twenty minute recess before classes began in the afternoon. Most of the teachers would use the time for preparation, although Miss Stevens and Miss Clark would linger over another cup of coffee and talk awhile.

"Time to get back to work," said Mrs. Janis, throwing her crumbled lunchbag in the wastebasket and bustling out the door. The others bowed their heads to say the thanksgiving prayers, then rose to clear the table.

Mrs. Janis was unlocking her office door when Fr. Rodriguez approached her.

"Mrs. Janis," he said. "Just the one I need to see."

She greeted him with a tight smile. "Hello, Fr. Rodriguez."

She looked at him critically. He didn't look like a priest.

Fr. Riley's attempts to make him dress like one had been unsuccessful. When he called the chancery, the bishop told him it wasn't important and that he was not to impose on Fr. Rodriguez. When Fr. Riley protested, Bishop Washinsky had been patronizing.

"Yes, yes, I understand your feelings, Tom. But that's not how Stefan feels, and you must be accepting of that."

Fr. Riley was not accepting of it at all, but there was nothing he could do about it then. It was just one more thing that he would add to his report to the Archbishop.

"I've come to ask a favor," said Fr. Rodriguez.

"Yes?" answered Mrs. Janis going over to her desk and scanning the afternoon schedule.

"I need to get into Laso's locker."

Mrs. Janis looked at him sharply, her suspicions roused.

"For what? We don't go into the students' lockers. We respect their privacy."

"You have locker checks, don't you? Come on now, I know you do."

"We announce our locker checks," she answered primly.

"It's nothing major," he said. "It's just that Laso has some things of mine in it, and I need them right away."

"I'll buzz Laso and have him get them for you."

"But that's the problem," he said smoothly. "Laso left with Mr. Fortunata to go to the hardware store." It was a lie. Laso was in the science lab, but Fr. Rodriguez was betting Mrs. Janis wouldn't call him on it. " And I really can't wait for him to come back," he added for emphasis.

Her general respect for priests overcoming her reluctance, the secretary opened her desk drawer and took out a little notebook. "Come on," she said, "I'll open it for you."

"That won't be necessary, Mrs. Janis. Just give me the locker number and the combination. I won't trouble you any further." He smiled at her ingratiatingly while she wrote the numbers on a piece of scrap paper and handed it to him.

"Thank you," he said, walking out the door, his black hair nearly reaching his shoulders in the back. He needs a haircut, thought Mrs. Janis, and turned on her computer.

Clasping the piece of paper in his hand, Fr. Rodriguez went to the high school wing and found locker #137. He twirled the combination lock, and it opened easily. Books were stacked neatly on the shelf and Laso's blue nylon jacket was hanging from the hook. On the floor were baseball shoes and a canvas bookbag.

Fr. Rodriguez looked around to make sure he was alone and then reached for the bag, bending down to unfasten the buckles. He slid his hand in and felt the smooth glass jars. He took them out carefully, checking the labels, then cradled them in his left arm against his chest. He closed the locker quietly and headed for the parking lot.

CHAPTER
13

Liberasti in brachio tuo populum tuum,
Filios Israel et Joseph

Catherine was walking out the door toward the playground where the elementary school girls were jumping rope when she saw Fr. Rodriguez hurry to his car. He was hunched over slightly and his trenchcoat was pulled tightly around him. He didn't see her. Arriving at his car, he opened the passenger door and laid something on the seat, then circled to the other side and got in.

He looked around, and seeing only the children at play, he turned on the ignition. The car lurched as he pulled out of the parking lot. Catherine watched him turn the corner. She was glad to see him go. They'd have a peaceful afternoon, at least. She brushed him out of her mind and went over to the play area.

Fr. Riley had engaged the boys in a game of touch football, and he was shouting encouragement to them as Rob O'Keefe ran down the field with the ball, dodging and ducking, and Jim Whittaker and Johnny Wasniak scrambled in vain to tag him.

The older girls were walking around the parking lot, although they would have preferred to gather at the picnic bench at the edge of the field. They had a lot to talk about. But the school rule was that they had to have some exercise at recess. They weren't required to play any games, but they had to be moving.

It would clear their minds for their studies, Fr. Riley said. He was a firm believer in exercise, and the girls were afraid if they didn't walk, he'd make them run instead. There was homework to discuss and teachers, new clothes, and the plans for the spring concert.

They were making their dresses themselves and some of the ladies from the Altar Society were helping them after school. The girls were excited about the dresses, royal blue for the Blessed Mother, in whose honor the concert was to be given. The formal gowns, their first, had high ruffled necks and long billowing sleeves with skirts flowing like a bride's. The patterns were difficult, and they were glad they didn't have to sew them by themselves.

Peggy Wasniak was telling Annie Whittaker about how hard it was to set in the sleeves, and Annie exclaimed, "Wait 'til you get to the collar!" Jeanne Pitlowski and Bernadette O'Keefe exchanged glaces. Annie always liked to have the last word. She tossed her long blond hair, and the sun caught the golden strands, framing her face like a halo. She looked more saintly than she was.

Three ninth graders, eager to be accepted by the older girls, skipped behind them, catching up, straining to hear what they were saying. It was hard with the wind. They came around the bend and saw Catherine walking over to the younger girls.

It was time to discuss the new principal.

"How long do you think her hair is?" asked Annie.

"Down to her waist, I bet," answered Peggy.

"Yeah, probably. You can tell by how thick the French twist is. It's pretty. I wish I had auburn hair like that instead of brown," said Jeanne. "She should wear it down."

"She can't, silly," said Bernadette. "She'd look like one of the students. She's got to look dignified."

"Do you think she's nice?" asked Annie.

"Seems to be," answered Peggy. "I was pretty worried about who we'd get when Fr. Riley said she was coming."

"What did you imagine?" asked Katie Hanenberg, one of the ninth graders.

"Somebody like Mrs. Carruthers," said Jeanne, making a face. They all groaned.

face. They all groaned.

"If she had been, Father would have gotten rid of her, too," said Annie decidedly, confident of Fr. Riley's protection.

"Hey, look!" exclaimed Jeanne, pointing. Dr. Anderson's jumping rope!"

The girls stopped walking and looked over. It was true. Mary Ellen Long and Julie Wasniak were twirling and Catherine was, indeed, skipping an intricate double step as the other girls lined up for their turn. She was holding her hair with one hand and keeping her skirt down with the other, laughing like a school-girl herself.

"She's pretty good," said Bernadette.

"I wonder what her husband looks like," said Jeanne looking away from the jump rope and over at the boys playing football.

"How do you know she's married?" asked Bernadette.

"She's wearing a wedding ring. Didn't you see it? It's nice. No diamonds, just gold." Jeanne held out her ringless left hand, trying to imagine how it would look with a wide gold band.

"Her husband's dead," said Annie.

"Dead!" exclaimed the girls in unison. "How do you know that?"

"My mother told me. She's been sewing the drapes for the Altar of Repose with Mrs. Fortunata, and Mrs. Fortunata told her."

"How did Mrs. Fortunata know?" asked Bernadette, letting the new information sink in. Jeanne dropped her outstretched fingers.

"Her daughter and Dr. Anderson are friends."

"Oh, my gosh," said Peggy. "That's awful. Does she have any kids?"

"No," said Annie. "Just us, I guess."

After her classes in the afternoon, Catherine went back to

her office to wait for Laso and noticed that the ivy needed watering. She was looking for the watering can when Laso knocked at the door. She motioned to him to come in.

"Hello, Dr. Anderson," he said.

"Hello, Laso. Please sit down." He sat straight in the visitor's chair, his shoulders not so rounded as before. He looked at her and felt the last trace of anger and resentment begin to fade. There was no way that this woman with her soft voice and graceful ways could be an enemy of the people. He couldn't believe it. Still, he should be wary. He'd been fooled before, he thought ruefully.

Catherine wished he would say something, but he sat silently, his head down, waiting for her. She groped for words. She wanted to reach out to him, help him in some way, but she didn't know how and wasn't even sure that help was wanted or would be accepted. But she had to try, for no other reason than to offset the influence of Fr. Rodriguez on this impressionable student. She plunged ahead.

"Laso, I just wanted to say that I saw you yesterday with Fr. Rodriguez and Sr. Agnes."

His head snapped up. How did she know about Sr. Agnes? What else did she know? He started to feel afraid, and she sensed it.

"It's all right, Laso."

"No, it's not all right." His voice was husky. "It's not all right now and maybe it never will be." She had disarmed him, and he felt his chest tightening. He took a deep breath, trying to loosen the spasm around his heart.

"Can you talk about it?"

"No. There is nothing to say. I do not belong here, that's all." He started to get up.

"Please, Laso, sit down. It's all right. Why don't you feel like you belong here?"

"Because I do not deserve to be here. So if you please, ma'am, just expel me and get it over with."

"I'm not going to expel you. Why would I do that?"

"Because you should. It is what I deserve."

"You're a good student and a credit to your family..."

"No! No! I am not! My father would be ashamed."

"Laso, please, what is it?"

Catherine had no idea how to reach the young man sitting in front of her, how to ease the anguish he was feeling. She was afraid that if she said the wrong thing, she would alienate him. But she knew that she had to say something or he'd retreat, and she'd never know what was bothering him. She tried again.

"I understand you're new here."

"Yes, I came over last year with my father."

"Your English is very good."

"Thank you. My mother taught me. She studied in London."

"I understand your mother did not come over with you..."

"No. My mother...my mother is in the hospital."

"Yes. I know. I'm awfully sorry. You must miss her a great deal."

"Yes. I do. It is pretty hard." Laso caught his breath as the searing memory burned his eyes. He and his mother, pretty, cultured Marija Bjalckevic Matov, had walked to the market for some potatoes and cabbage for dinner and were on their way home.

Laso had flung the bag of groceries over his shoulder, and they were climbing the hill to their house when they heard loud shouting. A barrage of shots rang out from behind the trees and from the rooftops.

Laso felt the impact on his back and he fell to the ground, his face driven into the dirt. Disoriented, he tried to clear his mind. He was surprised he felt no pain, and then he remembered the sack of potatoes...of course...the bullets had hit the bag. But his mother... He lifted his head from the ground and looked to his side. There she lay, motionless, three round red holes torn through her blouse and blood everywhere.

Laso shuddered at the memory.

"Are you all right, Laso?" Catherine was frightened by the way he looked.

"She was shot... and I... oh, God..." He couldn't say anymore. He felt so guilty. Why couldn't he have protected her? Why couldn't he be the one lying the hospital bed? He looked at Catherine. How could she understand? Americans were sheltered. They knew nothing of war on their own soil, in their own village, the bullets, the screams, the little children lying limp in their mothers' arms, and the fathers who never came back.

Catherine said nothing. She waited.

"They did not kill her, but she's paralyzed. From the neck down. The doctors say that here in America they might be able to help her. But we do not have enough money. My father... he is working all the time... saving, saving... but it grows slowly, like a pine tree in the rocks."

"And you wish you could do something to help."

"Yes. I have to do something. I cannot just sit still like a little boy on his papa's knee. I tried, Dr. Anderson... I tried... oh, what's the use? You could not understand."

"Give me a chance."

"No. You Americans. You live here in your nice warm houses with your green grass and your pretty flowers. Everybody drives a car, and the supermarkets have enough food in them to feed my village for a year. Things my people have never seen. All they know is fighting and constant fear. No work. No money. Hungry babies with swollen bellies crying, crying all the time. How could you understand? How could you?" He pounded the desk with his fist.

"Where are you from, Laso?"

"A village near Ljubljana -- that's in Slovenia," he said.

Catherine gasped. Her face blanched and her hands and knees shook violently like they had when the police called her that cold winter night when the mountain snow was piled high against the windows and the wind howled over the hills. "Oh, my God!"

150

she whispered silently. Laso looked at her, startled. Her eyes were wide open, the pupils black and empty. He wished she'd say something. She was scaring him.

"Laso," she said, forming her words carefully. Tears glistened in her eyes. "I think... I understand more than you know."

He sat quietly. He didn't want to argue, not when she looked like that. But how could she know?

"Laso... you see... my... my husband was killed in Slovenia. In the Julian Alps. In January." She looked down at her ring. "I know about war."

It was Laso's turn to be shocked into silence. He closed his eyes, and the tears he had fought so long began to fall.

He wept for her and for him and for his mother... for everyone who suffered from the savage war. His chest heaving, he laid his head down on the desk and gave himself up to his grief and his fear, sobbing as though his heart would break.

Catherine came over and stood by him, leaning against the desk and resting her hand on his shoulder, patting it like a mother soothing a little child. They stayed like that for awhile, and then Laso lifted his head. Catherine walked over to her chair.

"I'm sorry," he said, "for crying like that, like a baby."

"There's nothing to be sorry about. When something hurts so badly, you have to cry. That's why God made tears."

He had heard that expression before -- his mother used to say the same thing when he was hurt and embarrassed because he had cried. Laso took a deep breath and let it out slowly. Catherine's gentleness lay over his burning heart like a cool cloth against a fevered brow. He took out a handkerchief from his pocket and wiped his eyes. He felt foolish, but better.

"I guess you want to know about Fr. Rodriguez."

"If you want to tell me."

"I do. But I need to... I need to find Fr. Riley..."

Catherine raised an eyebrow.

"I need to go to confession."

Catherine reached for the intercom. Father Riley answered

on the second buzz.

"Yes..." he said..

She told him what she wanted.

"I'll be right over. Have him meet me in the church."

"Fine, Father," she said, turning off the intercom. "You heard him, Laso, get going." She shooed him out the door.

He turned around and faced her, feeling awkward. "Thank you, Dr. Anderson. I cannot tell you..."

"It's okay, Laso. Go on now, Father's waiting for you."

She stood in the doorway as he walked down the hall, and she could hear the children singing.

Carrie had brought them into the gym so they could practice from the new stage. Vito had set up the risers that morning, and she had spent the first fifteen minutes of practice getting everyone in the right order. She was sure they wouldn't remember where their places were, especially the little ones, so she was sitting on a folding chair, her notebook balanced on her lap, drawing a chart. Catherine came up behind her and gave her a little tap of greeting on the arm.

"Oh, Dr. Anderson, I didn't hear you come in."

"Don't let me interrupt you," said Catherine, "I heard them from the office, and I thought I'd come down."

"What do you think?"

"They sound good, don't they? " She longed to run up and sing with them. She listened to them, the yearning sweetness of the *Ave Maris Stella* lingering in the air. "How did you do it?" she asked Carrie, struck by the beauty of their voices.

"There's a lot of natural talent, there. The O'Keefes carry a lot of it, and Annie Whittaker is a really good soprano, but I don't tell her that. It would go straight to her head. She's vain enough as it is. Do you sing?"

"Yes."

"Alto?"

Catherine nodded. "Is everyone performing?" she asked, changing the subject and diverting it from herself.

"Just about. A couple of the boys will be stagehands."

"Laso?" He hadn't said anything about practice.

"Yes. He'll be working the lights."

"Doesn't he sing?"

"Yes, but I think he'd rather not. I think it makes him think too much of home. They were in the choir back there -- all his brothers. He's the youngest, the last one. Anyway, when he asked if he could handle the lights, I said all right. He's really the only one I'd trust. I'd be afraid some of the other boys would electrocute themselves or something."

Catherine laughed. "You're probably right," she said. They stopped talking as the children began the next song. She closed her eyes . It was difficult to come to a school in the middle of a year. It would have been hard enough if she were just one of the teachers, but being brought in as principal must not have been easy for the others.

The teachers had accepted her coming and that made her feel less apprehensive. more at home. She was grateful for that. As she listened to the music, she thought about how her life had changed in a few days. All these new people. And new ressponsi-bilities. The children. Laso.

When practice was over, she stayed and talked with Carrie for a few minutes.

"Well," said Carrie, "how do you like it here?"

"I like it a lot," said Catherine. "It's so different from the college."

"A lot more hectic, I bet."

"Yes," said Catherine, "But so much richer. Have you always been in the Catholic schools?"

"Yes," said Carrie.

"Well, try to imagine what it would be like not to be able to mention the Name of God all day. Or to eat lunch with atheists who were driven to spread their despair. Or to listen to conver-

153

sations filled with obscenities."

"Why did you stay?"

"I always wanted to teach, and I loved my field. And then, well, I didn't have any children, so I thought maybe I could help make things a little better for other young people, pass on a love of good literature and good writing to my students. I wasn't particularly successful, I guess, but I kept trying."

"Are you glad you came?"

"Oh, Carrie, I can't tell you...Yes, I'm very glad I came." She looked at her watch. " Well, I'd better get back to my office and finish up a few things."

"Do you have a car?" asked Carrie.

"Not yet. I need to get one pretty soon. I hate imposing on my mother-in-law every day. I have to call her when I get back to the office."

"I can give you a ride home."

"I don't want to take you out of your way."

"It's no bother," said Carrie.

"Thanks," Catherine answered. "I appreciate it."

"I'll fill you in some more on who does what around here," said Carrie.

"I need that! I can't wait until I've got everything and everyone in their right place. You feel so awkward when you're new."

"That's for sure. Well, I'll meet you in the front. I have to pick up my books from my classroom."

They walked down the gym together and parted at the door, each going in opposite directions down the hall. Catherine saw Laso at his locker as she headed back to her office. He looked up as she started to pass him and smiled, nodding his head at her in greeting.

"Back from the science lab?" she asked.

"Yes, ma'am. We are almost finished setting it up."

"Good," she said. "I'll see you tomorrow."

154

"Yes," he said. "And Dr. Anderson..."

"Yes, Laso?"

"Thank you."

"It's okay," she said. "Anytime."

She walked on past him. The afternoon sun was filtering through the Venetian blinds in the windows and the slatted light crisscrossed the floor. Laso bent down to get his book bag from the bottom of his locker, then decided to leave it where it was.

There wasn't anything he needed in it anyway, just his gym shoes and a tee shirt. He'd carry his books under his arm. That way, if Fr. Rodriguez started poking around the lab looking for the chemicals, he wouldn't find them. Laso wasn't taking any chances. He laid his baseball cap and mitt on top of the book bag.

The jars should be fine there, he thought, until it was safe to bring them back to the lab. If Mr. Corwin needed them for anything, he could always come and get them. He put on his jacket, grabbed his books, and closed the locker door. He started to walk away, then came back and doublechecked the lock. It was tight. He headed toward the door.

CHAPTER

14

Adjutor meus, et liberator meus esto;
Domine, ne tardaveris

Carrie dropped Catherine off at the Andersons'. Catherine stood in the driveway, the wind blowing her hair, and waved goodbye. She walked quickly around the back of the house and into the kitchen. Helen was cutting radishes for a salad.

"Hello, dear," said Helen. Catherine leaned over and kissed her cheek. She smelled of lemon and sugar. "How'd it go today?"

"Fine. I'm tired, though. This is a lot harder than teaching a few English classes at the college." She took off her coat and hung it in the closet. A pie sat cooling on the window sill, and Helen had just finished setting the kitchen table for dinner.

"You didn't leave anything for me to help you with," Catherine said.

"No, you don't need to bother yourself about helping in the kitchen. You have enough to do at the school. By the way, some of your things came today. They're still in the front hall. I left them for Dad to carry up. And don't you go doing it yourself, either," she said. "You can go through them right there."

"Okay," Catherine said. She took a knife from the drawer to slit open the packages and hurried to the front hall, eager to unpack the boxes. She knelt down and sliced deftly through the strapping tape, then reached in. There were some of her favorite books and her wedding album and the patchwork quilt she and Angie had made that she wanted to give to Helen. She lifted the

156

quilt out and laid it carefully on the deacon's bench. She reached again into the bottom of the box and her hand closed on the slim black case of her flute and drew it out.

Frank had given it to her for Christmas the first year they were married, replacing the old nickel plated one that she had carried around since the fourth grade. Smoothing her long skirt over her knees, she sat down cross legged on the floor and opened the case. The three silver pieces lay nestled in blue velvet and she ran her fingers over the smooth metal. Taking the pieces out, she twisted them together and laid the instrument across her lap, looking at it, turning it in her hands.

She pressed her fingers against the keys, tapped them, stopped, considered for a moment, then lifted the flute to her lips and began to play. In the kitchen, Helen turned off the running water and stood, listening, caught by the haunting melody coming from the hall.

Don came in the back door fifteen minutes later and Catherine laid down her flute and went into the kitchen.

"That was lovely, dear," said Helen. Catherine blushed. "I'm a little rusty," she said.

"Didn't sound rusty to me," said Don.

"Oh, Catherine, I forgot to tell you --there's a letter for you on the counter over by the phone." Catherine picked it up and recognized the neatly curved handwriting. "It's from Angie," she said excitedly as she tore open the envelope and started scanning the letter.

"Oh, she's coming for spring break! She'll be here Palm Sunday. Catherine's eyes slid down the page. "It seems that things are looking up with Rick," she said, continuing to read.

"Rick went to talk to the Air Force chaplain the other day," wrote Angie. *"I guess things are pretty scary over there , so he decided he'd better get his life in order ...in case he gets blown out of the sky, he said. I wish he wouldn't talk like that.*

157

But anyway, the chaplain, Major McGarry, says Mass every morning. They set it up in an old hangar off the side of the air field. Most of the squadron is Catholic and they take turns serving. Rick hadn't even known. Every morning, early, before he flies, he goes to Mass...oh, Catherine...pray for him."

She finished the letter and folded it back into the envelope. "I can't wait until she gets here," Catherine said. "You'll like her."

"Is she like her mother?" asked Helen.

Catherine laughed. "No, I'd say she's more like her father."

"Say, Catherine," said Don, leaving the kitchen for the den. "How'd you like to go look for a car tonight after dinner?"

"I'd like that," she answered. "I hate for Mother to have to be running around town for me every day."

"It's no inconvenience," said Helen.

"All the same..." said Catherine.

They arrived at the car dealership at seven twenty and by eight thirty, Catherine was buckling the seat belt of her sporty red Fanfare, bought off the lot .

"I'll meet you at home," she said, tuning in the classical radio station and putting the car in gear. Don and Helen watched her drive off. Don opened the car door for Helen.

"It's good to have her here," he said.

Wednesday in Passion Week dawned bright and clear. The grass was turning from gray to green and the maple and birch trees were budding, the warming air whispering hope of spring and life renewed. Catherine pulled her car out of the driveway and tried to keep her foot from pressing too hard on the accelerator. The Fanfare was built for speed, and she was in a hurry to get to school. Ten minutes later, she turned into the

Holy Martyrs parking lot. Clustered near the entrance to the school were three police cars, circled like wagons on the frontier.

"Oh, my God, what's happened?" Catherine thought, alarmed. She hoped there hadn't been a robbery. At least they were in front of the school and not the church. The Blessed Sacrament would be safe. But what could have happened in the school? There really wasn't that much to steal -- the computers maybe? Or the paintings?

She drove up next to the squad cars and threw the Fanfare into park. Six police officers got out of their cars and stood, legs planted solid on the pavement, arms tensed. Grabbing her purse and books, Catherine stepped out of the car.

"Good morning, officers," she said, her voice shaking. "What's going on?

A burly policeman approached her. "Are you Dr. Catherine Anderson?" he demanded.

"Yes," she answered, wondering how he knew her name.

"You're under arrest," he said, moving toward her and grabbing her arms. Catherine wanted to scream. This couldn't be happening. What in the world was going on? She forced herself not to struggle, but she wanted to kick the man who was pushing her back toward the car.

"Read her her rights," he commanded the young officer to his left, who pulled the Miranda card out of his pocket and droned out the words mindlessly. Catherine was growing frantic. The first officer slapped a pair of handcuffs on her wrists and they cut into her skin. She cried out in pain.

"Hurts, uh, lady? Well, how do you like it?" He opened the door of the squad car and shoved her into the back seat, narrowly missing her foot as he slammed the door

"What is the meaning of this?" she asked with all the dignity she could muster, looking at the two officers in the front seat through the mesh grill. The driver started the car and cocked his head at her.

"You oughta know, lady," he snarled. "You gotta learn

159

you can't do stuff like that in this town. Maybe you shoulda stayed in Colorado and played your games out there. Sick, really sick. Some Christian. Real religious, aren't ya?"

"What are you talking about?" she demanded. " I want to know why you're doing this to me."

"Child abuse, lady, as if you didn't know. You're gonna be locked up for a long time."

"Please," she said, "Let me go get Fr. Riley."

"You're not going anywhere, lady, except to jail."

"You must tell him, then, where you're taking me. I'm expected to be here."

"Ain't that tough. The little lady's got a job to do." The driver smirked at his partner. "You'll get your phone call at the station," he said. "Now shut up. We like a little peace in the morning."

The phone rang in the rectory and Fr. Riley picked it up. It was not a good morning. He was already late getting to the sacristy, Fr. Rodriguez was in bed and would probably sleep until noon, and Mrs. Janis had buzzed him on the intercom, saying that Catherine hadn't shown up yet.

"Yes," he barked into the phone.

There was no human voice on the other end, just a recording.

"Collect call from an inmate at the Dearborn Jail. Will you accept the charges? Press one and the pound sign for yes, two for no."

Oh, brother, he thought. Now what? He pressed one, and the connection was made.

"Fr. Riley here."

"Father..." a choked voice came over the line. A woman. That was odd. He thought one of the men had probably been out drinking and had gotten in trouble. There were a few in the parish he was thinking about.

"Yes. Who is this?"

"It's... it's Catherine," she stammered.

"Catherine!" Fr. Riley shouted, almost dropping the phone. "What in the world...!"

Catherine swallowed hard. The words wouldn't come out.

"Catherine? Are you there?"

"Yes...they arrested me, Father. They were in the parking lot waiting for me... They handcuffed and fingerprinted me and everything." She was crying.

"For what? What did they arrest you for?"

"Child abuse. They said I beat one of the students. There was a complaint lodged against me by one of the neighbors."

"Dear God in heaven," said Fr. Riley, gripping the phone. "I'll be right there."

"No -- after Mass," she said. "I'll be okay."

"Are you sure?"

"Positive. Don't postpone the Mass. I was just nervous until I could reach you. I was afraid you'd already gone over to the church."

"I'll see you in a little over an hour, then."

"Yes, Father. Thank you." A policewoman motioned to Catherine that her time was up and waited while she hung up the phone.

"Let's go," she said and led Catherine down a narrow green hall, through a security door, and down another short hall to the third door on the left. Catherine kept her face straight ahead. The policewoman unlocked the holding cell and pointed with her thumb for Catherine to go in. Numbly, Catherine obeyed and went over and sat on the thin cot by the wall, her head in her hands.

She jumped as the woman slammed the metal door shut, shaking it to make sure it was locked. Her footsteps receded down the hall, and Catherine started to shake uncontrollably. Haltingly, she walked over to the sink and splashed water on her face and looked around for a towel. There was none.

She wished she had her purse so she could get her handkerchief, but they had taken it from her. They had even removed her combs, and her hair had fallen loose. She pushed it away from her face, but had nothing to fasten it. All they let her keep was her rosary, which she pulled out of her pocket and wrapped around her hand, fingering the beads. She knelt down by the side of the cot to pray.

When Fr. Riley hung up the phone he ran over to the school and down the hall to the workroom.

"Vito!" he shouted. "Vito!"

Vito was locking his toolbox before heading for the church for Mass.

"Here, Father," he said. He turned around as Father Riley came storming through the door. "What..."

"Your son's a lawyer, isn't he?"

"Yes, Father, but..."

"Get him on the phone. See if he can get over here right away."

"Sure, Father, but..."

"Hurry!" Father Riley turned and was gone before Vito could say anything else.

He wiped his hands on his shirt and headed for the front office to call Nick. Now what in the world was he going to tell the kid? he wondered. He hardly ever even talked to him. Say, kid, if you're not too busy suing corporate bigwigs and doctors who make mistakes could you, you know, sort of speed over here? Why? I don't know. Don't have any idea. Just come, okay? Now. Be here in an hour... Vito played it out in his mind as he dialed the phone.

"Good morning. Fortunata, Swenson, Hughes, and Jacobowitz."

What a mouthful, Vito thought. "Hello, is Mr. Fortunata

there?"

"Yes, he is, but he is unable to come to the phone right now. May I take a message?"

"I gotta talk to him right now."

"Yes, sir, I understand , but he's not available. If you would please leave your name and number..."

"This is his father and I have to talk to him right now."

The secretary was smooth. "You say you're his father."

"I'm not *saying* it. I *am* his father!" Vito shouted. Now let me talk to him."

"And what did you say your name was, sir?"

"What do you think my name is if I'm Mr. Fortunata's father?" exploded Vito.

"Sir?"

"Fortunata. I'm Mr. Fortunata."

"I'll see if he can come to the phone. One moment please."

Vito drummed the desk. It was taking forever, and now he was late for Mass. It would sure be a lot easier if he knew what was going on.

"Fortunata here."

"Nick?"

"Dad?"

"Yeah, it's me. Didn't your secretary tell you?"

"Not exactly."

"Well, it's me. Can you do me a favor?"

"You're my father aren't you?"

"Yeah, and tell that secretary so, too, for me."

"What do you need?"

"I need you to come over here right away."

Nick tensed. "Are you in trouble?"

"No, not me. Somebody else."

"Who?"

"I don't know."

"What happened?:"

"I don't know that either."

"Wait a minute." Nick was getting annoyed. He'd been pulled out of a partners' meeting, and he didn't have times to play little games. Not even with his father. "You want me to come over because somebody is in trouble but you don't know who it is or what happened..."

"Yeah, that about sums it up. I wish I could tell you more. Fr. Riley came running into my workroom and told me to call you and see if you could come right away. That's all I know."

"Would this afternoon be all right?"

"I don't think so. I think it's urgent."

Nick sighed. "All right. I'll be right over. Give me an hour. I've got a few things to tie up."

"Nick?"

"Yes, Dad?"

"Thanks, son. I'll meet you in front."

Fifty minutes later, Nick Fortunata pulled his Mercedes into the parking lot. He had been there once, several years ago, when it first opened. It had been in bad shape then, but it looked pretty good now -- trimmed lawn, neat bushes, shining windows; and he realized that his father was responsible for most of the improvements. The old man always was a hard worker, he thought. He got out of the car and smoothed his hand-tailored Italian silk suit and straightened his tie. Looking up, he saw his father coming out of the church.

"Hey, Dad!"

Vito walked over and grabbed his son's arm and slapped him on the back.

"You're lookin' good, kid," he said. Nick flushed. He felt inadequate around his father, and graduating with honors from Harvard Law hadn't changed that.

"Where are we going?"

"To the jail. But we have to wait for Fr. Riley. He'll be

right out."

"Did you find out what's going on yet?"

"No. Father's been saying Mass."

Nick looked around. The children, followed by their teachers, started to walk quietly toward the school. He watched the line of them, their uniforms a plaid sea of blue and green, but each face distinct, startling, their individuality cracking his prejudices.

"Hey, Dad, I think I'll.." He stopped. Carrie Stevens walked in front of him, not seeing him. She was watching the children. Nick swallowed. He hadn't expected to see someone like that here. He thought everybody'd be old, retirees, that sort of thing. People on a nostalgia kick. But walking in front of him was the cutest young woman he had ever seen.

Her curls bounced around her heart-shaped pink and white face as she walked; and when she turned back toward one of the children who had fallen behind, he could see the deep dimples in her cheeks when she smiled and her tiny upturned nose. He stood watching her like an adolescent. He didn't know what to think.

In his circle of friends, among the sophisticated doctors and lawyers of the northern suburbs, Catholics were scorned as unenlightened relics of a more primitive, tactile time. His friends were not interested in God. They'd left their childhood faith at mama's house with their teddy bears and needed nothing but their own brilliance and drive and a few well placed friends to succeed. But that girl was no relic. He watched her as she went into the building, blond, neat, full of life.

Vito was waiting for Nick to finish his sentence.

"What were you saying, son?"

"Oh, nothing. Dad, who was that girl?"

"What girl?"

"That blond one who just went by..." Vito turned toward the school just as Carrie was going through the door.

"That's Miss Stevens."

"Miss?"

"Yeah, son, *Miss*. What's the matter, you want an introduction or something?"

Nick started to grunt disgustedly but stopped himself. "Yeah, Dad, an introduction."

Vito nodded. "It might be arranged." He was baiting him. "How about now?"

"We're waiting for Fr. Riley."

"Come on Dad, we've got time." Vito shrugged and hurried to the door.

"Miss Stevens!" She turned around.

"Good morning, Mr. Fortunata. How are you?"

"Miss Stevens, could here come here for a second?"

"Sure, what's up?" Carrie walked over to him.

"If you wouldn't mind..." he hesitated. She looked at him, waiting, but was impatient to rejoin her class.

Vito pulled at his collar. "Well, my son is outside, and...he saw you...and he...well, he..."

"Wants to meet me?"

"Yeah."

"I'd be honored to meet your son, Mr. Fortunata." If Vito could have blushed, he would have. As it was, he stood there, feeling foolish.

"Where is he?"

"You just passed him. He's outside."

"I didn't see him. Okay, lead the way. I've only got a minute."

They walked down the sidewalk to where Nick was standing. Carrie went right up to him. "Hi," she said perkily, her straight teeth white and shining, her eyes reflecting the blue spring sky. "I'm Carrie Stevens."

"Nick Fortunata."

"Nice to meet you, Nick. I haven't seen you around here before."

166

"No." He felt like a high school student, and she made him feel ashamed. His palms were sweating for heaven's sake.

"Oh." She was quiet. Her smile faded, and it saddened him. He shouldn't have insisted on the introduction. She'd never be interested in him, and he couldn't blame her. These people took their religion very seriously, and he was certainly not religious, not by any stretch of the imagination.

Vito interrupted them. "There's Fr. Riley!" and he left Nick and Carrie.

Nick kept looking at her, but couldn't say anything. Carrie spoke to ease his embarrassment. "I have to go to class, now, but if you ever come for Mass, maybe we could have coffee afterward or something..."

"I'd like that, Miss Stevens."

"Carrie."

"How about Sunday?" Nick couldn't believe the words were coming out of his mouth.

"That'd be fine. Palm Sunday."

"Uh...right." Boy, did he feel stupid, a *magna cum laude* jerk. "What time?"

"After the ten o'clock?"

"Great. I'll see you then." She turned and went toward the school, and he watched until he couldn't see her anymore through the glass door.

"Hey, Nick! You ready?" called Vito.

"Coming, Dad." He went to join his father and the priest.

"You remember Nick, don't you Father?"

"It's been a long time, Nick. Glad to see you."

"Good to see you too, Father." He shook Fr. Riley's hand. Vito looked at him. The kid looked nervous.

"All set?" asked Fr. Riley. "Let's get going."

They got into the Mercedes. Vito leaned forward from the back seat.

"What happened, Father?"

"You won't believe this, Vito. Dr. Anderson was arrested

this morning."

"Arrested? What'd she do, run a red light?"

"They're accusing her of child abuse. That's why I needed Nick. I don't know any more than that. They let her call me when they booked her. Apparently, a neighbor lodged a complaint."

"That's all it takes," said Nick. "Who's Dr. Anderson?"

"The school principal," said Fr. Riley.

"Married?"

"A widow." Nick pictured a white haired matron with sensible shoes and thick glasses patrolling the halls, slapping a pointer against her palms to scare the students into submission. He wondered if the charges were true. He half expected they were.

CHAPTER
15

Per signum Crucis de inimicis nostris libera nos

Officer Maddox ordered another vanilla cream donut and turned to Sam Oliver, his partner, a rookie.

"What'd ya think of that dolly we brought in this morning?" The waitress set the plate on the counter and slipped the two quarters left by the last customer into the pocket of her uniform. Maddox reached for the donut plate and slid it toward him. Oliver watched him.

"I don't know. She didn't look the type, you know."

"Can't tell nothing by looks."

Oliver stirred some sugar into his coffee. "Sometimes you can."

"Hooked ya, didn't she? Gotta be careful of that with good lookin' women. Get yourself in trouble that way." Maddox took a bite of the donut, and the whipped cream spilled out his mouth and down his chin. He caught it with the back of his hand, then groped for the napkin on his lap.

"Come on, Maddox, you know as well as I do that we've gotten false reports before about this sort of thing. Every time somebody's got a grievance against somebody, they turn them in for child abuse. She just looked, you know, ladylike, or something. Not the type to beat up kids."

"I tell you, you can't tell nothing by looks. She could be a serial killer for all we know. Why'd she leave Colorado, huh? Sounds suspicious to me. Maybe they ran her out of town..."

Oliver scratched at the palm of his hand. "I don't think so. Something bothers me. I don't like it."

"Toughen up. You're gonna see a lot worse than that on the Force."

"Yeah, maybe." He held out his cup for a refill, then swivelled half way around on the stool and looked out the window. He didn't want to talk about it anymore. He didn't think Maddox should have been so rough. Besides, he'd bet a week's pay there was more to it. Something didn't add up. That was a parochial school. Maybe it had something to do with religion.

His mother had been raised Catholic, and she said a lot of people hated Catholics. He'd seen on the news that there was some kind of commotion about something the Pope was doing, something about an Old Mass. He didn't know what it was all about, but he'd heard people were getting killed over it in Europe. Hard to imagine, but there were lots of strange things going on in the world now.

He was still thinking when another squad car pulled up, and Lt. Denny Long, a man of military bearing, got out and came toward the door. Oliver watched him with respect. The lieutenant hadn't let himself get paunchy like a lot of officers his age. He was a fair guy, too. Never saw him fly off the handle. That was the kind of cop he wanted to be.

"Hey, Maddox," the rookie said, elbowing his partner. "Lt. Long's here."

"Mind your manners, Oliver." Maddox laid his napkin on the counter. "Lieutenant!"

"Morning, gentlemen. How's it going?"

"Not bad. Not bad. We picked up some woman at a school a while ago."

"Yeah? For what?"

"Beating up a kid."

Lt. Long grimaced. He was disgusted by the way the country was falling apart. "Did you bring her in?"

"Yeah. Some classy dame. The kid's upset about it." He crooked his thumb at Sam Oliver.

"Why's that, son?" asked Denny Long, easing onto the next stool. He leaned against the short wood back and signalled the waitress.

Sam glared at his partner. He didn't want to be put on the spot like this in front of the lieutenant.

"I don't know, sir. "

"He's got a *feeling* about it," said Maddox.

"I didn't say anything about a feeling." He tightened his lips.

"What is it, Oliver?"

"She just didn't seem the type, you know. Her face. I can't explain it."

"Well, she'll have her day in court. That's the American way." The waitress came over and stood in front of him, hand on her hip. "Just coffee," he said. "Black." She slid a cup toward him and filled it. He turned toward Maddox. "Where'd you say you picked her up?"

"I didn't say. Some Catholic school. A weird name," he muttered under his breath. "Holy Martyrs or something." Lt. Long set his mug down so hard that coffee splashed on the counter. He grabbed a napkin and blotted it.

"What did you say?"

He repeated the name. Louder this time.

"Holy Martyrs?" Denny Long stared at him.

That's what I said, thought Maddox. "I can check the report if you want. I got it in the car."

"Who was the woman?" he demanded. Oliver was startled by the change in the lieutenant's voice.

"Don't remember her name...Let's see.."

"You better remember it fast, Officer!" Lt. Long stood over him, his hand gripping the back of the stool. Maddox sprang to attention, his memory jolted.

"Anderson, I think. Catherine Anderson."

Lt. Long slapped a dollar on the counter and strode toward the pay phone on the wall.

171

"What's with him?" asked Oliver.

"Beats me," his partner answered, draining his coffee cup and pushing it away.

Catherine was sitting on the cot, her head tilted, like a woman who had just asked a question and was waiting for an answer. Twisting her hands in her lap, she stared out beyond the green cinderblock walls, remembering the Roman martyrs, after whom the school was named. Felicity, locked in a dismal prison, awaiting death, her baby torn screaming from her arms. Her handmaiden, Perpetua, ready to die with her.

For Christ.

She thought of Symphorosa, forced to watch the murder of her seven sons, one by one, because they would not renounce the Faith, and then was killed herself, last, a mother yearning for her children, a woman dying for her God. Catherine closed her eyes. Thinking about them, she felt less frightened, her own plight less terrible.

She sat for a long time, thinking, and then stood up and started pacing back and forth, her head bowed, rubbing her palms together as she walked. She stopped when she heard footsteps approaching. It must be Fr. Riley, she thought, and tried to smooth her hair, but without her combs there was little she could do. She walked over to the door and rested her hands on the narrow window ledge. She had to stand on her toes to see out into the hall.

The policewoman led the way and Nick and Fr. Riley followed her. They hadn't let Vito come back, so he was reading the newspaper in the waiting area by the front desk. As the policewoman stepped up to unlock the door, Nick saw Catherine's face framed in the window, her hair falling over her shoulders and down her back like an auburn veil.

He caught his breath. Where was the overbearing gray matron of his imagination? This was the third surprise of the day. His father's phone call. Carrie Stevens. And, now, this woman who looked like a Florentine Madonna, locked in jail with the drunks and petty thieves. The policewoman opened the door.

"All right, Anderson, your lawyer's here. Brought the priest with him. It's up to you if you want to see them."

"Please," said Catherine.

"The priest, too?"

"Yes." She tried to smile at Fr. Riley, but seeing him made the tears fall again. Nick felt a pain in his chest looking at her.

"Catherine, this is Nick Fortunata."

"Fortunata?" She thought he looked familiar.

"He's Vito's son," said Fr. Riley.

"Thank you for coming," she said. "I've heard about you."

"Heard about me? From Dad?"

"No, from Angie."

"You know Angie?"

"Yes... She's my best friend, in fact."

"No kidding."

"No, no kidding. Did you know she was coming to Michigan? She'll be here Palm Sunday. "

Nick started to answer, but the policewoman interrupted him.

"My, my, it's Old Home Week. Well, you can come down to the visitor's room," said the policewoman. "You've got twenty minutes." She led them down the hall.

When they were seated at the table, Nick opened his briefcase and pulled out a yellow legal pad. He took his embossed fountain pen from his pocket and removed the cap carefully, then scribbled a few lines on the top of the page to check the ink flow.

"All set. Now what happened?"

Catherine started to tell him about the police cars in the parking lot.

"No, I mean, what happened? You know...what made them

173

think you had abused a child?"

Catherine shook her head. "I have no idea."

He looked at her quizzically. "None? Nothing that could have appeared to somebody as child abuse? A paddling? A smack? Something like that?"

"No. Nothing like that."

"Anybody have a grudge against you?"

"No. I've only been at the school since Thursday."

Nick was perplexed. Usually he could find some foundation in these sorts of charges. Maybe it was only a misinterpretation, but there was usually *something*. He bit on the end of his pen.

"Have you had to discipline any child since then?"

"Just Billy Pitlowski and Tommy Flanagan."

"What for?"

"Fighting."

"What did you do to them?"

"Kept them in at recess for a week and assigned some chores for them to do."

"Well," said Nick, capping his pen, "There's not much we can do. We'll have to wait for the hearing. If they don't have anything to back up their charges -- which it doesn't look like they will -- you should be out of here tomorrow."

Catherine took a deep breath, suppressing a cry.

"Now there are just a few more things I want to go over with you, so you'll know what to expect. ..Certain procedures...I have to file a motion for dismissal. There'll be a hearing in front of the judge tomorrow; and if he doesn't dismiss the charges, he may do one of three things: release you on your own recognizance, set bail, or refuse bail. And then you wait for the trial."

Trial! Catherine had never even gotten a detention slip or a traffic ticket, and now here she was in jail, possibly awaiting trial, then what? More jail? Her eyes widened and her imagination raced ahead -- newspaper headlines -- **Catholic School Principal Arrested for Child Abuse. Bail Set at One Hundred Thousand**

Dollars. She turned to Fr. Riley who had been sitting quietly, listening.

"I'm sorry," she whispered.

"Nothing for you to be sorry about. You didn't do anything wrong."

"It's what we expect, isn't it?"

"Yes," he said quietly. "Blame me for bringing you here. You could have stayed in Colorado and avoided these battles."

"And lose the grace that comes from them? No, thank you, Father!"

"It might not be over for a while."

"I know, Father. It's okay. "

"Remember the martyrs."

"I was thinking about them earlier. All things considered, this is nothing."

"That's the spirit. Don't forget to offer it up."

"I won't, Father. For the poor souls."

"Right."

Nick listened, not understanding much of what they were saying, especially that part at the end. He thought religious people were supposed to be fanatics -- that's what everyone said, anyway, but these two were as matter-of-fact as if they were discussing the weather. This had been a very different kind of day. He and Father Riley rose to leave.

"Your blessing, Father, please..." Fr. Riley nodded.

Nick couldn't believe what he was seeing as Catherine gracefully dropped to her knees right there on the chipped linoleum with the policewoman standing outside the door.

The priest raised his consecrated hand and made the sign of the cross over her. Curiously, Nick felt the weight of it. He tried to shake off the heaviness as Fr. Riley whispered something in Latin. Catherine rose and held out her hand to Nick.

"Thank you so much for your help," she said. He took her slender fingers in his own and was surprised by the firmness of her grip. He looked down at her radiant face. He'd never had a client like this before. He expected her to cry or complain or something. But, instead, all he felt was a soft and comforting peace.

CHAPTER

16

Deus, meus in te confido

The phone rang three times in the secretary's office and Mrs. Janis couldn't ignore it any longer. She stopped typing and reached for it.

"Holy Martyrs School," she said crossly.

"Evelyn? It's Denny Long."

"Good morning, Lieutenant."

"Is my wife around?"

"She's in class. Do you want me to get her?"

"Yes, I need to talk to her."

Mrs. Janis buzzed Judy Long's classroom. "Mrs. Long," she said into the machine. "There's a telephone call for you in the office."

Judy Long stopped in the middle of writing the homework assignment on the board and laid down the chalk.

"Billy Pitlowski," she said. "I'm putting you in charge while I'm gone. I expect y'all to behave, y' hear?"

"Yes, ma'am," the class answered in unison.

"I'll be right back. Billy, come up here and sit at my desk."

Billy drew back his shoulders and walked to the front of the room. He had never been in charge before.

Judy hurried to the front office, her stomach churning. With her husband on the police force, unexpected telephone calls made her nervous. Two of her friends had lost their husbands in the riot in the South End when they closed the steel plant and the workers went crazy. A depressed market, management said.

And another one had been shot when he pulled over a car thief. There was so much violence and turmoil now. You never knew what was going to happen. She quickened her steps. She went into the front office and headed straight for the phone. She nodded at Mrs. Janis as she lifted the receiver to her ear.

"Hello. .."

"Judy, it's me."

Thank God, she breathed. He's all right. But why would he be calling during school?

"Is everything okay, Denny?"

"That's what I wanted to ask you."

She was confused. "Yes, everything's okay."

"The kids are all right?"

"Yes. What's going on?"

Lt. Long leaned against the wall and cupped his hand over the receiver. He didn't want anyone to hear him. "Was there an incident of child beating at the school last week?"

"What in the world are you talking about? Of course not!"

"You're sure."

"Of course I'm sure. Who said there was?"

"They've got your principal down at the station."

Judy gripped the phone and looked at Mrs. Janis who continued to type. "Just a second." She laid her hand over the receiver. "Mrs. Janis, is Dr. Anderson in her office?"

"No," the secretary answered. "I don't know where she is. I told Fr. Riley she hadn't come in yet. I don't know what's going on. She didn't seem like the type who just wouldn't show up. But nowadays you never know..."

"Where's Fr. Riley?"

"I don't know that, either. Nobody tells me anything. He left right after Mass." She went back to her typing.

"Denny...what's going on? This is scary."

"Hang on a minute. I'll see what else I can find out." He called to the officers at the counter. "Hey, Maddox, get me that report, will you?"

"All right." Maddox turned to Sam Oliver. "You heard him. Get the report."

Oliver jumped off the stool and ran to the squad car. He grabbed the clipboard and brought it to the lieutenant.

"Thanks," he said. "After you finish your coffee, wait for me in your car."

"Yes, sir," Oliver answered and went back to the counter. He laid some money on the counter.

"It's on the house," said the waitress.

"Thanks, but we pay our way." He turned to Maddox. "I'll meet you in the car," he said. "The lieutenant wants us to wait for him."

"I heard him." Maddox hunched over his coffee.

Lt. Long was reading through the report while Judy waited.

"It seems a Mrs. Obertynski filed a complaint," he said. "Alleges that she saw one of the kids walking home from school and his shirt was covered with blood."

"What?"

"That's what it says. She questioned him and he refused to answer her, said this Dr. Anderson wouldn't want him to. I guess that's why she figured Dr. Anderson was the one who did it."

"Did what?"

"Beat him up."

"Oh, for heaven's sake. Did it say who the student was?"

"Let's see. The complainant couldn't remember his last name,just that it was Polish. Billy something..."

The episode with Billy and Tommy Flanagan flashed through her mind. She didn't know whether to laugh or cry. "Denny, this is absurd...but I can clear it up for you."

"Good. I'm listening."

"It was probably Billy Pitlowski. He's the only Billy we have. He's in my class. Anyway, Tommy Flanagan punched him and gave him a bloody nose because Tommy thought Billy tripped him. His shirt had a little blood on it, but it sure enough wasn't *covered*!"

179

"When was that?"

"Thursday."

Denny looked at the report and confirmed the date.

"Where were you when this happened?"

"In Catherine's...Dr. Anderson's office. She sent for the boys and I went back to my room. She made them both stay in for recess."

"That was it?"

"That was it."

"Thanks, Jude. I'll see you later. Gotta get back to work."

"Denny?"

"Yeah, Babe?"

"Take care of this, hear?"

"I'll do what I can. See you later."

She hung up the phone. Mrs. Janis was waiting for an explanation.

"That was Denny," Judy said. "The reason Dr. Anderson ₃n't here is...y'all're not going to believe this...they arrested her this morning."

"Denny did?"

not Denny. He just found out about it. "

"What'd they arrest her for?"

"Child abuse."

Mrs. Janis closed her eyes. "People don't like what we're doing," she said. "It's going to get worse."

"I'm afraid you're right."

"These are bad times." She pulled the sheet of paper from the typewriter.

Denny Long hung up the phone and went out to the squad car where the two officers were waiting. Maddox was smoking a cigarette. Lt. Long put his hands on the top of the car and leaned toward the open window.

"Oliver, I think you'll make a good cop."

"Sir?"

"Looks like your instincts were right about the Anderson woman." He told them what he had found out. Maddox glared at the steering wheel. "Follow me to the Obertynski house. I want to ask a few more questions myself. "

"Suit youself," said Maddox as Lt. Long got into his car and radioed headquarters.

Catherine was released that afternoon at two thirty, and the charges against her were dropped. Lt. Long met with her in his office and explained what had happened.

"That little Billy's quite a character," he said.

Fr. Riley had called Helen in the morning when he got back to the church, and she had stayed at home for the rest of the day, waiting for news. She sat restlessly in the den, trying to do some cross-stitch, a delicate table runner with an intricate pattern, but she couldnt concentrate.

The phone rang as she was ripping out a row of stitches and she jumped in her chair, pricking her finger with the needle. The cordless phone was by her side, and she picked it up with trembling fingers, fearing the worst, then sighed with relief when Denny told her of Catherine's release.

Helen folded her needlework and laid it in her basket. She hurried out to her car, nearly forgetting to lock the kitchen door. In fifteen minutes, she was waiting impatiently by the front desk of the police station while the officer on duty gave Catherine her purse and combs and belt.

"We're sorry, ma'am," said the officer at the desk as Catherine and the policewoman came through the door.

"It's all right," said Catherine. "You were just doing your job."

"Yeah, but it's stuff like this that makes people hate cops."

"I'm just glad you didn't keep me overnight. I was

181

dreading that."

Helen walked briskly over to Catherine and embraced her.

"Are you all right, dear?" she asked anxiously.

"Fine, now, Mother, " answered Catherine, "but that was one experience I wouldn't want to repeat!"

"I should say not," said Helen. "The idea! I wonder who the old busybody was who turned in the complaint."

"I don't know. It doesn't really matter. These things happen for God's own reasons." She held the door open for Helen. She laughed softly. "I was so proud of Billy. He wouldn't tell who hit him. He was protecting Tommy's good name. That's a lot of integrity for a little boy, I'd say."

Helen glanced over at her daughter-in-law. She was always saying surprising things. " I never would have thought about it like that," she said.

The two women walked outside. High pewter clouds obscured the sun and the wind was starting to pick up. It would be raining by morning. As Helen drove, Catherine brushed her hair and twisted it behind her head, securing it with her combs.

"That's better," she said, shuddering at the indignity of the search at the police station. She couldn't allow herself to dwell on it. The life of a Catholic was sometimes difficult, she thought, an arduous climb up a steep mountain. Smiling to herself, she spun the metaphor in her imagination: If a few rocks hit you and knocked you down along the way, well, it was to be expected. You had to get up, jam your pick into the rock with all the strength you could muster, wrap the rope around your waist, and inch up the ledge. You didn't get to heaven by limousine.

They arrived back at the school just as classes were dismissed and the students began pouring out the doors, looking forward to the evening's freedom, laughing as the wind swept their skirts and jackets.

"Thanks for picking me up," said Catherine, unlocking her door.

"Are you coming home now?" asked Helen.

"No, I've got some work to do. A lot, actually. Then, if you don't mind, I think I'll stay for the Mother of Perpetual Help devotions tonight. I'll grab some hamburgers on the way home."

"I can heat up your dinner. No sense filling yourself up with junk."

"I don't want to bother you...." Catherine felt she had caused enough disruption for one day.

"It's no bother. Then you can tell Dad and me all about what happened. About nine, then?"

"Yes. See you later.." Catherine closed the car door and walked toward the school. Helen watched her, her thoughts troubled. She had been raised to believe that if you followed the appropriate social conventions, were polite and well mannered, and did what you were supposed to do, that life would be pleasant and things like what had been happening to Catherine -- and what had happened to Frank -- wouldn't happen.

But all the neatly packaged niceties came crashing down; and in those brief moments of confusion, there was a shift in the depths of her soul. She began to abandon her dependence on the little proprieties of her class, and the seed of true faith which had lain dormant in her heart began to germinate, the husk breaking, and the life enclosed within pushing up and drinking the water that flowed from sorrow. Turning off the ignition, she got out of the car and walked over to the church.

CHAPTER

17

A viro iniquo libera me,
Qui cogitaverunt malitias in corde
Tota die constituebant praelia

It was good to be back at school, Catherine thought, cringing as she realized again how much worse things could have been. She shuddered to think of it. Heading down the main hall toward her office, Catherine felt a deep gratitude toward God sweep over her as a knowledge of His ways impressed itself upon her mind and illumined her thoughts like the welcome light of a lantern in a rolling fog, beckoning the sailor through the murky night.

The words of the ninetieth psalm, memorized long ago, came to her lips -- *Because he hoped in me I will deliver him: I will protect him because he hath known my name...*

She could feel God's protection and His love as she stopped for a moment, gazing at the large crucifix on the wall. Jesus nailed in agony for love of her. What were her little sufferings in comparison to that? She longed to reciprocate, to love back with the full force of her mind and soul, but her heart felt small and tight, inadequate for the demands of divine love.

Oh, to love like the saints loved! Catherine thought. She resolved to try. It would be the task of her life, she decided, to seek that grace. She lifted her eyes to the Crown of Thorns.

Her purse swung from her shoulder as she walked briskly down the hall, her steps quick and purposeful. She stopped short when she got to her office.

Fr. Rodriguez was sitting at her desk, the chair swivelled around and facing the window. He had a large manilla envelope in

184

ਪí

in his hand and he was on the phone, the receiver wedged under his chin. She flung the door open and stood with her hands on her hips, her face red with indignation. How dare he! He might be a priest, but he certainly didn't know how to act like one. What a contrast between him and Fr. Riley, she thought.

"Fr. Rodriguez!" she said peremptorily.

He turned around toward her, unfazed. "I'll call you back later," he said into the phone, "Something's come up." He replaced the phone. "Ah, Dr. Anderson, you have returned."

"Did you expect otherwise?"

"One never knows...I understand you ran into a little difficulty with the police..."

"Who told you?"

"It doesn't matter. Perhaps you are regretting coming to Holy Martyrs."

"The only thing I regret is the fact that you are sitting at my desk."

"I needed to use the phone."

"Who let you in?"

"Who else would have the key? Mrs. Janis, of course."

I'll have to talk to her, Catherine thought. Mrs. Janis must not allow herself to be intimidated by this...this *person*. "No one may use my office without my permission."

"My, my, aren't you the queen? Where is your sense of *sharing*? You have an obligation, you know, in Christian charity..."

"I have no obligation to share my office with you."

"We'll see about that," he said, rising from the desk and sliding past her and out the door. He stopped and put his head through the partly open door. "A little lesson for you -- the needs of the community supersede those of the individual. That's the teaching of the Church."

"Not quite," she said to no one. Fr. Rodriguez had left. Catherine closed the door and locked it. She walked over to the desk and picked up the manilla envelope he had forgotten. She debated whether to open it. It was unsealed. She felt its thickness, wondering what was in it. These papers might be mine, she thought, and I need to know if he's been going through my desk as well as sitting at it. She considered what to do. If it's his and it's private, but he left it in my office when he wasn't supposed to be in here, can I look at it? Or do I have to respect his privacy? She didn't know. She pressed the intercom to the rectory.

"Fr. Riley?"

"Ah, Catherine, you're back."

"Yes. Thank you for everything. "

"Is something wrong?"

"No. It's just that Fr. Rodriguez was in my office when I got here."

"What?"

"Mrs. Janis let him in."

"That is not to be permitted. I'll speak with him...and with her." Good, thought Catherine, I won't have to talk to her myself. She paused, sliding her fingers along the edge of the envelope.

"He left an envelope on my desk."

"What is it?"

"I don't know. I didn't open it. I didn't think I should. But, Father, he makes me nervous. There's something creepy about him."

"That's one way of putting it. I'll be right over. I'll take responsibility for the envelope."

He arrived within minutes. She forgot she had locked the door and looked up to see him standing there. Embarrassed, she rose to unlock it.

"I'm sorry, Father. I'm a little edgy, I guess."

"With good reason."

She turned back toward her desk and picked up the envelope. He took it from her hand.

"Thanks. I'll take care of this." And he was gone. Catherine turned to her work. A biography of Jane Austen and

Hamish Poynter's, *Jane Austen: Style and Meaning*, were at her elbow. She was taking notes on *Pride and Prejudice* for Wednesday's lecture when the door flew open. Fr. Rodriguez walked up to her desk without a word and started moving her papers.

"Stop that!" Catherine demanded. "Move away from my desk immediately."

He ignored her.

"I said, leave my things alone!"

"Where's my envelope?"

Catherine clenched her teeth and gripped the edge of her desk..

"If you hadn't been where you weren't supposed to be, you'd have your envelope now."

"Don't get smart."

"It's true."

"Where is it?"

Catherine stood up, wrapping her fingers around an agate paperweight. "Leave my office now!"

Fr. Rodriguez looked at her, his eyes narrowing. "What have you done with it?"

"I gave it to Fr. Riley."

Fr. Rodriguez snarled. "I'll teach you, you little..." and he swept his arm across her desk sending her papers, books, and pens flying across the room. Catherine moved around him, her eyes blazing.

"You may leave now," she said, standing at the door.

"You'll regret this," he said as he rushed out, hitting against her shoulder.

That's what I get for forgetting to relock it, she thought, rubbing her arm. If he weren't a priest, I would have tripped him. She bent down to pick up her books and a question slipped into her mind, making her straighten up quickly, clutching the books in her arms. .

What if he really isn't a priest? She laid her books on the desk and decided not to think about it.

Fr. Riley bent over his desk, the papers from the manilla envelope spread out before him. The first page was entitled *Planning Commission* and twenty names were listed. He read through them, not recognizing any except for Fr. Rodriguez and Sr. Agnes Hopaluk. Fr. Dan Gregson, Fr. Jaime Rivera, Fr. Rodriguez, Sr. Agnes, Sr. Anne Hodgson, Fr. Jeff Van Meter.

His eyes came to the bottom of the list. "Approved by the Chairman, Bishop Edwin Washinsky, this fourteenth day of March." *The Bishop!* Fr. Riley stared at the paper. That explained a lot.

But what was it they were planning? Was it merely some committee like countless others over the past thirty years organized to reform the liturgy and impose the endless changes? Or was this something different? There was no way to tell. He glanced at the next page. *Targeted Parishes.* Third on the list was Holy Martyrs. It was the only one listed from the diocese. The others were out of state.

He took the first two sheets to the copy machine and ran them off, placing the copies in his drawer. The remaining pages were form letters to bishops. He started to scan them and quickly recognized the familiar style of the revolutionaries. Tendentious drivel, he thought, if only it weren't so dangerous. His mouth tightened in disgust. "Your Excellency," the first began...

"We, The People of God, vigorously oppose the recent misinterpretation and distortion of the Gospel in various Sees in this country, namely, Detroit, and, to a lesser extent, Orlando and Providence.

As you know, we are organizing *Marches of the People*, parish hall meetings, and talk show programs to let our feelings be known. We trust that you will join us in our resistance to the unilateral imposition of obsolete religious practices. As mature Christians, we have the right to choose what we believe and how we express those beliefs.

Therefore, we shall follow the same program as our brothers and sisters in Italy, France, and Spain. We are in contact with major television networks and have key people in communications media throughout the country.

We demand that you resist following the so-called return to tradition which only leads to divisiveness and alienation among the People of God. Unless you join us, you can be assured that we will urge the faithful in your diocese to revolt against you and the dead religion of Innocent XIV with its superstititions and childish mysteries.

We reject the emergence of a new and dangerous religious fundamentalism that seeks to interpret literally every word from the Vatican, as though the Pope, who is no different than any other man, were speaking for God Himself.

The so-called *return to tradition* is an egregious attempt to divert the course of History and we must rise up against it. **THE EVOLUTION OF TRUTH MUST CONTINUE.**

We refuse to return to the dark days when the ignorant masses considered the pope to be a sort of Vicar of Christ, a special emissary of Jesus, our brother, who, like us, struggled to achieve divinity amidst contradiction and violence. Innocent and his followers are Pharisees, but **WE ARE THE CHILDREN OF THE KINGDOM.**

We remind you that truth can only be found in the consensus of the faithful. The pope is first among equals, with no authority beyond our own, for example, without the approval of the People. The operative word is equal, and this must be recognized by all bishops. The doctrine of collegiality as revealed by the Spirit of Vatican II demands it.

Therefore, we must not assign any weight to those

189

pronouncements coming from Rome which would thwart the growth of the past half century. We trust that you agree.

The Restoration of Tradition is a direct attack on you and the National Catholic Conference of Bishops. It is a bid for power, and we refuse this foreign interference. You must act immediately to assure that there is no suppression of the liturgy given to us after Vatican II and developed into maturity over the past three decades. The new liturgy is the celebration of the Christ within us.

We reject any notion of a God Above whom we must placate with sacrifice and servile prayers in a dead language.

The reform must continue so that the Spirit will lead us to the true meaning of Church.

The letter was signed by leading theologians, seminary rectors, heads of religious orders, and university professors. After them came the Parish Worship Committee Chairmen, the Society of Eucharistic Ministers, the Diocesan Educational Directors -- Fr. Riley spotted Sr. Mary Anne Whittaker's name -- religious publishing companies, magazine and newspaper editors and then the long long list of those without titles. There were nine pages of signatures in all, closely spaced.

The storm troopers of the revolution, mused Fr. Riley. He was not surprised. He had expected it. This was the sort of thing which had gone on for years, pressure placed on the bishops to make sure they did nothing to preserve and pass on the venerable traditions of the Catholic Church. The threat to each bishop himself was clear.

And those men -- insecure in the face of the group, fearful of being different. and ashamed of their religion and what they saw as the *primitiveness* of it -- had smashed the face of Christ by their failure to safeguard His Mystical Body, the Church.

The Catholic Church was a broken thing, now, beaten and

betrayed, and Fr. Riley wondered whether it was too late, whether Innocent XIV could rebuild the ravaged household of faith.

Or was the end near? he wondered, thinking of the hatred that clawed at the Church. He heard the words of the Saviour penetrating the struggles of the twenty-first century Christians, *"And you shall be hated by all men for my name's sake. But he that shall endure unto the end, he shall be saved."*

He shuffled through the rest of the papers. There were several petitions like the first, then slicks for newspaper ads. He couldn't bring himself to read them closely. Maybe later, he thought, as he ran off more copies. He put the originals back in the manilla envelope and locked the duplicates in his drawer.

Turning on his word processor, he began a letter to the Archbishop. He thought he would hand deliver it. The most important thing at this point was to get Fr. Rodriguez out of Holy Martyrs as soon as possible. He was glad he hadn't called Bishop Washinsky again, knowing what he knew now. He rubbed his chin as he tried to figure out how to start. He was staring at the blank screen when Fr. Rodriguez opened the door. Fr. Riley turned toward him.

"It is customary to knock," he said.

"Look, your little rules and customs make me sick." He spotted the manilla envelope on the desk. "I believe that is mine."

"Is it?"

"Yes."

"How did you come to misplace it?"

"I left it in your sweet little principal's office."

"And what were you doing there?"

Fr. Rodriguez was growing tired of the questions. "It's none of your concern."

"Everything that happens here is my concern," said Fr. Riley, his words hard and cold.

"Ah, yes, I had forgotten. The priest as *paterfamilias*. Daddy in Charge."

Fr. Riley looked at him, sizing him up. He wondered if Fr. Rodriguez had ever had a vocation. Had he ever wanted to serve God? Had he ever loved the Church? He doubted it. He wondered who had ordained him, whether it was valid.

"You may have your papers back."

Fr. Rodrguez hadn't expected that. He grabbed them off the desk before Fr. Riley could change his mind.

He started to walk out the door, but Fr. Riley stopped him.

"I want you out of here in an hour," he said. "Pack your things and leave."

"I'm not going anywhere. I'm here on assignment from the bishop."

"You have sixty minutes to clear out."

"You can't make me." He sounded like a whining child.

"Can't I? Don't push me. Now, get out." Fr. Riley stood up, his size and manner conveying his authority.

Fr. Rodriguez didn't argue further but turned and went out the door, slamming it behind him. He considered that it would be better if he appeared to comply with the expulsion. He was cornered. Furious and driven by a thirst for revenge, he hurried to his room to call the bishop.

"Good afternoon, Bishop Washinsky's office," answered the secretary. She hooked the receiver under her chin so that she could continue to file her nails.

"Rita, it's Stefan."

"Oh, hi, Stefan, how's it going?"

"I've got to talk to the bishop."

"Sorry, he's at a meeting in Cancún."

"Terrific. When will he be back?"

"Not for ten days. Good Friday. He'll have a nice tan for Easter."

"Yeah, not like us peons stuck here in Detroit..."

"Gloomy, isn't it?"

"Yeah, and not just the weather."

She laughed sardonically. "Maybe we could arrange an All

Faiths Leadership Conference in Majorca or something. ."

"Yeah, why don't you book the reservations? Put it on the bishop's American Express card. We deserve a break.

"Don't I know it...You wouldn't believe the calls I've been getting. From all over. St. Alan's, St. Cletus, Holy Family, St. Joseph's. People are mad that their priest isn't being *obedient*, that he hasn't started the Old Mass up again and they're demanding to talk to the Archbishop. All they know how to do is complain.

"They don't like the new lectionary, they don't want eucharistic ministers, they want to *kneel* for communion, for heaven's sake. Probably want to stick out their tongues, too. I really don't get it. After all we've done to make the liturgy more meaningful for people, this is the thanks we get. One speech from the pope and they're all right back where they were in the sixties."

"Most of humanity is stupid," answered Fr. Rodriguez. "That's why they need leaders. They really can't think for themselves. We'll have to educate them all over again."

"I thought we were done with that."

"Education is a lifelong process. We can't stop now -- there's too much at stake."

"I guess you're right, but you don't have to listen to all these crybabies."

"Just remember, they haven't evolved. They haven't taken the giant step, the quantum leap into superconsciousness. They're part of the old humanity."

Fr. Rodriguez was warming up. The new theology, with its power and glory for people like himself, was exhilerating. He had just finished Ernesto Sanchez' *On Man Becoming God*, and he was inflamed. There was no need for God except for the God man was becoming. He intended to be in the forefront.

The secretary continued to complain. "They're certainly annoying."

193

"They're like children, Rita, or animals. They'll learn, some of them anyway. If they don't, they'll have to be eliminated. They cannot be allowed to obstruct the work of the Spirit."

"Well I wish you'd hurry up and eliminate them. They bore me."

"Patience, Rita," he said before hanging up the phone.

He packed his clothes and the few books he had brought and took his jacket out of the closet. Checking the dresser drawers, his eyes fell on the car keys and wallet lying on a wooden valet tray below the mirror. Keys. He had almost forgotten. He would need need keys to the building while he was gone. He had to have access. He sat down on the edge of the bed to think. He was certain someone would have an extra set.

These people were so organized and careful that they must have provided for lost keys. He leaned against the headboard, stroking his beard. Suddenly he bolted off the bed and over to the dresser. Taking a credit card out of his wallet and a miniature screwdriver off his keychain, he headed back for the school. Dr. Anderson was still in her office, so the outer doors probably hadn't been locked yet.

Fr. Rodriguez went in the main entrance and hurried toward the secretary's office. Mrs. Janis had already left. Looking around to make sure he wasn't seen, Fr. Rodriguez pulled the credit card out of his pocket and slid it along the edge of the door, trying to spring the lock. His first attempts were unsuccessful. He pried the screwdriver against the latch and angled it, then slid the credit card down again. The latch gave way, and he opened the door quickly before the bolt sprang back.

It was dusk and Mrs. Janis hadn't drawn the blinds, so there was enough light for him to see without flicking the switch. He didn't want to draw attention to himself. Now it was just a question of finding the extra keys that he was sure had to be here.

He pulled at the the desk drawers and tried the file cabinets. Locked. He'd pick the locks if he had to. There was a cabinet under the printer. Nothing there. He started to sweat, and his black hair clung in damp clusters at the back of his neck.

He started to breathe heavily. There was a blue sweater on the chair that a child had left behind, and he picked it up and threw it against the wall, knocking a picture of the St. Philomena askew. He glanced at it and grimaced.

As he walked pantherlike around the desk, he noticed the teachers' mailboxes. He scanned the names on the compartments and reached his hand far into the back of the cubbyhole marked *E. Janis*. Triumphantly, he pulled out a ring of keys, each carefully labelled with a little paper tag. He chortled as he shoved them into his pocket.

Pleased with his success, he opened the office door slightly and looked down the hall to make sure no one was there. It was deserted. He turned the lock on the door handle and shut the door quietly, shaking it slightly to make sure it was locked behind him. Trying to appear nonchalant, Fr. Rodriguez walked slowly back to the rectory for his suitcase, thinking that he would call an emergency meeting of the planning commission when he got to his apartment to discuss the latest developments.

Fr. Riley looked out his living room window and saw him walking toward the parking lot, his canvas jacket over his arm, suitcase in hand. He was relieved and glad to have a respite from the turmoil stirred up by the visitor, but he knew the problem wasn't over. He sat down in an easy chair and turned on the light to read, but he couldn't concentrate.

Instead he thought about the recent events at Holy Martyrs and wondered how they were connected. Sr. Agnes' imposture, the rebellious priest who seemed more like a revolutionary than a cleric, Laso's regretted involvement with Fr. Rodriguez, the threatening phone call, Catherine's arrest. It was bizarre. Fr. Riley wondered how he could even make his report believable. He only hoped he'd have a chance to talk to Archbishop Stagniak before anyone else got to him.

He shut the book that lay open and unread on his lap. The housekeeper would be calling him soon for dinner.

CHAPTER

18

Benedictus es in templo sancto gloriae tuae
Et laudabilis, et gloriosis in saecula

Palm Sunday dawned blue-gold and the supple limbs of the trees swept gently back and forth in the soft wind, banishing the rainy gloom of the past three days. It was one of those rare April mornings when the humidity wasn't too high, the musty ground had dried, and the fragrance of new spring flowers floated on the breeze.

It would be a long service at Holy Martyrs that day with the blessing of the palms and the procession marking the triumphal entry of Jesus into Jerusalem. And then the solemn reminder in the Gospel of the sadness of the week ahead, the holiest seven days of the year, when the Passion and Death of the Lord would be commemorated, relived, brought forward into the lives of the faithful Catholics who now kissed the palm that the priest placed in their hands and wept in their hearts over the fickleness of man.

The Andersons arrived early. Helen was saying her rosary and Catherine was marking the places in her missal. To Helen's surprise, Don had wanted to come with them again and he knelt at his wife's side, his head bowed, as the scores of parishioners quietly filed into their pews. Palms were banked on the credence table in preparation for the blessing, and there were no flowers on the altar. Instead, tall vases were filled with palms, the statues still covered in purple.

Groups of young parents with small children took their places, trying to keep the toddlers from climbing and the babies quiet while older sisters smoothed their skirts and said their prayers.

Stan and Stella Tomaszewski slipped into the front pew, joined by his sister, her husband, and a neighbor. The Fortunatas were behind them, Teresa on the end. Angie had arrived the night before. Her dark brown hair was covered by a light rose mantilla that matched her suit, and she knelt between her parents, tiny as a young girl, and prayed for Rick across the ocean flying over countries gripped by war. Trying not to think of the terrible danger he faced from antiaircraft missiles and landmines hidden along landing strips, she entrusted him to his guardian angel.

Beside her, Teresa was beseeching the help of the Blessed Mother for her children, especially the ones who had fallen from the faith, Nick and Marty and Rose. Vito read the prayers before communion in his missal.

Jewelled light from the stained glass windows suffused the church and the altar candles burned with an ivory flame. In the still morning silence, the faithful poured out their cares before the Throne of God, to Jesus in the Blessed Sacrament, hidden behind the tabernacle veil. Comforted by the Real Presence of their Saviour, the people waited for Mass to begin.

Teresa blessed herself and reached behind her for the white leather missal that she had had since her wedding. As she opened the prayerbook, she felt a tap on her shoulder, the signal that someone wanted her to move down so he could enter the pew.

She slid to the right, nudging Angie to move farther in, and without looking up, began to read her missal. She felt the person next to her move closer, so she started to push against Angie again. Angie looked up, and her eyes opened wide. She elbowed her mother gently.

Teresa was annoyed and started to remonstrate silently. Angie elbowed her again and pointed for her mother to look to the side. Teresa sighed and looked. *Nick*! She almost dropped her missal. She reached over and briefly squeezed his hand, then went back to her prayers, her heart full and her eyes swimming with tears.

198

From the choir loft, Carrie saw Nick come in. She looked quickly down at her music.

It was ten o'clock on Monday morning in Holy Week, and Catherine sat at her desk, leafing through some papers, planning the week. There would be classes through Wednesday, but the children were to report in uniform to the school for Mass on Maunday Thursday and the *Tre Ore* on Good Friday. She was preparing a notice to be sent home to the parents as a reminder. There was a knock at the door, and she looked up to see Carrie standing there. She smiled and motioned her to come in.

"Hi," Carrie said, coming through the door. "Do you have a minute?"

"Sure," said Catherine, motioning her to sit down. "Don't you have class now?"

"Father came and took them. He's putting them to work for an hour to get things ready for Holy Thursday. The girls are helping the ladies iron the altar cloths and surplices, and the boys are polishing brass." She bit her lip. "I should probably be at my desk doing some work."

Catherine waited.

"This is really silly..."

"What is?"

"Coming down here like a flighty teenager... I shouldn't be interrupting you."

"I'm nearly finished. I just have to bring this notice down to Mrs. Janis."

"I'll take it to her on my way back."

Catherine handed the paper to her. "Thanks. So now that you've saved me a few minutes, what did you want to talk about?"

"Nick."

"Nick?" Catherine thought over the class lists. She didn't remember any of the students being named Nick.

199

"Nick Fortunata."

Catherine's curiosity was aroused.   "Vito's son?" she asked.

"Yes...I met him the day...well, the day you were ..."

"The day I was arrested?   Was he here?"

"Yes...In the parking lot.   He was with Mr. Fortunata, waiting for Fr. Riley.   He wanted to meet me," she said shyly.

"I can see why," said Catherine.   Carrie blushed.

"He came to church yesterday, and we went out to eat afterwards with his parents.   His mother kept crying all through breakfast."

"Was something wrong?"

"No, she was happy."

"I thought maybe she didn't want her son having breakfast with you," Catherine teased.

"Very funny," said Carrie, tossing her head.   "Anyway, Nick hadn't been to Mass since college, so Mrs. Fortunata was really happy that he came.   Especially since it was Palm Sunday and Easter coming and everything.

"I felt kind of funny.   I mean, I had just met him, and he brings me along with his parents....can you imagine?   It went okay, though.   Mr. Fortunata's really nice.   We started talking about the concert.   Then Mrs. Fortunata told me how Nick sang at Harvard...he's really interested in music.   He even thought of majoring in it for awhile, but I guess he was afraid he couldn't make a living singing, and he sure didn't want to teach."

"Sounds like you've found out a lot about him already," said Catherine.

"Oh, Catherine, I really, really like him!"

Catherine laughed, amused by Carrie's impetuousness.   She seemed so young and fresh, as though life stretched before her like a cloudless sky.

"I mean, I've only known him for three hours, really, and I can't stop thinking about him.   That's why I came down here.   I just had to tell you."

"I'm glad you did. Are you going to see him again?"

"Yes. We're going out to dinner tonight."

"Things are moving right along, then, for you..."

"Stop making fun of me! He's coming to the concert. I'll be so nervous! Will you come by practice tonight and tell me what you think?"

"I'd be happy to."

"I want to make sure I'm not missing anything."

"You'll be fine. They sounded wonderful every time I've heard them."

"Thanks. They are good, aren't they? Oh, I almost forgot...the most important part! Guess what?" She paused, waiting for Catherine to guess.

Catherine shook her head. "I give. What?"

"Nick's going to talk to Fr. Riley. He wants to come back to church."

"You've had quite an influence on him in just three hours."

"Oh, I didn't have anything to do with that part. It was his mother's prayers that got him back, I think. She told me she can't even count how many novenas she's made for him over the past ten years. Well, I guess I'd better get back to my room. See you after school. Thanks for listening to me...I must sound like like I'm fifteen..."

Catherine laughed softly. "Thanks for telling me. I love news like that." Carrie's happiness reminded her of the day she had met Frank. It was the first time she had thought of him without pain. She closed her eyes and could still see him standing at the front of the lecture hall at the University of Colorado where she was a graduate student.

Frank had just won the Pulitzer Prize for a series he had done on the resurgence of Communism, now called the *Vox Populi,* in the countries of the former Soviet Union. The chairman of the English department had invited him to be the guest

201

lecturer at a writing seminar.

She listened to him raptly that afternoon, thinking she had never heard anyone so fascinating in all her life. He was good looking, too, tall and broad shouldered, with longish dark blond hair brushed back from his forehead, thick and wavy in the back. He was dressed in jeans and a corduroy jacket, his plaid button down shirt open at the collar. Catherine leaned back in her chair, her memory summoning his voice, his thoughtful brown eyes, his soaring intelligence.

He had noticed her, too, because after class he came up to her in the hall and invited her for coffee. She went, and that was the beginning. Eight months later, they were married. Catherine smiled, remembering their wedding at the little chapel in Colorado.

Fr. Riley had flown in to perform the ceremony, and Angie was maid of honor. Frank had stood at the altar in a morning coat and pinstriped trousers, his shoes gleaming, a gray ascot at his neck; and she, in her grandmother's white satin gown with a cathedral train and her mother's veil, had begun her life as his bride.

And now she was a widow. How old that word made her feel. But she knew that that was what she would be for the rest of her life. She would never marry again. There could never be anyone for her but Frank. She would see him again, she hoped, in Heaven, where she could love him for all eternity. She would just have to be patient and wait. In the meantime, she had work to do.

Catherine pulled a thick folder of notes from the bottom drawer of her desk. She had some ideas that she wanted to present at the upcoming teachers' meeting, and she wanted them to be clear. Rereading what she had written, she made a face. It wasn't good enough. Too pedantic.

She turned on the word processor and began to type. The lunch bell rang as she finished the outlines that she was preparing for the teachers. She slipped a disk in the computer to store what she had written and leaned back in her chair, rubbing her temples and trying to focus after staring at the screen so long, while the printer shot out the pages.

After gathering her things for lunch, Catherine closed her door and started to walk down toward the teachers' lounge when she stopped and decided she should lock it. She never would have thought it necessary in a school like this, but after the events of the past few days, she was going to be very careful. The keys jangled as she locked the door. Slipping them into her purse, she turned and ran into Laso.

He reached out his arm, stopping her from colliding too heavily. She smiled sheepishly.

"I'm sorry, Laso, I wasn't looking where I was going."

"It's all right, Dr. Anderson. I should not have been in your way. Never be in the path of a principal deep in thought."

"It could be dangerous," she said. She looked at the young man in front of her. He seemed more mature, and the hard sullen look that had troubled her when she first arrived was gone. In its place was a new gentleness. She saw it toward her, and she noticed it as the students left the building after school. The elementary school boys would circle him, clamoring for his attention; and he would throw a ball or listen to a story as he walked, the younger boys clustered around him.

"I was coming to see if I could set up an appointment to talk to you."

"Of course, Laso. " She wondered what he wanted. "I'm free after lunch today, during the recess. If you want to give up your football game, that is." Her eyes twinkled.

"We are playing baseball now. Unless Fr. Riley comes over, then we have to play football." Laso had played soccer in Slovenia and was intrigued by American football.

"He used to play college ball, you know."

"No, I didn't know that."

"At Michigan State. He and my husband were on the same team. Fr. Riley was All American."

"You're kidding.

"No, I'm serious. You'd better pay attention to what he says. He knows what he's doing."

" That is impressive, " Laso said, shaking his head. Fr. Riley grew even larger in his estimation. "Anyway, I don't mind missing baseball. Are you sure you have time?"

"Yes, I'll see you in half an hour."

She walked down to the teachers' lounge. At the table, the teachers were talking over their day. Catherine sat down and pulled her sandwich out of the bag. Judy was standing by the coffee pot.

"Want some?"

"Thanks, yes." Judy poured the coffee and handed the mug to Catherine over Barbara's head. Catherine set it down and turned to Mr. Corwin, "I understand the science lab is all set up."

"Yes," he said. "Rob O'Keefe wants to start a Science Club. What do you think?"

"I think it's a good idea. Would you sponsor it?"

"Why not?" he said. "Rob and Laso would be doing most of the work. They've already started a notebook of experiments for different age levels."

Catherine nodded approval. "Is everything all set for the concert?" she asked Carrie.

"Yes. I can't believe it...only two more weeks...I'm so nervous. You're coming over to hear them today, aren't you?"

"I wouldn't miss it." Catherine spent a few minutes going over specific projects and lessons with each teacher, and then their conversation turned to other, lighter topics. They were laughing and talking quietly when Mrs. Janis came bustling in, breathing hard, her brown hair wisping around her forehead and her small eyes darting around the room.

"Good day, Evelyn," said Mr. Corwin. "You're late for lunch. Come, join us."

"No lunch for me today. Too busy." She went over to the counter and started opening and shutting the drawers, then pulled out the wastebasket and peered into it. Barbara Clark watched her quizzically.

"Lose something, Mrs. Janis?" she asked.

"I never lose things." She opened the closet.

"I wish I could say that," said Catherine.

"I was always taught that you take care of things. Put them where they belong and then they'll be there when you need them."

"Well, then, what are you doing going through the drawers and closet?"

"Just looking."

"But you didn't lose anything?" asked Mr. Corwin.

"Of course not. I told you, I never lose things."

"Everybody loses things once in a while." said Judy.

"I don't," Evelyn said and walked out of the room. Where are those keys? she wondered, gritting her teeth. Somebody must have taken them. Probably Brandon O'Keefe. Everybody thought he was such an angel. You have to watch those sweet faced boys. The door closed behind her.

Barbara shrugged her shoulders. "Wonder what that was all about?"

"Who knows?" said Judy.

Catherine remained silent, feeling edgy, irritated by Mrs. Janis' smugness. Why was she being so secretive? Why wouldn't she tell what she was looking for? It was peculiar. Catherine laid down her sandwich, unable to finish it, her stomach in knots.

CHAPTER
19

Confundantur superbi
Quia injuste iniquitatem fecerunt in me;
Ego autem in mandatis tuis exercebor

After lunch, Catherine hurried back to her office and unlocked the door. She was still thinking about the episode in the lunchroom when Laso arrived.

"Please sit down," Catherine said to Laso, motioning to the chair.

"I wanted to thank you," he said. "For the other day. And for forgiving me for being rude when you first got here. I'm sorry."

"It's all right..."

"I went to confession...I don't know how I got involved with Fr. Rodriguez."

"You were lonely and homesick and he befriended you. He played on those feelings."

"Still, I should have known. It was like I did know, deep down, in here..." he pointed to his heart. "But I went along with him."

"He's a priest..."

"Yes."

"There are many like him now, I'm afraid. Men caught up in revolutionary new ideas with no understanding of the past."

Laso was silent. He was thinking of home and the havoc which had been wrought by men like Rodriguez.

"I got a letter from my grandfather yesterday."

"About your mother?"

"Yes. He had good news to tell. She can move her hands. Soon she'll be able to write to me herself."

"That's wonderful, Laso. Maybe she won't have to come to America, after all, and your father can go home." She didn't say that he could go home, just his father. An intuition, a presentiment, had seized her and somehow she knew that Laso wasn't going back to Slovenia.

"He called the doctors yesterday, and they have more hope now. Father is not happy here. He should return."

"And you, Laso?" Catherine looked across the desk at the intense young man who sat with his hands resting on his knees, his shoulders square. The roundness had disappeared and a new strength could be seen, a resolve that showed itself in his posture.

"I want to stay here." He struggled with himself. "Does that sound like I do not love my mother?"

"No. It sounds like you're a young man whose life is opening up before him, and who sees the road that he must follow."

"I shall never forget her. I'll go and visit. I'll bring her here. But Dr. Anderson, I have to stay."

"I'm sure she would understand, Laso. No mother wants her child to live for her. I imagine it would cause her great pain if she felt that you couldn't live a full life because of her. She would hate that. She would want you to do what you must do. A mother's happiness comes from seeing goodness in her children, virtue, and holiness -- not from keeping them tied to her."

"I'm not staying just so I can be a rich American."

"I didn't think you were, Laso." She waited, not wanting to pressure him to say more than he was ready to tell her.

"I want to be a priest."

Catherine thought back to her other conversation with Laso and his first attempt at entering the seminary.

"I have not mentioned it to anyone yet, just you, not even Fr. Riley or my father. I hadn't thought it all out yet. I had it all wrong the first time, so I wanted to get it right now."

"And you have?"

"I'm trying. I think I have a vocation. Is it prideful to say that?"

"No."

" I want to serve God. I want to give my life to Him. Not like that bargain I tried last time. That was the work of a silly schoolboy."

"You were young. You've changed since then."

"Do you think so?"

"Yes. However unfortunate your involvement was with Fr. Rodriguez, you came through it well, with a greater maturity. And, I think, a deeper understanding of your faith..."

"How did you know?"

"You can see it in how you behave, how you look."

"Do you think my mother will understand?"

"I think your mother will think it's the best gift you could have given her."

"I am worried to tell her."

"Laso, your mother raised you, she helped form your character. Long before you could even think of the priesthood , she watered the seeds of your vocation by her own faith and her love of you.

"Knowing you, I can perhaps know a little bit about your mother, and I think she'll be proud. I would be. For most mothers, Laso, having their son become a priest is one of the greatest joys of their lives. It's a privilege that women treasure like gold."

Laso pondered what Catherine was saying. "I am going to write to her tonight, but I wanted to talk to you first." He paused, looking down at his hands, then raised his eyes. "You are a lot like her," he said.

Pressing the compliment to her heart, Catherine felt the sweet warmth of maternal joy. She understood, then, how nuns and other childless women could fulfill their dreams of motherhood in other, sometimes richer, ways. A maternity of the soul.

"I must go now," Laso said. "I have to arrange with Fr. Riley about altar boy practice tonight."

"You're serving again?"

"Yes, ma'am."

"I'm glad, Laso." She looked at him, and his dark brown eyes met her own, softly, like a boy looks at his mother.

Later that afternoon, Catherine greeted the eleventh and twelfth grade students as they rose when she came into the room for their English class.

"I have a task for you," she said, motioning them to be seated. Annie rolled her eyes and glanced at Jeanne. More homework. Jeanne shrugged.

"We have a problem."

Bernadette tensed. No one was quite sure about the new principal. While she seemed like a good teacher and everyone said she was nice, which was high praise among teenagers, the students didn't want to trust her too soon. They were wary because of the chaos and disintegration of the society around them.

Betrayed by adults, they were not quick to accept what someone told them. Before Holy Martyrs opened, many of the older students had spent their early years in schools where learning was sporadic and discipline harsh under the guise of a new, enlightened multiculturalism.

They were pushed and prodded into abandoning their beliefs; and if they did not, they were sent to social workers and psychologists and, eventually, relegated to the back of the class where they were either ignored or ridiculed. They drew apart from their classmates whose rebellious attitudes and brazen immorality shocked them. Consequently, the Christian students were isolated with few friends and fewer joys.

There were alarming gaps in their education. They had never been taught the fundamental things, and the teachers at Holy Martyrs worked to fill in the empty spaces. It was not easy.

Catherine surveyed the classroom. Most of the boys were looking down at their desks or out the window, but the girls met her gaze, then dropped their eyes. Their minds were not on English, but drifted like sand, their thoughts light and frivolous.

Jeanne Pitlowski sat right in front of Catherine's desk, and she felt like someone had captured her and put her on display. Deciding she had better look up so she wouldn't get into trouble, she rested her chin on her hands and spent the first minutes of class evaluating Catherine. She scrutinized her jacket and the fall of her skirt and decided that an emerald green blazer would have looked better than navy. It would have brought out the red highlights of her hair.

Annie Whittaker, seated behind Jeanne, hated studying English, hated studying anything, in fact. She loved to sing and to draw and to sew. but lines of words in a book left her cold. Leafing through her copy of *Pride and Prejudice*, she tried to picture Catherine as a teenager.

Dr. Anderson seemed a little prim to her, and she wondered if she had always been like that. Too much Jane Austen, probably. Annie thought that she would rather be like Miss Stevens, but maybe that was because she wasn't smart enough to be like Dr. Anderson. She couldn't imagine going to college for eight years. High school was bad enough.

Near the window, Bernadette had opened her notebook, ready to take notes, and in the last row, Laso sat, preoccupied, forcing himself to pay attention. It was important that he do well, and English was his most difficult subject.

Catherine continued speaking. "Now, the problem. You are here to study literature which, to my mind, is the most interesting of all subjects, but we are presented with a dilemma.."

She looked from row to row. The boys and girls, young men and women, actually, appeared attentive, at least. She drew her breath, trying to form her ideas in ways they would understand. There was nothing she dreaded more than blank stares on the faces of a classroomful of students.

"Like painting and music and architecture, literature can be high art," she said. "It is through poetry and novels and drama that you can reach beyond the confines of your own life and begin to understand the thoughts and aspirations of those who have lived before you or in places far from you. At its best, literature is ennobling. It can lift the human mind."

She paused, hoping they were still listening. She felt the importance of what she was saying so deeply, and she wanted to pass on her own understanding to them. The students sat quietly. She continued.

"But that's where the problem for us comes in. You see, no matter how wonderfully written English literature is -- and there is no language like English for the full expression of ideas -- it is still largely non-Catholic. Because of that, it does not ring true to us. It does not capture our imaginations and draw us beyond ourselves. The best of it contains the scent of Christianity -- its mores, its influence on manners and culture -- but, unfortunately, some of it -- powerfully and brilliantly written -- is anti-Catholic. We'll go into that more, later."

She wondered if they understood what she was saying. She closed her eyes briefly, then plunged ahead.

"Unlike continental literature -- Spanish and French and Italian, for instance- - there has been no solid Catholic literary tradition among English speaking people for the past five hundred years. A few wonderful writers, yes -- Chesterton, and Newman and Belloc. Joyce Kilmer, who was killed in World War I before his writing could mature. More recently there was the Jesuit poet Gerard Manley Hopkins. But they are the exceptions. Can anyone tell me why that is?"

Annie slouched down in her seat, hoping Catherine wouldn't call on her. Jeanne looked blankly ahead.

"No ideas? Bernadette?"

"I don't know." She wished she did. It was an interesting question.

Catherine sighed. "Mike?" He shook his head. "Dan?" Another blank stare. "Laso?"

"Because England isn't a Catholic country," he answered.

"It isn't?" said Annie.

Oh, dear, thought Catherine, trying to be patient. "Not since the sixteenth century. And you're right, Laso. We face the same thing in America. The literature of a country reflects its philosophy, its religion. Religion is the tree; art is the blossom."

"Is that why so many books published now are bad?" asked Bernadette who loved to read but was repulsed by the garish covers of the novels on the racks at the drugstore and super-market. She didn't dare leaf through them, much less buy one.

"Yes," said Catherine. "They paint the godlessness and irreligion of the modern age. That's the problem I wanted to talk to you about. I don't think it's enough to read things from the past like some do with the sole purpose of criticizing and analyzing. You must understand what you read and learn to appreciate fine writing.

"And then some of you must become the artists and crafts-men of the future. The Catholic writers. Just as the Holy Father is working to restore the beauty of our religion and the traditions that we love, it is our task to begin to restore our own little corner of the world. And in this class, that means that you must learn to write. And write well."

Catherine walked up and down the aisles as she spoke, looking over her students. "I hope someday to walk into a bookstore and pick up a novel that one of you has written, or a book of poems, or go to the theater to see your play performed. So..." she said, closing the book she was holding in her hands and tapping her palm against the cover, "We are not going to spend all our time buried in books that do not touch your souls. You will learn to recognize what is good and what is not. You will read like you eat, for nourishment, so your mind can grow.

There is pleasure in good reading.   Too many students think it's a bore."

Annie was startled. She felt like Catherine was reading her mind.   Catherine caught her look.

"I assure you, it is not. You will fine tune your critical ear, but not to the point that you stifle your own desire to write, to give expression to your thoughts and dreams. That happens too often to students. I don't want it to happen to you. God loves to make things, and I want you to love to make good things, too."

She had their full attention now. This was entirely different from previous English classes where they had sat listening to dull lectures and reading dry books, never understanding why they weren't moved by them.

The class stirred. Catherine had sparked their interest. They felt older when she talked, less like children; and she made them want to accomplish great things, to reach farther and higher than they had ever reached before.

Bernadette O'Keefe was especially intrigued by Catherine's challenge. A few poems that she had been working on were folded and tucked in the back of her notebook, and she wondered whether she should show them to Dr. Anderson. She thought she would. Her pen poised over a clean sheet of paper, Bernadette made up her mind that she would be one of those writers of the future. She leaned forward so she wouldn't miss anything else the new teacher had to say.

At three o'clock the dismissal bell rang and Catherine went back to her office. She was tired. Teaching was exhilerating, but exhausting, she thought, as she dropped her books on her desk and sat down, sliding her feet out of her shoes and wiggling her toes. She slipped her shoes on again and leaned back against her chair, her eyes closed.

The school grew quiet. Far down the hall, she could hear the children begin to sing. In a few minutes she would join them, as she had promised Carrie. For now, though, she wanted to bask in the silence for a little while. She reached down for her briefcase to begin packing her papers and noticed an envelope lying on the corner of her desk with a pale blue note clipped to it.

J.M.J.
Catherine, this came after you checked your mailbox today.
Thought you might want it before tomorrow.
Evelyn

She is certainly efficent, thought Catherine, as she slit open the envelope, wishing she hadn't gotten so annoyed with Mrs. Janis in the lunchroom. Standing by her desk, she unfolded the single sheet of paper, not paying too much attention, just assuming the note was routine. She dropped her eyes to the bottom of the page to see who had written it before she began reading.

The signature startled her. It was signed, *People of God on the March.*

She scanned the lines quickly.

*Ms. Anderson...*Catherine read, shuddering at the hated title. *You don't learn very fast, do you? You were warned once. Your religion belongs back in the tomb where we put it. If you think you can stop the forward movement of History, you are mistaken. We will eliminate you and anyone else who gets in the way. We are the Voice of the People.*

What in the world? thought Catherine, feeling limp. The color drained from her face. Who were these *People of God on the March?* And that expression -- the Voice of the People. *Vox Populi.* The European neo-Communists. Were they in America too? Gaining power against the Church? Remembering the fire-bombs that had destroyed the cathedrals in Europe, she shook the paper from her hand as though it burned to the touch. For several minutes, she sat staring at it, unable to move.

So the person who had threatened her on the phone was not working alone. She had known that, of course. But she didn't want to admit that this was a network, a -- she forced herself to use

214

the word -- a conspiracy. Probably worldwide.

A conspiracy against Christ as evil as the plotting of the Pharisees, the betrayal of Judas, and the judgment of the San-hedrin against Him. The full force of the modern onslaught against the Church hit her in the face, and she shuddered at the intensity of anger toward her and toward the school because of the Faith she loved and the Incarnate God they served.

She wondered what was happening in other parishes where the True Faith was kept. Were they going through the same thing? It reminded her of the Reign of Terror after the French Revolution. How bad was it going to get? she wondered. Would blood be shed? Could she face that? The fiery rage seared the Church from top to bottom, and she feared for the Holy Father.

Just the night before there had been a man dressed in the red robes of a cardinal, skullcap askew, who had hidden a hunting knife under his cassock and was walking through St. Peter's Square. The handle of the knife protruded from the side pocket slit and a perceptive Swiss guard had apprehended him.

The spirit of Antichrist stalked the world.

Catherine stared blankly at the note. She hated to bother Fr. Riley again and was tempted to crumble the paper and throw it away, but knew she couldn't. It might just be intimidation, empty threats, an attempt to frighten her into running away. But on the other hand, the danger could be real.

She had had some bitter lessons about man's capacity for evil and would not pretend now that nothing had happened. She had children to protect. Fr. Riley had to be told. Sighing, she lifted the receiver and buzzed him on the intercom. No answer. She slipped the note into her desk drawer and locked it. The joy of the day's work was crushed under the weight of a thin sheet of paper.

Catherine finished loading her briefcase with her books and papers and went to the closet for her coat, which she draped over her arm. While she had been looking forward to hearing the children practice after school for the concert, her heart was heavy now and she wished she could go home. But as she locked her door, a sound like the seraphim, the sweet soprano of Brandon O'Keefe, floated down the corridor.

Ora pro nobis... nobis peccatoribus... Nunc et in hora .... *mortis nostrae...*

Catherine stood listening, not wanting to move as he held the final perfect note of the *Ave Maria* and then was quiet.

Pray for us, Dear Mother, she whispered, *Oh, pray for us.*

"Miss Stevens, Miss Stevens," called Billy Pitlowski as Catherine opened the door to the gym. "Dr. Anderson's here!" The high school ensemble had gathered on the stage, ready to sing and, baton in hand, Carrie was reminding Annie Whittaker to watch her vowel sounds. Annie could sing, but her Americanized Latin grated Carrie's ears. Carrie turned and smiled at Catherine.

"I'll be right with you."

"Just keep going," said Catherine. "I'll sit back here." She sat down on a folding chair and three little girls came and sat beside her. Billy Pitlowski grinned and rejoined the boys in the front row who would be performing next. There were some empty spaces. Laso had come to get the torch bearers and the acolytes for altar boy practice in the church, and they weren't expected back for awhile.

An old walnut upright piano stood below the stage, and Bernadette sat straight and still on the hard bench, ready to accompany the singers. Lying on a chair near the piano was a flute and a sheaf of music. Catherine's fingers itched as she looked at it. She folded her hands in her lap. On the stage, the girls began to sing the *Ave Maris Stella* and Julie Flanagan, a first grader, leaned her head against Catherine's arm and hummed quietly along.

When they finished the song, they looked expectantly at Carrie.

"That was fine, girls," she said.

"Ask Dr. Anderson what she thought," said Jeanne.

Catherine rose and walked toward them. "Beautiful," she said and the girls glowed with pleasure, then walked off the stage and took their seats.

"Who plays the flute?" Catherine asked.

"Nobody," said Jeanne.

"Nobody?" Catherine looked puzzled. She pointed at the flute.

"That's Bernadette's," said Annie. "She's trying to teach herself to play." Bernadette blushed and tried to hide her face.

"Her aunt gave her the flute. It used to be her daughter's, but her daughter never liked it, and she told her mother to give it to Bernadette because she's good at music."

"And everything else, " said Danny.

"Anyway," continued Jeanne while Bernadette wished she could disappear, "Her cousin said if she could play the piano, she could play the flute."

Catherine laughed. "That sounds like something someone would say who didn't know how to play either one."

Bernadette looked quickly at her, an expression of relief spreading over her face. She hadn't been making much progress with the new instrument.

"Knowing how to read music will make it easier for her to learn, but someone will have to teach her how to breathe, how to finger." Catherine walked over to the flute and picked it up. "May I?" she asked. Bernadette nodded. Catherine drew a clean linen handkerchief from her pocket and wiped the mouthpiece, then lifted the instrument to her lips and began to play.

The high school girls got up from their chairs and circled around Catherine. The younger ones followed, and the boys looked over from their side of the gym, shrugged, and joined them. Coming down the steps of the stage, Carrie moved her wrist keeping time, her baton in miniature motion against her left palm. Catherine played for several minutes, the music soothing her frazzled nerves, and then, nodding at Bernadatte, she began

Schubert's *Ave Maria.*

Bernadette flipped the pages of her music and joined her teacher on the fifth measure. They played as though they had played together long before; and when the last chord on the piano struck and the last lingering note of the flute hung in the air, the students began to clap. Flushed, Catherine, laid down the flute.

"Bravo!" said Fr. Riley coming through the door, altar boys in tow.

Carrie motioned to the boys to take their places on the stage, and Catherine walked over to Fr. Riley.

"I didn't know you played," he said.

"Yes," she said. "Since I was a child."

"You're very good."

"Thank you. It's a beautiful instrument. When I think of Heaven, I always imagine flutes and lyres."

"No harps?"

She laughed, then dropped her voice. "Father, I received another threat today."

The broad smile disappeared from his face. "Phone call?"

"A note this time."

"Do you have it with you?"

"It's in my desk. I'll go get it."

"I'll come with you," he said, frowning, his jaw tight.

Catherine walked up to Carrie and nudged her gently. "I have to go back to my office now," she said. "I'll try to come back tomorow. I want to hear the boys, too."

"That'd be nice. I'm getting so nervous. It's nice to have you sit in."

Back at her office, Catherine unlocked her desk drawer and picked up the small piece of paper lying on top of an attendance folder. She handed it to Fr. Riley who stood by the open door, scowling as he read the note. He walked over to the chair and sat down, rubbing his temples. Catherine watched him from across the desk.

"They're certainly trying to scare you."

218

"They're succeeding."

He looked at her sharply. "Are you all right?"

"Yes. I just have trouble accepting things like this. It doesn't seem possible. We're not bothering anyone."

"Oh, yes, we are," he said. "We're bothering a good many. More than you can imagine. And the one we're bothering the most is the devil. He's not about to take this sitting down. We've got a real battle on our hands, and we'd better be ready. I thought I had accomplished something sending Fr. Rodriguez packing... Unfortunately, I seem to have made it worse. I might have pushed somebody over the edge."

Fr. Riley was certain that the priest and his *Planning Commission* were behind the threats. He only wished he knew exactly what it was they were planning. He rose. "I'll think about this," he said, folding the note and walking toward the door.

"Good bye, Father."

"You're sure you want to stick it out?"

"No doubt in my mind," she said firmly.

He smiled at her spirit and shook his head. "Glutton for punishment, are you?" he teased, then stopped and grew serious. "Catherine, it could get pretty bad. A village church in England was firebombed last night."

"Oh, no! Was anyone..."

"The curate. He was making a holy hour before the Blessed Sacrament at midnight."

"Oh, dear God..."

He paused. When he started to speak again, there was a catch in his voice. "Remember the friend I told you about, Fr. Boccatello, the one arrested in Italy for treason?"

"Yes."

"He was executed last night. The bishop, too. Stephano Andreoni."

Catherine dropped her head into her hands.

219

"Still game?" he asked gently. "The stakes are pretty high."

She looked up, her green eyes glistening with tears, her face pale against her auburn hair. "I'm in," she said.

CHAPTER

20

Confitemini Domino, et invocate Nomen ejus:
Annuntiate inter gentes opera ejus

There was a car in the driveway when Catherine got home. She parked in the street and walked around to the back door. Clumps of daffodils ready to bloom filled the spaces between the yews along the side of the house, and the blue green junipers perfumed the early evening breeze. Catherine ran up the back steps and opened the kitchen door. Helen and Teresa Fortunata were sitting at the kitchen table. Teresa was crocheting a pink and yellow afghan for her daughter Rose's baby and Helen was threading her needle with red silk, her cross-stitch table runner lying across her lap.

"Hello, dear," said Helen and Catherine leaned over to kiss her cheek.

"Hi, Mrs. Fortunata," she said, turning to Teresa. "How are you?"

"Fine, fine. We've been having a good time."

Catherine pulled up a chair.

"Did you have a good day?" asked Helen, snipping the thread from the spool with tiny silver plated scissors.

"It was interesting," she said. What else could she say? She would tell Helen later what had happened. "How was yours?"

"Good. It's a small world," said Helen. "Guess what? I went to school with Teresa's older sister -- Rosa Maria. They were the Miriani girls. Five of them. We all went to Sacred Heart, but Teresa wasn't there yet when I graduated. She was still at St. Sebastian's. We've been reminiscing. Remember Sr. James

GLORY OF THE OLIVE

Matthew? The religion teacher?"

Teresa started to laugh. "Oh, you should have seen her, Catherine. She must have been six feet tall! "

"And the sisters wore that high coif, so it made her even taller."

Catherine tried to imagine tiny Helen Girard next to the nun.

"She'd walk up and down the aisle and we'd shake in our shoes. No one peeped in that class," said Teresa.

"And she had this funny laugh. Like a little girl's giggle. It didn't fit her at all. "

"She died before the changes."

"Lucky for her..."

The older women were silent, thinking of the past, when the phone rang.

"I'll get it," said Catherine, feeling apprehensive. "Hello," she said, waiting for trouble, then broke into a huge smile and clasped the receiver with both hands as she heard the voice at the other end. "Angie!"

"Catherine, it's so good to hear you."

"When did you get in?"

"Early yesterday morning. I saw you yesterday at church, but we left before you could separate yourself from all those kids around you after Mass."

"They had some things to tell me."

"You've got a way with students. You always did."

"You flatter me. Anyway, when are you free?"

"Now."

"Your mother's here."

"She is? I wondered where she was. I went out to lunch with Nick, and she was gone when I got back. "

"How is Nick? Did he tell you what happened?"

"All about it. He thought you behaved *regally*."

"Don't be silly. It was awful. I was certainly grateful for his help."

Angie laughed. "Turns out he thinks you're the one who did him a favor. If it hadn't been for you he wouldn't have met Carrie."

"He likes her?"

"He didn't talk about anything else all through lunch. She'd better be good to him...He's got it bad."

Catherine laughed at Angie's protectiveness of her brother. "I don't think you have to worry about that. She's not exactly indifferent to his charms."

"Really? It's not just hopeful thinking on his part?"

"Not a bit."

"That's a relief. You know how men can get."

"No, how?"

"Stop it, Catherine, you know what I mean. What's she like?"

"All American girl type. Blond, vivacious."

"Not empty headed, I hope."

"This is like being on the witness stand. No, not empty-headed. Artistic. A history major. Musical. Sings in the choir."

"All right."

"Does she pass?"

"Very funny. You can't be too careful these days."

"You'll like her. Instead of sitting here talking on the phone, why don't you come over?" She looked at Helen questioningly. Helen nodded, knowing what she meant. "Have dinner with us."

"Are you sure?"

"Please come."

"Ask my mother if she minds."

Catherine turned to Teresa. "Would it be all right if Angie had dinner with us?"

Teresa smiled. Catherine thought she had the warmest, most motherly smile she had ever seen.

"That's fine."

Helen interrupted. "Why don't you and Vito come, too?"

she asked.

"Oh, we couldn't..." said Teresa.

"That way you'll be able to see more of your daughter. Besides, the roast is plenty big for all of us. I'll just add a few more potatoes. "

"I'd like to stay," she said. "Thank you."

Catherine lifted the receiver back to her ear. "She says it's fine. Is your dad there? Mother thought maybe your parents would like to join us."

"Yes, he's here. Just a second." She came back in less than a minute. "We'll be there."

"Great," said Catherine. "We usually eat at six-thirty. Can you make it by then?"

"No problem."

"I can't wait to see you. We've got so much to talk about."

Helen rose to peel some more potatoes and Teresa began another row of the afghan, the dainty shell stitches falling like cotton lace through her fingers.

"If you'll excuse me," said Catherine. "I'm going to run upstairs and put my things away."

"That's fine, dear," said Helen.

"Then I'll come down and set the table."

Helen dropped the potatoes in the pan of boiling water on the stove, then opened the oven door and pricked the beef with a fork.

"Smells good," said Teresa.

"It should be done right on time," Helen said.

Forty minutes later, the potatoes mashed and the table set, Catherine stood stirring the gravy while Helen sliced the roast. She was putting it back in the oven to keep it warm when Don came in the kitchen door, followed by Angie and Vito.

"Perfect timing," said Helen, lifting her cheek to Don to be kissed. Catherine set the whisk down on the spoon rest and turned to welcome Angie.

"We'll get out of your way," said Don, leading Vito into the den.

"How long are you staying?" asked Catherine.

"Only until tomorrow," said Angie. "You know the state schools. No Easter vacation. Just spring break. I'm just glad it fell this week. Usually it's earlier. They changed the schedule this year."

"How's Rick?"

"Good." Angie hesitated, looking at her mother. "I guess now is as good a time as any to tell you..."

Teresa caught her daughter's eye, knowing what she was about to say and feeling a tug at her heart.

"We're getting married."

Catherine clasped her friend's hands. "Oh, Angie! When?"

"As soon as he gets leave. He's put in for the second week in May, but we won't hear for a few days whether it's approved." She paused, looking hesitantly at her mother. "I may have to meet him in England."

Teresa looked down, her eyes burning. Life was like that. Joy mixed with sorrow. New beginnings and old things ended. Separation, always separation.

"Mama?" said Angie, worried.

"It's okay, Angelina, it's okay. I'm happy for you. If you have to go there to marry this young man of yours, well, you have to, that's all."

"We didn't want to wait any longer."

"No."

"The world is too uncertain. It'll be a Catholic wedding," she said, sensing Teresa's unspoken fear. "The Air Force chaplain will marry us. We can have a reception later, when things have settled down. You do understand, don't you Mama?" Angie leaned over her mother's shoulders and put her face next to hers.

"What's to understand? You're a woman now, not a little girl." She snipped the yarn and tucked the end in the skein.

Later, when dinner was over, Helen chased Angie and Catherine out of the kitchen.

"Teresa and I will do the dishes," she said. "You two have a lot to talk about."

Laughing like school girls, Angie and Catherine ran up the stairs to Catherine's room. Angie sat on the edge of the bed, resting her feet on the baseboard and clasping her hands around her knees. Catherine pulled out the Chippendale chair from the writing desk and turned it to face her. Kicking off her shoes, she propped her feet up against the side of the mattress.

"So you decided to do it..." said Catherine.

"Yes. Am I being a fool?" asked Angie.

"Of course not."

"But, Catherine...you know...what if...what if he dies?"

"There's no guarantee about that no matter where you are."

"You know what I mean. Will it be worse? Harder because we were married?"

Catherine was silent. She stood up and walked over to the window, drawing back the curtain and gazing far off, trying to pierce the dark domed sky which rested black and impenetrable over the earth.

"Yes," she said finally. "Much harder."

"That's what I thought."

"But worth it." She leaned against the bed poster. "Worth every tear and every lonely night," she said, her voice choked and low.

Angie twisted her hair between her fingers . "You didn't mind my asking...?"

"No," said Catherine.

"I didn't want to make it worse for you....bring back memories..."

"They're always right there, Angie. They have to be. I

wouldn't have it any other way. I want to remember. It hurts a little less as time goes on, thank God."

"You loved Frank a lot, didn't you?"

"More than I could ever say. I still do, and I always will. You know how when you're a little girl, you have an idea in your mind of the man you want to marry someday? How over the years, you keep adding more things to that image? And you knew from the beginning you would never be happy if you didn't find him?"

Angie nodded.

"Well, I found him." Catherine sat back down. "I had more happiness in those seven years than most women have in a lifetime. I wouldn't change it for anything."

"You're strong."

"No, I'm not. I'm like a skittish colt, and life is the bridle. It's the Good Lord who tames the fearful wildness."

"Oh, Catherine... I'm so scared."

"I know, Angie. There's a lot to be afraid of..."

"Sometimes I wonder why it has to be this way, why the world is so torn apart now."

"You know, of course..."

"No, I really don't."

"It's the Apostasy," Catherine said as simply as if she had said, "It's Monday."

"Do you really think so?"

"Actually, I think we're nearing the end of it."

"Surely you can't mean..."

"What?"

"That Our Lord will be coming again soon..."

"I don't know. We can't know when. It seems like it. I guess we can't even know if this is the Great Apostasy or just a foreshadowing of it. But think about it. The whole world has been convulsed for the past five years with war and terror and famine like never before in history. There is no safety anywhere. Not even here in this peaceful city where things have always been so quiet and predictable." Catherine shook her head ruefully thinking of the events of the past week."Worst of all, the Faith has just about been extinguished everywhere except for the little pockets of Catholics scattered over the earth, holding on for dear life. Who believes anymore? And think of what the older people have been through --fighting this thing since before we were born. It's been nearly forty years now."

"Forty years of being lost."

Catherine nodded. "Ever since the Council. And what does the forty mean? Forty years in the desert for the Hebrews. Forty days from the Nativity to the Presentation. Forty days fasting for Our Lord. Forty days of Lent. Forty days from Easter to the Ascension. Forty, always forty. And now, it's almost forty years since the Council, since the changes."

Angie looked puzzled. "But why else? Maybe it'd be a different length of time now. How do you know?"

Catherine walked back over to her chair and sat down, an unfathomable depth in her eyes, her face a bride's face, roseate in the lamplight. "Because the True Faith has been restored," she whispered. She looked straight ahead at something unseen. "Because the Barque of Peter has weathered the storm, that's why."

"But people aren't accepting it."

"I know. But now the choice is clear. The lines are drawn. It's not so confusing anymore. You're either in or you're out. The faithlessness on the outside will increase, but the Church they thought they'd killed has risen, fair and beautiful."

Angie looked thoughtfully at her friend. She had always known that Catherine was a deep thinker, more reflective than anyone she had ever known. She marvelled that someone only two years older than she could understand so much.

"What do you think will happen next?"

"The bad will get worse and the good will get better."

Angie kicked at Catherine's foot. "Come on, I'm serious..."

"I'm serious, too."

"Do you think the war will spread?" Angie asked, her voice tremulous.

"Yes."

Angie looked away, frightened. "Poor Rick."

"No one will really be safe, Ange, you know that. He's going to need you more than ever."

"Why does it have to be this way? Look at us. Why couldn't we have a normal life like other women?"

"That's just an illusion, Angie. There's never been a time since Adam that people didn't suffer. This cross seems heavy because it's ours. We don't have to carry anybody else's, so we don't know how hard that would be. For myself, I'm glad we live in these times. Things are sharply defined. And the pain is just for a little while."

"I suppose you're right. But what do we do?"

"We just keep doing what has to be done. Each day. We're part of the Church Militant, remember. The troops have to keep marching forward."

"Like we're in the war, too..."

"On the front lines, Angie."

"I feel funny talking this way. I mean, nobody else says things like this." She looked thoughtfully at her friend, trying to understand how the words could come so naturally to Catherine, ideas that the world ignored, and figures of speech that others mocked. Angie wished she could lift herself up and meet Catherine on her own level. " All we discuss at school is government funding and tenure."

"I know how that goes..." said Catherine, remembering her years at the community college.

"But back to my question...what happens next?"

"I think..oh, Angie, I don't want to sound ridiculous..."

"You never sound ridiculous. Incomprehensible, maybe, but never ridiculous."

Catherine sighed. "I think we shall soon see the Antichrist emerge from the shadows and take center stage."

"Oh, no! Catherine, why do you say that? That's too frightening to even think about."

"I know, but look, Angie...Everything is in place. The world is torn apart. There are no standards of right and wrong anywhere. People are starving and killing each other. Civilization is in ruins and everybody's fighting. People are tired and desperate for peace. So they'll accept the Antichrist when he promises them the world.

"Most people have no faith, nothing to believe in, nothing to live for beyond themselves. They have to have a god. Since they've rejected Our Lord, they're ripe for the Man of Sin. They'll worship him instead."

"But things have been like this for years. Why do you think his time is near now?"

"Because of Innocent XIV. Christ's vicar has thrown down the gauntlet."

Angie looked wide-eyed at her friend.

"It's like in literature, Angie...the events build to an inevitable climax. Human life is God's own drama."

"All the world's a stage," Angie quoted softly.

"And all the men and women merely players..."

The two friends were quiet, their understanding of the evil that threatened the world clearer, more immediate. Man had turned his back on God for too long, and the fruits of his infidelity hung heavy on the vine.

CHAPTER

21

Popule meus, quid feci tibi?
Aut in quo contristabi te? Responde mihi.

Cars began pulling into the parking lot at eleven thirty on Good Friday, as the people of Holy Martyrs arrived for the *Tre Ore* to kneel and weep for their dying God and kiss His Holy Wounds. He would not be forsaken in His agony. Those who loved Him drew close, their hearts heavy, as they prepared to relive the most sorrowful day in human history, taking their place among those who had kept the watch over the centuries, mourning their crucified Saviour.

Thick black clouds rolled heavily across the sky and the wind howled through the bending trees. As the parishioners hurried from their cars, the rain began to fall, ice cold and sharp, and the people bent forward against its bite. All was quiet save the roar of the wind and the staccato fall of the rain as creation shuddered under the shadow of the Cross.

Catherine knelt in the front pew with the first grade children. The hours passed swiftly -- the readings, the Adoration of the Cross, the choir singing the *Crux Fidelis* as the people filed two by two to the altar, genuflecting three times as they approached, then bent to kiss the Crucifix.

Dulce lignum, dulces clavos...Dulce pondus sustinet... On and on the choir sang as the people moved soundlessly up the aisle. *Faithful Cross! above all other, One and only noble Tree!* The Procession, the Mass of the Presanctified. Swiftly one ceremony followed another, until again, there was silence. Fr. Riley and the altar boys filed out and the people buried their heads in their hands. It was two thirty when they came back in for the Stations of the Cross, the priest flanked by the two acolytes carrying lighted candles, the heavy candlestick balanced in one palm, the other hand gripping it near the top.

"We adore Thee, Oh, Christ, and we bless Thee," intoned Fr. Riley.

"Because by Thy Holy Cross Thou hast redeemed the world," answered the people, as they began the fourteen stations, the prayers of St. Alphonsus Liguouri on their lips, giving form to their love and their sorrow.

"I love Thee, oh my beloved Jesus, I love Thee more than myself..." Catherine recited the prayers by heart and at her side, little Mary Pitlowski traced the words in the prayerbook with her finger trying to pronounce them.

Soon it was over. Fr. Riley went back up into the sanctuary and began the customary prayers for the intentions of the Holy Father, the people answering. When they were finished, he made the sign of the cross, replaced his biretta, and followed the altar boys to the sacristy.

Catherine motioned to the children to remain seated while the rest of the parishioners gathered their missals and umbrellas and began to leave the church. The rain had not stopped and the wind pressed ominously against the darkened stained glass windows. Catherine wasn't anxious to leave.

Just then, the sacristy door flew open and Fr. Riley rushed back into the sanctuary, genuflected quickly, then turned to the people, his arms upraised.

"Stop!" he commanded.

Startled, the departing parishioners turned around.

"Please," he continued. "Be seated again. Would some of you in the back please go tell those who are already outside to kindly come back in?"

Everyone looked at each other questioningly as Fr. Riley climbed the pulpit steps. He stood above the congregation, his face ashen and drawn. Catherine looked at him, alarmed.

"What's wrong, Dr. Anderson?" Mary Pitlowski whispered.

Catherine drew her finger to her lips to motion Mary to be quiet, then squeezed her hand to reassure her. The schoolchildren stirred nervously. Fr. Riley waited as people came back into the church and took their places. He looked from right to left , then down at the pulpit. No one moved. After a few moments, Fr. Riley looked up again.

"My dear people," he said, his voice breaking. "I have terrible news. The Holy Father has been shot."

"No...no..." a low groan spread through the pews.

"Oh, God," whispered Vito.

Helen Anderson grasped Don's hand and Stella and Stan looked at each other in disbelief. Catherine dropped her head in her hands and began to cry

"I don't know many details," continued Fr. Riley, struggling with emotion, trying to remain calm for the sake of his people. "Apparently he had come out on the balcony before _Tenebrae,_ which was just before noon our time. It was most unusual. But he had an announcement to make to the world."

Catherine drew her breath in sharply. _The Fatima Message._ There had been rumors that the pope was going to reveal the Third Secret on Good Friday. She remembered talking about it with the other teachers. "Oh, dear Lord, don't let him die," she prayed silently. "We need him."

She felt her heart tighten, caught in the vise of triumphant evil. She beat back the feelings of despair that broke like the waves of the sea over her soul. It would be all right, it had to be. _All things work together unto good for those who love God and are called according to His purposes,_ she reminded herself.

Who was she to question the unsearchable ways of God? Hadn't there been prophecies about the pope with the voice of thunder who would be killed after restoring the ancient disciplines of the church? Hadn't they known that a new age of martyrs was approaching? Would he be the first? Pope St. Innocent XIV, Martyr? She choked back a sob. The little children huddled closer together.

"He has not regained consciousness," continued Fr. Riley, "and the prognosis is grim. Those of you who can stay, please do. We will say a rosary now for our Holy Father."

He paused, then went down the pulpit steps and knelt before the barren altar, his shoulders dropping under the weight of the news. He drew out his black beads and began the sorrowful mysteries of the rosary, the devotion given to the people by the Mother of God herself hundreds of years ago. No one left. With soft voices and breaking hearts they prayed. Outside, a mournful wind blew and the sky grew black.

After the rosary, Catherine led the tired children back to the school to gather their books and jackets. She sat at her desk for a few minutes after they left and listened to the cars pulling out of the parking lot and the last of the teachers going out the door. She didn't want to talk to anyone and was glad no one had stopped by her office on the way out. Sitting back in her chair, she closed her eyes as burning tears streamed down her face.

Everyone was gone and the building was dark, but Catherine didn't notice. She was thinking about the Fatima message and wondering if the person who shot the Pope had known about it. Or was he shot because of restoring the Mass? She shook her head, appalled at the magnitude of the evil that stalked the world. It was just like she had told Angie a few nights before. No one was safe who tried to do what was right and good. The Prince of Darkness would brook no opposition now.

"But, oh God, " she sobbed, "What will we do without him? Will everything he tried to do be lost?"

A feeling of despair washed over her again, and she fought it, refusing to give in to hopelessness. No, she decided. it could not be. God would not permit it. Even if the Holy Father died, what he had begun could not perish. She wiped her eyes and straightened her desk, preparing to leave.

The rain had finally stopped. Catherine drew her coat tightly against her and walked out into the wind and darkness.

She was preoccupied as she drove home, hardly noticing the passing traffic and the changing signals.

She drove mechanically, her mind on the life of Innocent XIV and the crisis which was gripping the church. There hadn't been enough time for the restoration to take root. Too many things had changed and two generations of Catholics had grown up in the new ways, ignorant of their rich heritage. If the pope should die, who would be elected to succeed him? Could they continue the course he had set?

The lights were on at the Andersons, and there were several cars parked in front when Catherine pulled into the driveway. She hurried in the back door. Helen was setting out coffee cups as Catherine came into the kitchen. A plate of tuna sandwiches and a bowl of potato chips were lying on a tray. Helen looked tired. Her dark hair had flattened in the rain and deep lines ran along the sides of her mouth. Her eyelids were heavy, and for the first time in Catherine's memory, she looked her age.

"Any news?" asked Catherine.

"No," said Helen. "There's no change. Everybody's in the living room. We're just going to have a light supper before we go back to church. "

"I'll give you a hand," said Catherine, hanging up her coat and walking over to the sink to wash her hands. She let the cool water run over her wrists for a minute, then dried them briskly with a towel. "Who's here?" she asked.

"Stan and Stella, the Fortunatas..."

"Angie?"

"Yes...and the son, the lawyer."

"Nick?"

"He's with a teacher from your school."

"Carrie..." Catherine thought about how curious life was. While momentous events riveted their attention, unrolled before their eyes like a panoramic screen, engaging them, touching them, uniting them, the scenes of each person's life played on, birth and marriage and death. The triumphs and defeats of daily life. She forced her attention back to the kitchen and the coffee cups. Helen was stacking paper plates and napkins.

"And there's a boy here, too. He came with Vito. An older boy... with an accent. His name sounded like Lazarus or something."

"Laso."

"Where's he from?"

Catherine paused, then spoke softly. "Slovenia," she said.

Helen's jaw tightened, and Catherine reached over and put her arm around her mother-in-law's shoulders.

"I'm all right, dear," Helen said quickly as she pulled the sandwich tray toward her.

Catherine let her hand rest where it was for a moment, and she began to tell Helen about Laso's mother. Helen closed her eyes and dropped her head, laying her palms flat on the counter, pressing her weight against them. "Oh, the poor boy," she murmured. "When is this going to end?"

"Not any time soon, I'm afraid," said Catherine gently. "Come on, let's feed the troops."

"There's another tray on top of the refrigerator for the coffee."

Everyone had gathered around the fireplace. Don had lit the gas logs and the flames cast an orange-rose light on the ivory walls. The radio was on, set low to a news station. No one felt like talking. Catherine handed them their coffee and Helen passed the sandwiches. Grace said, they ate, not hungrily, but for strength, balancing their plates on their laps. Catherine broke the silence.

"Any further word?"

"No," said Don.

Vito took a deep breath as though talking would exhaust him. He ran his hands through his hair. "They're going nuts over there."

Catherine was startled. "Who's going nuts? What do you mean?"

Don took his wife's hand. "Somebody bombed the American Embassy in Rome."

"No."

"And the U.S. Naval Hospital in Spain is on fire."

"Arson?"

"Probably."

"Do you think it's connected to the pope?"

"They don't know," said Stan.

"I'd say the same people shot the pope burned the embassy," said Vito. He looked around the room. "Revolutionaries. They're all tied together."

"Come on, Dad," said Nick. "You're not going into that secret societies conspiracy theory, are you?"

"You got a better idea?"

"Isolated acts of terrorism."

"Yeah, you sound like the newspapers."

"There's no indication they're connected."

Vito looked hard at his son. "You don't think they're go-going to let you see the connection, do you? That's why they're called *secret societies*. They're no dummies. They've been at this for three hundred years. They're out to destroy everything so they can have more power. I didn't go to Harvard Law but I can see what's in front of my face."

"That's not it, Dad."

"What do you think the *Vox Populi* is all about? They're the muscle. Puppets. The secret societies are the brains."

Nick wished he wouldn't talk like that. He didn't think it was credible. Vito saw the look on his face.

"Look, kid, not everybody who believes there are people planning to overthrow our government and our religion is a right wing nut. Sure, there's a bunch of fanatics and schizos who believe it, but there's crazies who think the sky is blue, too, and that doesn't make it not blue because some crazyman agrees with you."

Don chuckled. "Good point, Vito," he said.

237

"What about the Muslim terrorists?" asked Carrie.

"That's what I'd guess, that radical group in Iran," said Stan.

"Nah." Vito shook his head and took a bite of his sandwich. "They'd be calling up the papers and claiming responsibility by now if it was them. Yelling for publicity. That's how they intimidate people, push them around. Scare tactics. Makes them seem stronger than they are."

"We'll probably never know," said Stella.

"Yeah, that's what I'm telling you," said Vito. "They keep it secret." Across the room, Laso nodded in agreement.

"Yes," he said softly, and the adults turned to him, surprised. He had been so quiet they had forgotten he was there. "I've seen them. How do you say it in America? I have personal experience of how they operate?"

Catherine leaned back and rested her cup on her knee, thinking how much suffering was behind Laso's calm statement.

"More coffee, anyone?" asked Helen, rising from the piano bench where she had been sitting.

"Please," Nick said and held out his cup.

"Me, too," said Vito, "Thanks." Don reached for the sugar bowl on the end table and handed it to Nick.

A break was heard in the professionally bland voice droning from the radio. Don hurried over to it and turned up the volume. Everyone turned toward the radio.

"We interrupt this program for a special report from Rome."

No one breathed in the Anderson living room. Catherine froze in her chair

"Vatican spokesmen confirm that Pope Innocent XIV has died from a gunshot wound to the heart. The pontiff, who has raised a storm of controversy since imposing unpopular changes in the Roman Catholic Church, was shot today at 5:46 p.m., Rome time, as he prepared to address the world from the balcony in St. Peter's Square. There are no suspects in the shooting. We return you now to our regular programming."

Don shut off the radio. Although the little group of Catholics gathered together that Good Friday had expected the worst, the news stunned them. Vito hit his fist against his palm, and Teresa and Stella sat in shocked silence. Stan stared at the now silent radio in stony desolation.

Outside the windows, the darkness deepened and the wind moaned, caught by the corners of the house and the eaves; and the night-blackened branches of the old silver maple scratched against the roof. Don's shoulders slumped as he came back to the sofa, and he looked over at Laso, who sat with his head bowed, rubbing his eyes. Carrie started to cry, and Nick reached over and closed his hand over hers. Helen began gathering the cups and plates, and Teresa rose to help her. No one spoke. Finally, Catherine looked up.

"Let's head back to church now," she said.

"The dishes..." said Helen.

"They can wait." Don said as he picked up the coffee cups and followed Helen into the kitchen. Catherine went to the hall closet for the coats and stood handing them out at the front door.

"We'll see you there," she said as everyone hurried out to their cars. Catherine locked the front door and turned on the porch light, then walked back down the hall to the kitchen. Helen opened the back closet door, took out her coat, and slipped it on. She handed Catherine's to Don, who stood holding it as Catherine rejoined them.

"Here you go, girl," he said, as he held the coat for her.

"Thanks," Catherine murmured, sliding her arms in the sleeves and buttoning it up to her neck, but no coat could protect against the cold touch of advancing evil.

239

CHAPTER

22

Confitemini Domino, et invocate nomen ejus
Annuntiate inter gentes opera ejus

It was fitting, Catherine thought, as she entered the church on Easter Monday. The black bunting of a church in mourning draped above the entrance and, inside, the reminders of the Resurrection: The glorious white lilies flanking the altar and the steps. The golden candelabras and the tall white candles. The roses before the side altars. Statues of the saints, Our Lady fair above them all. The representation on earth of the court of heaven. And hidden in the tabernacle, the Body and Blood, Soul, and Divinity of Jesus Christ, God dwelling among his broken people. Catherine knelt and the pain in her heart was assuaged by the Presence of the Saviour.

After Mass, she lingered awhile in silent prayer, begging the Mercy of God on the world. Comforted and at peace, she left the church and went over to the school. She was alone in the building. The children and teachers would be on Easter vacation until the following Monday, and Catherine welcomed the quiet. She hadn't had much time to prepare for her new responsibilities, and she was eager to get to work. It would take her mind off the sad events of the past three days.

She was preparing a lesson on the poems of Emily Dickinson, and she laid her book open on the desk and began to read. She was never quite sure whether she liked the poems or not. What was the problem? she wondered. Maybe it was the trenchant style? Or was it the underlying bitterness? Catherine didn't know. She almost felt like the poet was mocking the reader and it annoyed her. She tapped the desk with her pen.

There was a knock at her door, and she looked up, startled. Fr. Riley opened the door.

"What are you doing here?" he asked.

"Not much," she said, starting to rise. He motioned to her to remain seated.

"I'm just trying to get a jump on next week's lessons."

He looked at the book lying on her desk. "Dickinson."

"Yes."

"Life goes on." He stood up and walked over to the window, his hands clasped behind his back, his Roman collar crisp and white against his black cassock. "What do you think, Catherine?" he asked.

"About what?"

"Are we going to be able to continue?"

The question was rhetorical, she knew. He would press forward, she had no doubt about that. But against what opposition? Would the next pope continue what Innocent XIV had so valiantly begun? Or would everything be undone?

"God willing," she said softly.

Fr. Riley leaned his head forward against the window. He wanted to move, take action, strike out against the enemies of the church. He clenched his fist.

"We have to carry on," he said. "There's no turning back. Whatever it takes. I will not let this be destroyed." He paced back and forth a few times, then stopped himself and sat down. "Are you ready for what lies ahead?"

"You don't have much hope, do you?"

"No. Dear God, no. I wish I did. Do you?"

Catherine looked down at her papers. She didn't want to say what was in her heart, that she was afraid. "I'm trying to be hopeful," she said. "But I'm not succeeding very well."

"The Modernists are gloating. They think their way is clear now."

"Yes, but..."

"Right. I know. They're not in charge." For the first time since he was a boy, Fr. Riley was struggling with uncertainty and fear. He didn't like the feeling. "I saw you come over from the church, and I thought I should come and talk to you for a minute." He looked down at his hands. "You know I'm glad you came to Holy Martyrs. The school needs you. But now..."

"But now what?"

"We don't know, do we?"

"No, we don't. But, then, we never do, do we?"

He stood up and started to pace again. "You don't have to stay. Your life has been disrupted coming here. Who knows, oh, God, who knows what's going to happen now? Maybe it's not too late for you to go back to Summit County in the fall."

Catherine stared at him and felt her face redden.

"Fr. Riley! How can you say such a thing? I'm not going anywhere."

"If things go back to the way they were..."

"And if they do? Holy Martyrs won't change, will it?"

"Of course not."

"Then I'm staying right here where I belong, come what may."

"It might get ugly."

"It already has."

Fr. Riley relaxed a little and smiled. He began to feel better. It was one of the greatest joys of his priesthood -- one the world couldn't understand -- to see the effects of grace in the souls of his people; and he marvelled at the goodness of God. He stopped pacing and stood at the open door.

"Thank you, Catherine."

She dropped her eyes, embarrassed by his gratitude. She felt undeserving of it. "I'm the one who should thank you."

"How's that?" he asked, waiting, his hand on the brass knob.

"It's hard to say, it sounds so maudlin, but, don't you see? Coming here has given my life a purpose again. I was floun-

242

dering after Frank died. I was so lonely, and I didn't feel like I was doing anything, well, to do my part...When Frank was alive, I was content. I knew I was doing God's will, caring for my husband, creating a home for him. The teaching was secondary. But, then, after he was killed..."

Catherine paused, composing herself, "After he was killed, the main part of my life was gone and I was just filling in time. It was like I was split in two. My religion and my work. The college was --oh, how can I saw this without sounding like I'm whining? It was like a desert and there was an oasis nearby, but nobody cared. They *liked* the desert. I didn't realize how thirsty I was. Being here, having a chance to be part of Holy Martyrs, a part of the restoration -- a chance to serve Our Lord and give my life to Him -- I could never go back...

Her face was peaceful. "I've put my hand to the plow-share," she finished lightly.

"Good," he said. "I won't bring it up again." He was quiet for a moment. "I never realized when we named this place that we'd be living in a new age of martyrs."

He looked up as though he could see beyond the ceiling and the sky, and in his eyes was the strength of the martyrs, the courage of the saints.

"Peter's won the crown," he said, his voice low. Catherine wondered whether he yearned for it himself. " I hope..."

"Yes, Father?"

"Nothing. The Archbishop has left for Rome. "

"The funeral is tomorrow, isn't it?"

"Yes."

"And then the Conclave..."

"Yes. Pray that the Almighty will spare us a modernist pope."

Catherine nodded. "Speaking of modernists, what's happening with Fr. Rodriguez? Is he gone for good?"

"I hope so. I brought my report to the Archbishop, but I doubt that he's had a chance to look at it." He thought about

243

the papers that had been in the envelope Catherine had given him, the revolutionary plans, the hatred against the church that spilled from the pages. He didn't trust that Rodriguez wouldn't be back. "I'll leave you to your work," he said. "Keep your chin up. Remember the martyrs."

"That should be our battle cry."

He chuckled. "That's good," he said, leaving, and she turned back to her books.

The time until the concert passed quickly and the interregnum continued. Each day the world waited expectantly for the white smoke proclaiming the election of the new pope and each day ended in disappointment. Sixty-three times the ballot had been cast and sixty-three times the smoke was gray. The reporters and cameramen who had clustered daily around the Vatican lost interest and turned their attention to other things.

There had been a spattering of bombings since the American Embassy in Rome had been hit -- an Army barracks in Saudi Arabia, an American oil company in Jordan. An attempt to blow up the Golden Gate Bridge was thwarted at the last minute. Heads of government were on edge, thrusting their fingers at the television screens as though jabbing an opponent's chest. Impassioned threats of retaliation filled the airwaves.

The countries of the United Nations sat powerless to combat the escalating terror and locked themselves in verbal battle, forced to admit that their grand idea of global peace had crumbled before their eyes. The world floundered in its moral bankruptcy.

But at Holy Martyrs life continued peacefully. To Catherine's great relief, Fr. Rodriguez had not returned, and there had been no further notes or phone calls to frighten her. The days passed uneventfully. Her classes were going well, especially the senior literature class. She delighted in the work of her students.

Bernadette came to the principal's office the day before the concert to show her her poems.   Catherine smiled as she read them. Sitting at her desk, red pen in hand, she taught Bernadette to polish the edges and tame the adolescent unruliness so the music could be heard, and the girl pulled out her pen and opened her notebook, taking notes.

"I think this one's finished," Catherine said to Bernadette, handing back the neatly typed poem, unmarred by red ink. "It's good." Bernadette's face flushed under her freckles.

"Do you really like it?"

"Yes." Bernadette wished Catherine would say more, but she was sorting through her file folder. "Tuck that one away and start on this one." Catherine scanned the lines. "The diction needs to be tightened."

"Too prosy?"

"Yes. But it's basically quite good. You just ramble on too much. Tighten it up." She handed the piece of paper across the desk, then leaned forward, resting her elbows on the desk. "What would say about starting a literary magazine in the high school?"

"Oh, Dr. Anderson! That would be terrific! Could we really?"

"We can talk about it in class next week...see if there's any interest."

"I'm sure there will be. You've got everybody carrying around little notebooks and scribbling in them between classes."

"Is that right?"

"Yes. Jeanne's working on a short story. I'm probably not supposed to say anything...Oh, well, too late now. Anyway, it's really good. And, get this..." Bernadette leaned her head forfward conspiratorially. "Rob is working on something. He won't say what. Can you believe it? I never thought I'd see my brother writing something. I thought he was just interested in guinea pigs and frogs. It's funny. He doesn't use a notebook. He goes down to the science lab and Mr. Corwin lets him use the computer. I think he's working on some kind of essay on ethics in research."

245

"Oh? That's quite an undertaking."

"But don't tell them I told you."

"I won't." Catherine recapped her pen. "Well, we can talk about this in class next week."

"Why not tomorrow?"

"We're not having English tomorrow."

"Why not?"

"Practice. Remember?"

"I forgot... The dress rehearsal. Now I'm getting nervous."

"That'll go away once you start to play."

"I know. But this is different from my other recitals."

"How's that?" Catherine slipped her papers back into the folder and walked over to the file cabinet.

"This seems more important somehow..."

Catherine closed the file drawer and turned back toward Bernadette. "In what way?"

"Because it's... oh, I sound stupid."

Catherine walked back over to her chair and sat back down, leaning against the high back and resting her hands in her lap. She waited, studying Bernadette's face -- the deep blue eyes in a sea of freckles, the artist's soul shining through. Catherine recognized the sensitivity that would seem exaggerated to most people, the acute receptiveness to everything -- feelings, people, ideas. What would she be? Catherine wondered. A pianist? A poet? How would she use her gifts?

Finally Bernadette spoke. "Did you ever feel that some things were weighted somehow?" she asked in a tremulous voice. She looked away, afraid that she sounded foolish, and was surprised when Catherine answered.

"Yes," she said simply.

"You know, then."

Catherine nodded. "I always saw it as some things being fraught with meaning. You could feel the heaviness somehow."

"Yes, that's it! I knew you'd understand. I tried to tell Annie about it once, but she thought I was nuts, and when I told my mother, she told me to dry the dishes."

Catherine laughed. "That's exactly what she should have told you. The best antidote to an imagination like yours -- and like mine -- is a hearty dose of daily life."

"But I thought you wanted us to develop our imaginations.-

"Part of developing them is taming them. Otherwise you'll take yourself and your feelings too seriously."

Bernadette was disappointed. She wanted to talk about what she felt and it seemed like Catherine wasn't interested.

"But you said you felt like that, too, that some things are weighted, that there's some meaning attached to them beyond the appearances."

"Yes," she said. "I did." The curious thing was, she was beginning to feel the same way about the concert and didn't want to admit it to herself, because she thought she was being silly. She had been bothered by a feeling of apprehension that didn't seem like normal stage fright. She pushed the thought away.

Bernadette wanted to keep talking about it. "It's like ... Well, it's like there's all these unseen people listening..."

Catherine laughed lightly. "Well, Bernadette, there are! The concert is dedicated to Our Lady. You didn't think the Blessed Mother wouldn't hear the voices of her children, did you?"

"I hope she likes it."

"Does your mother like to hear you play?"

"Yes."

"Well."

"It's wonderful to be a Catholic, isn't it, Dr. Anderson? It makes you feel so good inside to know God loves you. I think about it a lot. I wonder, why me? Why am I here in this school where I can learn about Our Lord and receive Him in Holy Communion and have friends who love Him like I do? There's so many kids in the world. Why did God choose *me* to be here?

"Everything is so mixed up and awful nowadays. When I leave here, I feel like I'm going to another planet or something. I don't fit in anywhere else." Bernadette looked at her teacher's eyes, gentle and understanding. "I'm glad you understand," she said simply. "I guess I'd better go now and help my mother make dinner."

"Good. She'll appreciate that. I'll see you tomorrow."

Bernadette gathered her books. "Do you think I'll ever be a poet?"

"Yes, Bernadette, I do. But..."

"But what?" Anxiety tightened her face.

"You are very gifted. I want you to remember where those gifts come from and use them to reflect the beauty you see. Reach high with your writing so others can learn to love what you do."

"That's what I want, Dr. Anderson. I want to write for the Glory of God."

"May God bless your efforts, Bernadette." Catherine stood up. "Now go help your mother. Come on, I'll walk out with you."

Spring had finally come to Michigan. The lilacs were in bloom and bright red tulips lined the front walks of the houses across the street. It was still light and Catherine breathed deeply of the fresh warm air. At the parking lot, she headed for her car, and Bernadette turned left to go around the school to her street.

"I'll see you tomorrow," she said.

"Be good," said Catherine, as she got into her car.

Bernadette was walking up the sidewalk along the east side of the school, going over her conversation with her teacher and hugging the words to herself, when she saw a man duck around the corner toward the back door. She wondered who it was.

No one ever used the back door except for fire drills. Frightened, she turned back to tell Dr. Anderson, but she was too late. Catherine had already pulled out onto the street and was heading home.

Bernadette decided to keep walking as though she hadn't seen anything. She crossed the street, ready to run to a nearby

248

house if someone approached her. By the time she was even with the back of the school, whoever she had seen had disappeared.

She wondered whether he had gone into the school, and she decided to cross back toward the building and check the door. Her breath quickened. Looking closely at the bushes and behind the trees that lined the sidewalk, Bernadette ran to the door and pulled at the handle. It was locked. Satisfied that the man couldn't have gotten into the school, Bernadette crossed back over to the other side of the street and continued on her way home. Her heart began to beat normally again.

Thursday morning Catherine turned on the radio as she drove to school to hear if there was any news about the papal election. Impatiently she listened to the traffic and weather reports for the Detroit area followed by a loud commercial for diet cola. She switched the channel, punching the buttons quickly, one station after another. The news finally came on, but there was no word from Rome. The multisided war raged on in Europe, and the famine in the Baltic states deepened.

Suddenly her attention was drawn to the report of a movement for the restoration of the monarchy in France. She drew her breath in sharply, struck by the announcer's words. Everything was fitting together. Turning up the volume, she remembered the ancient prophecies about the Great Monarch.

It was said that during the end times before the Second Coming of Christ, when the world was plunged into infidelity and despair, a great king would rise in Europe and lead the forces of good, in union with a strong and mighty Pope. When the Antichrist came, the Monarch would oppose him. France, the eldest daughter of the Church, had long believed that the king would be hers. He would be known by the cross he wore on his breast and the virtue and valor of his life. Pious legends, some said. But Catherine wondered.

Because now a man claiming to be a descendent of Louis XIV and heir to the French throne, had emerged as a popular political leader. The man was known as Henri, Fils du Lys -- Son of the Lily -- but no one was sure just who he was. They said he was a duke, his family hidden for over two hundred years, since the time of the Revolution.

He had captured the imagination and the longings of the people who staggered under an impoverished and godless social- ist regime, their hopes as parched and dry as the brown fields of the relentless drought.

Henri rode through the streets of the villages and the roads of the countryside on a white stallion, wearing a finespun linen tunic emblazoned with a cross, and a fleur de lys embroidered on the back. Sophisticated people laughed at him and said he was crazy, but the French government was worried. Secret meetings were held and a campaign instituted to discredit him, but the crowds contined to throng around him, waving the white and gold flag of Catholic France. Children petted his horse and brought apples and sugar lumps, and women sat on benches at the edges of towns waiting for him to pass by.

Catherine was intrigued. Henri had met in private audience with Innocent XIV the week before the shooting, but there were no reports about what had been said. So he continued to ride, a romantic figure from the past, his gold-brown hair caught by the wind as he leaned forward on his mount and traversed the coun- tryside.

The newscaster turned to sports with the final results of the Pistons game and Catherine switched off the radio.

The school day passed quickly in a swirl of activity. Not much classwork was done, as the final preparations for the even- ing's concert were completed. Catherine ran into Judy Long on her way to the teachers' lounge after school.

"Everything all set for tonight?"

"I think so. Carrie's running them through a few last minute instructions."

250

"Y'all've worked hard." Judy shifted her books from one arm to the other. "We should have a pretty good crowd. I hope Denny can get off this evening."

"Is he scheduled to work?"

"No, but he's been investigating some sort of terrorist ring..."

"Here? In Dearborn?" Catherine was startled.

Judy shrugged. "They're everywhere..."

Catherine opened the door to the teachers' lounge. "There hasn't been any problem, has there?"

"Nothing major. There've been some phone calls and threatening letters, suspicious people lurking around. They found a few pipe bombs before they went off. That sort of thing."

Catherine caught her breath. "That's all though? What makes them think it's a ring?"

"I don't know... Denny can't say too much." Judy poured herself a cup of coffee. "Want some?"

"No thanks."

"Denny said there was a threat against the Archbishop. They caught some guy following him around the day before he left for Rome. He's in custody now...a big fat guy who claims to be a priest. Fr. Gregson from California. Says he's an admirer of the Archbishop and didn't do anything. He was carrying a gun, though. Some priest. But he'll probably be released..." Judy sighed.

Catherine shook her head. "There's no end to it, I'm afraid. She joined Judy at the table as Barbara Clark came in the door and tossed her purse on the counter.

"What a day!" she said. "I couldn't get those kids settled down for anything. I'll be glad when this concert is over. Maybe we can get some work done."

Judy sipped her coffee. "No way. We'll just get this finished and then it'll be June and no one will want to do any work then either...too close to the end."

"True. But then...two whole months to recover! And I'm

off to Montana to see my folks."

Judy got up and rinsed out her cup. "Well, I've got to see if Vito is through with my children so we can go home and get some food in them before we head back here."

"What are they doing?" asked Catherine.

"Jimmy's helping Laso set up the lights and Denny Bob and Mary Ellen are sitting in the chairs and calling out if they're working or not." She picked up her books and balanced them on her hip. "See y'all tonight."

"Right," said Barbara, leaning back in her chair and stretching her legs out in front of her. "You going home?" she asked Catherine.

"No, I'm going to stay here. No point going home and turning right around and coming back again. How about you?"

"I'm going to take a quick run to the library and stop at MacDonald's. You want anything?"

"No, thanks. I brought a sandwich."

"Well, I'm off, then. See you later."

CHAPTER

23

Miserere mihi, Domine, quoniam tribulor
Libera me, et eripe me de manibus inimicorum meorum

By a quarter to seven, the gym was nearly full. Heavy red drapes hid the stage, and there was the low sound of quiet conversation as the people waited for the concert to begin. Soon the lights dimmed and the curtains opened onto a softly lit backdrop of St. Peter's Square.

Laso and Denny Bob Long had done the construction, and Jeanne Pitlowski had sketched the outline. They enlisted the help of four of the eighth and ninth graders, and the seven students had spent the past two weeks painting it. Yellow and white footlights illuminated the familiar scene giving the appearance of a sunny day in Rome.

The crowd grew still, then rose silently as Fr. Riley walked onstage and approached the microphone in front of the newly painted risers.

"Good evening, my friends."

"Good evening, Father," the audience replied.

"Let us pray." Father Riley led them in the Our Father, Hail Mary, and Glory Be.

"Mary Queen of Heaven..."

"Pray for us."

"Holy Martyrs..."

"Pray for us." They made the sign of the cross and settled back down into their seats.

"I'm sure you're all looking forward to this concert as much as I am," said Fr. Riley, his face brightened by the foot-

253

lights, "so I'll turn the microphone over now to our principal, Dr. Catherine Anderson."

Catherine came onstage to acknowledge the polite applause, graceful in a navy skirt that swirled around her ankles as she walked. She wore a fitted white jacket with navy trim over a high collared white blouse, and her long braid was wound into a circlet of auburn at the base of her neck, held in place by a comb of clustered pearls. She was wearing the small diamond earrings Frank had given her before leaving for Europe on his last trip, and they caught the light, tiny sparkles dancing on each side of her face.

In the fourth row, Don and Helen Anderson watched her proudly. With them were the Tomaszewskis who had put their house in Chicago up for sale and stored their furniture. It was their first day back. They sat quietly waiting for the program to begin. Vito was backstage and Teresa sat next to Stella. Angie had left for Europe after finishing the spring term. She met Rick in England, and they were married by the Air Force chaplain. After Rick's five day leave, Angie would come back to Dearborn and stay with her parents for the summer.

It was warm in the gym, and Stella fanned herself with the program. Onstage, Catherine was introducing Carrie Stevens. Sitting in a center aisle seat in the front row, Nick Fortunata watched in fascination as Carrie took the microphone and Catherine slipped backstage to line up the children.

Like the high school girls, Carrie was dressed in a long royal blue gown, tightwaisted and full, with puffed sleeves tapering to the wrist. Her golden curls gleamed in the light as she stepped forward and gripped the microphone, greeting the audience in her lilting voice and capturing the heart of Nick Fortunata.

Carrie held out her arm as the first performers filed onto the risers, the elementary school choir who would sing, "Mother Dear, Oh Pray for Me," their sweet young voices soaring to the ear of their Mother in heaven. Bernadette played the accompaniment and backstage, Laso worked the lights, shining a sky blue spotlight on the three rows of singers. Catherine stood backstage with the high school ensemble who would go on next.

"Til in Heaven eternally, Thy love and bliss I share..." sang the littlest ones. Then led by Billy Pitlowski and Tommy Flanagan, with Mary Ann Haneghan and tiny Mary Ellen Long at the end, they stepped down the risers and exited stage right as the high school singers came in from the left and Bernadette played an interlude. Laso readjusted the lighting, switching to white. The concert continued, one song after another, for forty minutes. Carrie watched nervously from the wings and began to chew her fingernails.

Across the stage, Catherine gestured encouragingly to her, and Carrie smiled back, dropping her fingertips from her mouth and hugging her elbows instead. She peeked out trying to see if she could see Nick in the audience as the stage emptied and Laso shone a single spotlight on the emptiness. Brendan O'Keefe, holding himself as straight and tall as his four foot eight would allow, slowly walked to the center. Carrie whispered to him to walk slowly.

"Easy...ready...slowly...take a breath...that's a boy..."

Bernadette waited for him, her hands poised above the keys, then began to play.

Brandon O'Keefe sang the *Ave Maria* in a voice as clear as leaded glass. The pure notes soared and swelled, and no one, hearing, wanted to breathe.

"Nunc et in hora mortis nostrae...Now and at the hour of our death...Amen..."

Suddenly a thunderous explosion rocked the gym and plunged it into darkness. Stunned by the impact, Brandon dropped to his face. The students gathered with Carrie in the wings began to scream and cry.

The parents leaped to their feet and groped their way toward the stage, searching for their children in the dark. Overtaken by fear, they frantically shouted their names. In the audience, Helen and Teresa gripped each other, and Fr. Riley ran to the front and jumped onto the stage. He lifted Brandon and carried him to the edge and handed him down to Nick.

"He'll be okay," said Fr. Riley. He's coming to now. Take him outside in the fresh air." Nick grasped the frightened child and pressed his hand firmly against the back of Brandon's head, supporting it as though he could will strength to flow to the boy through his own bone and muscle.

The backdrop was in flames and Vito ran for the fire extinguisher. Rob O'Keefe found a flashlight and handed it to Fr. Riley.

"Quiet!" Fr. Riley shouted, turning toward the people. "Everyone, please remain calm. File out the back of the gym immediately. The children are all right. They are coming down the steps now. The explosion was on the other side." He shone the light on the steps as they began to feel their way down. Women cried out as they recognized their children and men shouted for their sons as they embraced and hurried out the back door.

The fire was spreading, and Fr. Riley yanked down the heavy curtains and beat back the flames. The back wall of the gym leading to the maintenance closet had a door-sized hole in it. Fr. Riley looked around. The people had cleared out of the gym, and he prepared to leave himself. He ran to check where the children had gathered in the wings after their performance to make sure that everyone had gotten out. There was no one there.

He ran his hand through his hair and took a deep breath, then leaned forward, eyes closed, resting his hands on his thighs and dropping his head, letting the blood flow. He stood back up and sprinted to the other side of the stage for a final check, then stopped short, stunned, his heart pounding wildly.

Laso lay still and bleeding on a bed of glass amidst the broken lights and crumbling wall. By his head knelt Catherine, her face black and her suit torn, her hair falling down her back and her hands covered with blood. She had found a piece of cloth and was wrapping Laso's head with it, trying to stop the bleeding.

Tears streamed down her face and she lifted his head and laid it across her lap, cradling it in the curve of her left arm and wiping his face and smoothing back his hair. She stroked his cold gray cheek.

"Oh, my God!" Fr. Riley bent over and took Laso's wrist, feeling for a pulse. Catherine watched him, her eyes huge and searching, her face glazed in silent agony.

"He's alive."

"Thank God," Catherine choked out the words. There was a deep gash on her upper arm where a falling board had struck her, tearing through her sleeve into the muscle.

"Are you all right?"

"Yes."

"I'm going to anoint him. I'll be right back." Catherine nodded, pressing the cloth harder against Laso's head. The wound was large and gaping and Catherine tried to hold the edges together to stanch the flow of blood which now spilled over her skirt and on the floor. Fr. Riley came back with a purple stole around his neck carrying the Holy Chrism. Catherine was too weak to kneel, so she sat back on her heels, her hands crossed over her heart, as Fr. Riley gave Laso the Last Rites of the Church, anointing the young man lying motionless on the floor, the wood blackened by fire and reddened by blood.

Outside the sound of sirens drew near.

Father Riley had finished administering the Sacrament and was wiping the oil from his thumb with an alcohol pad when two EMS men burst through the door pulling a stretcher. They looked questioningly at the priest, and he nodded and moved out of their way. Expertly they lifted Laso onto the stretcher, strapped him on, and covered him with a gray blanket. Catherine sat on the floor watching them, still in shock, and Fr. Riley came and helped her into a chair.

"You wait right there. There'll be another crew coming for you."

"I'm fine," Catherine said.

"Hardly. Don't move."

"I won't."

Fr. Riley started to clear away some of the debris and Catherine watched him without expression. Police officers filled the gym and Denny Long came backstage where Catherine and Fr. Riley were waiting.

"You all right back here?" Lt. Long asked, shuddering at the devastated scene, the backdrop split by flames, St. Peter's rent in two, the risers charred.

"They just took Laso out."

Denny looked over at Catherine.

"They'll be back for Dr. Anderson," said Fr. Riley. "I don't want her trying to walk."

"What a mess," said Denny. The fire trucks arrived, sirens screaming, and men in slick black coats and boots ran toward the gym pulling hoses.

"You in charge here?" one of them yelled to Fr. Riley after shouting instructions to his partner.

"Yes."

"Can you get that lady out of here?"

"The EMS should be here any minute."

"Well, move her out of the way!" He yanked the heavy hose under his arm and sprayed the smoldering backdrop, the colors of St. Peter's running together, the image lost in the stream of water. Fr. Riley helped Catherine to her feet, and Denny Long held out his arm and led her into the hall just as the paramedics arrived with a stretcher. Catherine sat back on it, still dazed. Her face was scratched and her right eye was beginning to swell. They laid her back on the stretcher and cut away the sleeve of her blouse. She winced as they probed the wound.

"She'll be okay, Father," said the technician.

"Where are you taking her?"

"Oakwood."

"The boy?"

258

"Same place."

"I'll be there as soon as I can."

By this time, Don and Helen realized that Catherine had not come out with the other teachers, and Don was running back into the building when a policeman stopped him.

"Where you going, Mister?"

"My daughter-in-law...she's still in there," he gasped.

"Go on back outside."

"But I have to find her...my wife..."

A young officer stepped up to Mr. Anderson. "Go on now, sir," he said . "I'll see if I can find her. What's her name?"

"Anderson. Dr. Catherine Anderson. She's the principal here."

Sam Oliver caught his breath. He remembered her; he'd never forget her. The graceful lady with the false arrest. He remembered that day, here in this same parking lot. "Don't worry. I'll find her. Go back with your wife." He headed down the hall toward the gym. "I owe her," he said to himself. He turned back toward Don. "I'll be out as soon as I know anything."

"Thanks, Officer, I appreciate it." Don wiped his forehead with the back of his hand, trying not to give in to the dread that was sweeping over him. He turned and walked back outside. Helen searched his face anxiously.

"They'll let us know when they find her," he said, putting his arm around his wife's shoulders and drawing her close to him. Helen stood staring at the school, not saying a word. Teresa slipped away from Nick and Carrie and came to stand by Helen as the paramedics brought a stretcher out of the building. Don strained to see who it was, but his view was blocked.

"Anderson! Mr. Anderson!" Don looked up at the young officer hurrying toward him.

"She's okay," he called, not waiting until he got closer. "They're taking her to the hospital."

Helen's knees buckled, and she started to fall forward. Don

held her tightly.

"What happened?"

"She was backstage on the side that got hit. She and a kid."

"How bad?" whispered Helen.

"She's in shock. Got a few bruises and bumps and a nasty cut on her arm. The kid wasn't so lucky."

Helen looked up, her face white.

"Is he?"

Oliver shook his head. "He's still alive but just barely, I guess."

"Who was it?"

"A foreign boy...Lazarus or something."

"Laso. Oh, dear God..."

"Guess your daughter-in-law saved his life. He would've bled to death if she hadn't been there. She got it stopped. Bad head wound."

Helen's face crumbled and she bit at her fist.

"Thanks, Officer," said Don. "We won't keep you from your work. Where'd they take Catherine?"

"Oakwood."

"Thanks. Come on, Mother," he said, turning her toward the car. "Let's go see our girl."

Sam Oliver headed back into the building and ran into Fr. Riley and Lt. Long in the hallway.

"Did you find her folks?" asked Denny.

"Yes, sir. They're going to the hospital now."

"Good. Come on back here with us." Lt. Long led the priest and the policeman to the supply room next to the gym. It had been cordoned off with yellow ribbon and a tall heavy set officer stood at the door.

"Evening, Lieutenant."

"Evening, Jones."

"You going in?"

"Yes." He motioned to Fr. Riley to follow him. He

pointed across the room. Sprawled on the floor was a body covered with a sheet. Fr. Riley fought a wave of nausea. The violence, the destruction, the horror of the evening rushed over him.

"Looks like the culprit didn't get away," said Denny, bending over the body and uncovering the face. "Know him?"

Fr. Riley looked down at the contorted face, the death-filled eyes and sneering mouth locked in an expression of perpetual hatred. The priest reeled back and turned his head away, filled with disgust.

"God help him...yes, I know him. The name's Rodriguez. Fr. Stefan Rodriguez. I'll notify the bishop." Fighting his loathhing and revulsion, Fr. Riley knelt beside the dead man and began to pray

The young officer watched him unblinking. Fr. Riley stood up and walked over to Denny, and Sam Oliver came up behind them. "Father?"

"Yes?"

"Sorry to bother you... but when this is all cleared up... well, I'd like to talk to you."

"Sure, son. Anytime."

"Oliver?" said Lt. Long.

"Yes, sir?"

"Go outside and let the people know everything's all right...try to fend off the reporters. They should be jumping the barricades any minute now."

"Yes, sir."

Lt. Long turned to Fr. Riley. "Well, that's about it."

"What do you think happened?"

"We'll have to get the bomb squad in here, but it looks like an amateur job. Nitric acid and glycerol, I'd guess. We found some smashed bottles. Looks like he didn't make himself a long enough fuse."

Fr. Riley shook his head and walked slowly down the hall, his cassock covered with soot and his cuffs edged with Laso's blood.

It was the Feast of St. Venantius, Martyr, and Catherine sat in the chair by her hospital bed, her bandaged arm in a sling. The wound was deep, and her arm had to be immobilized in a soft cast. Her blood pressure was too low and her head throbbed. She was pale from worry about Laso, who had not regained consciousness. The nurse came in to take her temperature and Catherine opened her mouth obediently.

"Normal yet?" asked Catherine, hoping she could go home.

"Yup, infection's gone, but the pressure's way too low. Looks like you'll be staying around a little longer."

Catherine sighed, disappointed. The nurse turned to hurry to the next patient.

"Nurse," said Catherine, interrupting her exit.

"What?"

"Is it all right...May I walk down and see Laso?"

"I don't think he can have any visitors."

"Could you check please?"

"I'll ask Dr. O'Neill. But don't get your hopes up." Five minutes later, the nurse poked her head through the door, her stethoscope hanging from her neck.

"The doctor says it's all right, Catherine."

"Thanks," she said.

Catherine walked over to the closet and pulled out the simple cotton dress Helen had brought over for her the day before when she thought she was going to be discharged. She dressed quickly and readjusted her sling, then walked down the hall through the double doors to the intensive care unit. It was a frightening place. The heavy doors. The incessant beeping of machines. The hiss of oxygen and the moans of the gravely ill. She stood outside Laso's room, summoning her courage. She was met by a nurse.

"Dr. O'Neill said I could sit with him," she said.

"Go ahead," said the nurse, moving aside.

Catherine slipped through the door and sat down by Laso's bedside. He was hooked to an electronic monitor, and bottles hung by his head with tubes running to his arms. His face was still a deathly gray. His long lashes rested on his cheeks, and he looked vulnerable, like a child.

Reaching through the bars, she closed her fingers around his hand lying limply by his side. She looked at him with an aching heart. Letting go of his hand, she pulled her rosary from her pocket and began the Glorious Mysteries, whispering the prayers softly. Her fingers slid quickly over the beads and she finished the last decade, then closed her eyes.

"Most Sorrowful and Immaculate Heart of Mary..." she prayed, her voice catching in her throat and her eyes burning.

"Pray for us..." Laso whispered.

Catherine's eyes flew open and she made the sign of the cross and tucked the rosary back into her pocket, never taking her eyes off Laso. He smiled weakly at her.

"I thought you were an angel."

Catherine laughed softly. "Sorry."

"It's okay." His breathing was labored.

"Don't try to talk." He smiled again and this time a flush of color came into his face. Catherine touched his arm.

"I should tell the nurse you're awake. I'll be right back." She hurried to the nurses' station, her steps light. A dark haired nurse sat amidst a stack of charts, recording her notes. She was annoyed at being interrupted.

"Laso's conscious," Catherine said.

The nurse's irritation disappeared. She got up quickly. "Are you sure?"

"Yes."

"I'll be right there."

Catherine went back to the room and was sitting in the chair again when the nurse and Dr. O'Neill came in. Catherine rose to leave.

The doctor bent over Laso, pulling back his eyelids, checking his pupils. "Well, well," he said. "So you decided to wake up."

"My mother doesn't like me to sleep in," he said.

"How do you feel?"

"Not so good. My head aches."

"It will for awhile. Let me take a look at you..." The nurse drew the curtain around the bed, and Catherine went out into the hall. She decided not to return to her room. She wanted to stay with Laso a little longer if she could. She sat down in a chair several feet from the door. In a few minutes, Dr. O'Neill came out the door followed by the nurse.

"He's going to be all right," he said. "We'll do some tests later after he's rested awhile. But I think he's out of danger now."

"Thank God."

"I think he wants to see you."

"Thank you, Doctor, for all you've done."

The elderly physician patted her arm and walked away.

Dr. O'Neill had removed some of the monitors, and Laso looked more comfortable. Catherine sat back down beside the bed.

"How long was I unconscious?"

"Six days."

"I'm sorry for the trouble."

Catherine smoothed the wool blanket, turning the sheet over the end of it so that the cool cotton would rest against his face.

"Don't be silly."

"What happened, Dr. Anderson?"

"Do you remember any of it?"

"No. The last thing I remember I was on the ladder adjusting the spotlight for Brandon."

"There was an explosion."

264

"What kind?"

"A bomb."

The color drained from Laso's face, alarming Catherine.

"Not nitric acid and glycerol?"

"That's what they think. How did you know?"

In a halting voice, Laso told her about Fr. Rodriguez. "But I didn't give him the jars. I put them back in my locker because I was afraid he was planning something like this."

"He must have gotten them out of there. Or he might have gotten them somewhere else."

"It's my fault."

"No. You weren't responsible. Quite the contrary. You tried to prevent it."

"How did he do it?"

"He attached an M80 to the jars, lengthened the fuse somehow, and set it up in the maintenance closet. Then he went to the supply room, lit it, and blew up the back wall of the gym."

"How'd he set that up without Mr. Fortunata knowing?"

"He must have done it during the night. He had keys to the school. They were in his pocket."

"Stolen?"

"What else? They were Mrs. Janis' extra set. She kept them hidden in the back of her mailbox, and he found them."

"Did the police catch him?"

Catherine bit her lip. "He's dead. He was caught in the explosion."

"Some priest," Laso said bitterly.

"Yes," whispered Catherine.

Mrs. Johnson, the afternoon nurse, a plump middle-aged R.N. with a happy face, bustled over to the bedside.

"How are we doing, young man?"

"Much better, Nurse, thank you."

She wrapped the blood pressure cuff around his arm. It's moving day for you, son. They're going to wheel you down to the Med-Surg wing. No more intensive care for you." She glanced over at Catherine. "What happened to you?"

"I caught some shrapnel."

The nurse chuckled. "Plucky bunch, aren't you?"

Catherine rose to leave.

"I'll come back later this evening," she said.

"Thanks...Dr. Anderson?"

"Yes, Laso?"

"Does my mother know?"

"Not yet. Your father wanted to wait a while and see if you regained consciousness."

Laso's face showed his relief. "I am glad. Now there will be good news to send to Ljubljana."

Oakwood Hospital was a red brick building set back from the road. A winding entrance curved through a line of oak and maple trees which had stood silent guard for fifty years. The sun set behind the hospital, brushing the roof red and gold, and the trees swayed in the evening breeze.

Fr. Riley drove quickly to the entrance and parked his car. He had just returned from a meeting at the police station when he got the message from the hospital about Laso. He was anxious to see him.

A prim volunteer in a pink pinafore sat at the information desk.

"May I help you, Father?"

"I'm here to see Laso Matov."

"Room 321B," she said, twirling her roll-a-dex. She handed him a pass.

"Thanks."

"The elevator is around the corner to the right."

"Thanks, but I'll take the stairs."

"They're across the hall..."

"Yes, I know. Thanks." Alone in the stairwell, Fr. Riley ran up the stairs, two at a time. It was faster than the elevator. At the top, he straightened his Roman collar and opened the door into the hallway where he was greeted with the familiar hospital smell of ammonia and alcohol. A spare young nurse's aide, her thin face and chiselled features forged by two hundred years of Appalachian poverty, greeted him.

"Evenin', Father." She blew a wisp of hair from her eyes.

He nodded. "Good evening."

"Who you looking for?"

"Laso Matov."

"He's down there. Third door on the left." Tucking her pen in her pocket, she sighed, "I wish everybody was like him."

"Why's that?"

"He just woke up, you know."

"I know."

"He thanked me for helping him. Talked real nice and quiet like." She shook her head. "Makes your shift a lot easier."

"I'm sure it does."

"Is all your people like that?"

Fr. Riley smiled ruefully. "They try."

"Cause that other patient that come down to visit him a while ago... That lady with the pretty hair and green eyes. You know who I mean?"

"Yes."

"She's just like him. You bring her soup and you'd think you was bringing her gold the way her face lights up and all."

Fr. Riley smiled. "Yes, she's like that. Say, could you do me a favor?"

"Sure, Father. What'd'ya need?"

"I'm going to talk to Laso for awhile. But could you ask Dr. Anderson -- that's the lady you were talking about -- to come down to his room?"

"Sure."

"In fifteen minutes?"

"Gotcha." She grabbed her cart and pushed it down the hall, leaning over it as though it were a wheelbarrow.

A quarter hour later, Catherine knocked at Laso's door.

267

"Ah, Catherine. Come in," said Fr. Riley. He stood up and pulled a chair over from the other side of the room. "I'm glad to see you're both recovering."

"I'm going home in the morning. Dr. O'Neill just told me."

"I wanted to talk to you together." Fr. Riley reached in his pocket for a small notebook. "I just got back from the police station."

Catherine looked at him expectantly.

"I know you both had some problems with Fr. Rodriguez, so what I'm going to tell you might ease your minds. I'll try to make it short. I had some suspicions about him."

Catherine listened, remembering her own questions.

"So, I started doing some research. Since the Archbishop's in Rome, I talked to the auxiliary, and he told me to notify the police, which I did. They just confirmed my information this afternoon. I wish I could have known sooner. Maybe I could have done something to prevent what happened." He rubbed his forehead.

Laso waited, wondering what Fr. Riley could have found out.

"Fr. Rodriguez was not a priest." Fr. Riley waited for a reaction. Neither Catherine nor Laso looked surprised.

"This comes as no shock, I take it?"

"No, Father," said Catherine. "Not really. The question had crossed my mind more than once."

"Laso?"

"I am more relieved than surprised. I did not understand how someone in Holy Orders could do what he was doing..."

"So if wasn't a priest, what was he?" Catherine asked.

"He had been in the seminary in California. San Diego. But he was never ordained. He and a group of fellow students were expelled for subversive activities two months before ordination. They were part of a revolutionary network in Southern California with connections in Mexico and Nicaragua.."

268

"The *Vox Populi*?" asked Catherine.

"Yes. Anyway, he was never ordained. The credentials he brought here were stolen."

"Like the keys."

"And the chemicals," said Laso.

"And even the name... He was really Emilio Rodriguez. Fr. Stefan Rodriguez...the real one...was his cousin. They were about the same age and could pass for twins. Anyway, Fr. Stefan Rodriguez was posted in Albuquerque but was killed three years ago in a car accident. After the funeral, Emilio went through his cousin's papers and took what he needed. And so the masquerade began. His orders were to move back here and infiltrate the Archdiocese after the restoration."

Catherine closed her eyes.

Laso was strengthened by the news. "At least the betrayal was not so bad as if he had been a priest."

"No," said Fr. Riley

"I was troubled by it, the way he was. It made me wonder..."

"Wonder what Laso?"

"Whether..." Laso looked at Catherine who prodded him.

"Tell him," she said.

"All right you two. What's going on?"

"I want to go to the seminary. I wish to be a priest."

Fr. Riley broke into a wide grin. "I'm glad to hear that, Laso." He leaned back in his chair and clasped his hands over his stomach, a look of satisfaction on his face. "Well, you can't say you don't know what might be in store for you..."

"I would be proud to face whatever comes for Our Lord."

"Were you planning to go back to Slovenia to study?"

"No, Father. I want to stay here."

"Good. When you get out of here, we'll get to work." Fr. Riley looked at the young man propped up against the pillows and remembered the early stirrings of his own vocation when he was a college student on a football scholarship at Michigan State heading for the pros.

Construction at Holy Martyrs had begun. All classes were moved to the elementary wing. The debris littering the gym had been cleared out and four panel trucks were parked in front of the school when Catherine arrived the next afternoon. The workers were sitting under a tree eating lunch.

"Afternoon, Miss," a carpenter greeted her.

"Hello. How's it going?"

"Good," answered the crew foreman. "We've got the studs up. Be good as new in a couple of days." He pointed his thumb at her sling. "They got ya, huh?"

"What's that?"

"It was in all the papers. Some big terrorist ring out of California. Bunch of Commies. You must be the one saved the kid's life."

"No," she said. "The Good Lord spared him. He's got some work for him to do."

The foreman looked at the carpenter and shrugged. All these people talked funny.

"See you," Catherine said, walking into the building. She hurried to her office, anxious to be back. No one was in the hall. She put down her purse and briefcase so that she could put the key in the lock with her good hand. Holding the door open with her back, she bent down and picked up her things and brought them over to her desk.

A row of notes lined the blotter. She glanced over them quickly and stacked them in a pile to tackle them one by one. An hour went by and she was on the last note when there was knock at the door.

"Come in," she said, not looking up.

"What are you doing here?" It was Fr. Riley.

Catherine was embarrassed. "Oh, Father. I'm sorry. I thought you were one of the children."

"So what are you doing here?"

"I'm working."

"So I see. But you were supposed to take a break."

"I had a break in the hospital. I was anxious to get back."

"Do you have a minute?"

"Yes."

He sat down in the chair by the open door and looked at his hands. She waited for him to speak. "I wanted to thank you, . You've done a remarkable job," he said finally, looking up at her, then dropping his eyes, "And... well... you've been through a lot."

"We all have, Father."

"What I mean is, I wouldn't blame you if you wanted to call it quits at the end of the semester."

"We talked about this before, Father. You promised you wouldn't bring it up again. You can't get rid of me that easily."

"Are you sure?"

"There's nowhere on earth I would rather be than here."

"Explosions and all?"

"Yes." Catherine grew pensive. Fr. Riley stood up and walked over to the window. Two workmen were unloading dry-wall from their truck.

"They're making good progress."

"Yes."

"You seem quiet, Catherine."

"I know."

"Well?"

"I just have this funny feeling, Father."

"What's that?"

"You'll want to reconsider my contract if I tell you..."

"Never."

"It's a feeling of expectancy..." She paused, considering how to say what she meant. "Maybe it's just waiting for the new pope...That's all."

"Really? I don't think so." He waited for her to say more.

271

She traced her finger along her bandaged arm. "I feel a little foolish."

"No need to."

"All right then. You really want to hear?"

"Please."

Her eyes looked beyond him as she spoke. "It's a feeling of events snowballing, escalating. Moving toward a climax. I keep listening to the news, waiting, expecting something momentous, something cataclysmic. Especially..."

"What?"

"Oh, you know. The prophecies about the Great Monarch. The restoration of Tradition... the Apostasy.... the last Pope... I just have this feeling of anticipation. Can it be possible? Could these be the End Times? Might we live to see Our Lord return?"

"*Watch ye therefore, because you know not what hour your Lord will come,*" said Fr. Riley solemnly.

"Yes," said Catherine. Her face clouded. "But before He comes..." The room suddenly felt very cold. She shivered.

"The Antichrist."

"Yes."

" Pray God we may have the grace to withstand him," he said.

Catherine lifted her head and gazed at the crucifix hanging on the wall across from her desk. "Yes," she whispered.

"It's the eleventh hour," said Fr. Riley, turning to leave.

EPILOGUE

Tu es Petrus
Et super hanc petram aedificabo Ecclesiam meam

The faithful gathered in St. Peter's Square. For the past two weeks, there had been few pilgrims, but today, called by an unseen voice, these had come. It was June 29, the Feast of Sts. Peter and Paul. The people waited, clustered under the balcony. In the center of the crowd stood a tall sun-bronzed man in a white tunic and crimson breeches. There was a red cross over his heart and a fleur de lys at his back. He was alone and spoke to no one, watching expectantly.

Suddenly another man pushed past the Swiss Guard. Black haired and olive skinned, he elbowed through the throngs of people, then stood still, his mouth curled and his face hard. His gold watch glinted in the sun and his diamond rings were heavy on his hands. Darkness lurked behind his eyes and the people close by shrank from him. He scanned the crowd until his eyes caught those of Henri, Fils du Lys, and locked in a cold stare.

Henri met the look, unafraid. He recognized his adversary: The Man of Sin. The Antichrist.

It was time.

At twelve o'clock white smoke rose and drifted like a single cloud in the blue summer sky, and the joyous cry sounded over the square.

"*Habemus Papam!*"

A roar went through the crowd.

"We have a Pope!

Viva il Papa!

Viva! Viva!"

The man in the tunic with the gold-brown hair moved for-

273

ward. People stepped back to let him pass, and soon he was at the front of the crowd just below the balcony. He looked straight ahead, his face resolute. There was strength in his bearing. He fingered the large wood beads of the rosary that hung from the cincture around his waist. His right hand rested on his heart.

The door of the balcony opened, and the new pontiff, white robed and majestic, stepped out into the sunlight. Henri, heir to the throne of France, sank to his knees and bowed his head, and the people did the same, except for the swarthy man in the gray suit who pushed his way out through the crowd. The gate shut behind him and two Swiss guards barred the entrance.

His Holiness Peter II raised his hand in benediction.

THE END